Praise for Sagnier

"*Sagnier builds characters as solid, gritty, and as broken as a DC street, with prose that lights up like monuments on a starry night.*"
— Michael J. Sullivan, best-selling author of The Riyria Revelations

"*As soon as I finished it, I wanted more; this is a real page-turner! The characters are well-developed and the story moves quickly.*"
— laurie from an Amazon review

"*One can only imagine how Sagnier gets so far into these people's heads. They are vivid and compelling in a story that turns, twists, and reveals so much of what lives in the darkness behind the white stone of Washington DC's monuments.*"
— Amanda Marsico

"*It is a story of the consequences of drug use and the age old adage of you reap what you sow. But these familiar themes are conveyed in an honest, gritty crime thriller set in the Nation's Capital. Each character will haunt you well after you have turned the final page.*"
— Donald Murphy

"*This is the perfect example of a skilled writer using a familiar literary form---in this case the mystery/crime genre---to plunge far below the surface and dig deep into those corners of our national life that we usually prefer to keep from the light. Combined with a fine prose style and an unflinching eye, Sagnier manages to keep the pace at top speed.*"
— An Amazon reviewer

The characters and events in this book are fictitious. Any similarity to real persons, living or dead, is coincidental and not intended by the author.

In accordance with the U.S. Copyright Act of 1976, the copying, scanning, uploading, and electronic sharing of any part of this book (other than for review purposes) without permission is unlawful piracy and theft of the author's intellectual property. If you would like to use material from this book, prior written permission can be obtained by contacting the author at thierry@sagnier.com. Thank you for your support of the author's rights.

PIGASUS BOOKS
Thirst Copyright © 2015 by Thierry Sagnier
Cover design © 2015 Michael J. Sullivan
Previously released as: The Girl, the Drugs, and the Man Who Couldn't Drink (2013) and Wasted Miracles (2012)
All rights reserved.
Third version: May 2015

Learn more about Thierry's writings at www.sagnier.com
To contact Thierry, email him at thierry@sagnier.com.

Thierry's Writings Include:
Thirst, a novel
Writing About People Places a Things, a collection of blog posts
Bike! Motorcycles and the People Who Ride Them
Washington at Night, a guidebook
The IFO Report, a novel

THIRST

By
Thierry Sagnier

Author's Note

Thirst was first published online in 2012 under the title of *Wasted Miracles*. Following a re-edit, it was published a second time and retitled *The Girl, the Drugs, and the Man Who Could Not Drink*.

In 2015, Robin and Michael Sullivan suggested further edits and a shorter title.

My thanks to Lori Sullivan (no relation to Michael & Robin), friend and wordsmith, whose editing skills I could not have done without. Kudos to Michael Klein and the Arlington Writers' Group, for providing a venue where critiquing is not a contact sport. And lastly, my unending gratitude to Paul Lavrakas for decades of friendship, inspiration, wisdom, and humor.

I am indebted to Robin, editor extraordinaire, and Michael, author of more books than I can count, for their efforts and willingness to make *Thirst* a better and more satisfying read.

— Thierry Sagnier, March 2015

Prologue

The Man Who Wouldn't Die

They drove Herbie through Rock Creek Park toward Beach Drive to do what they had to do, which was extract one or two pieces of information from him prior to finishing him off. But then things went wrong.

First, Akim accidentally stabbed Herbie in the chest when he was just trying to draw a little blood but the van hit a giant ragged crater of a pothole. The knife, thin as paper and sharp as cut glass, slid in. It caused more pain than damage and Herbie roared through the pillowcase and garbage bag. This shook Akim. He was new at this, barely twenty years old, and the whole thing was supposed to be a trial run. He hadn't anticipated any difficulties, had paced through the assignment a hundred times in his head. But Herbie's scream unnerved him, and Herbie's blood made him squeamish. So Akim stabbed Herbie two more times, trying to quiet him down. Herbie roared again, kicked out, somehow got an arm loose, flailed, and connected with a wild right fist that knocked the young man down. The driver, Comfort by name, an older man who'd done this

THIRST

type of thing in eight cities on three continents prior to coming to Washington, stopped the van and clambered back to help his colleague. Herbie, acting out of rage, instinct, and primal fear, was now trying to claw the garbage bag from his head. In the confines of the van, his struggle took up a lot of space. He was moaning and spraying blood, displaying an awesome strength for such an inconsequential man; the van was beginning to smell like a Third World slaughterhouse and rocking on its axles. Akim took out his gun, a slim Beretta he'd never yet fired.

Earlier in the day, as he and Comfort were reminiscing about their respective childhoods, Comfort had told him how, when he was a small boy in his native Nigerian village, there had been men who wouldn't die no matter the harm done them. The youth had listened wide-eyed and dry-mouthed. Now, right here, there was such a man. He fired the Beretta point blank into Herbie's chest. The sound was enormous inside the van, louder than anything the men had ever heard, and for an eternity all three were frozen in place. Then Herbie made an unearthly howl, a banshee shriek that tore their ears. Akim cried, "He is one of them! He cannot die!" Then he shot Herbie three more times without aiming.

Herbie did die then. The first bullet had merely nicked an artery, but the second one cut clean as a scalpel. Akim was vaguely pleased—this was *not* one of those men who couldn't die—but whatever satisfaction he derived from this realization was short-lived. Herbie was gone and the information they were supposed to get from him was gone too. This was very bad news, a major screw-up. And the van was a mess. Another screw-up.

Without a word, Comfort got back into the driver's seat, started the van, and pulled away. He drove only a few minutes until he found a spot near the dead end of Klingle Road, where barriers had been put up by the city to keep the blacks and Latinos out of the richer Cathedral neighborhood. There was no traffic there and with a bit of luck Herbie's body wouldn't be found for a while. They carried Herbie out, heaved him into a ditch, piled a few dead leaves on top of him, and drove away.

But it really was a luckless night for the Nigerians, the sort to make superstitious men believe in myths and spirits.

Not five minutes later a U.S. Park Police officer stopped his cruiser almost exactly in the same spot. He did this most nights he was on duty. It was quiet there, the traffic from adjacent residential roads made a low humming sound, and if you looked up, you could see stars. The officer looked forward to a Seven-Eleven Quarter Pound Big Bite and cradled a large paper cup of coffee in his lap. When he reached for the dome light, the coffee spilled and scalded his thighs and crotch. He yelled, leaped out of the police car, and tried to pull the fabric of his pants away from his legs. He tripped, fell, rolled, and came face to pillowcase with Herbie.

Chapter One

Josie found out about Herbie when she walked into a hive of cops. She'd gotten up early, flagged a cab on Lee Highway, and paid a purse full of money to get to Herbie's apartment. The cabby knew where he was going, zipped down 66, across Roosevelt Bridge, and onto Rock Creek Parkway. They drove up 18th Street, past the Ethiopian places and the Clint Eastwood house in the movie where he played a Secret Service man. The street was grungy from the night before, people sleeping in doorways, and the trash from all the restaurants hadn't yet been collected. Josie wondered how people could like living there, all the crime and the dirt and the noise.

She was going to surprise Herbie, give him a piece of her mind. He was supposed to call and hadn't, and she'd stayed up way too late waiting. Sleep had done little to dissipate her anger; if anything, her rage had turned colder and brittle. She almost hoped Herbie'd been with a woman, almost hoped she'd find some skanky fish with him at the apartment, then she could really cut loose because the truth of the matter was she was getting a bit tired of Herbie. He'd been fun at the start. They had a lot in common and talked late into the night the first few times they were together. The fact that he hadn't tried anything right away had impressed her. She'd even written him a *love poem* for God's sake!

But the thing was, Herbie was fast becoming a bore. She'd wanted to believe his wild tales about their going away together, just the two of them loaded with the cash he swore he'd have soon, be patient. She'd *really* wanted to believe. But she didn't, not *really*. It made for nice daydreams, but more and more the idea of going anywhere with Herbie, even with a lot of cash, lacked substance. He was kind of pudgy, made noises and farted when he slept, and wasn't all that tidy or—and this she hated—clean. He washed his hair every three days and by then it had a musty smell. When he made love to her with him on top, her nose was stuck in his scalp. It killed anything she felt below. And anyway, he wasn't that hot in bed, though of course she didn't tell him that.

ಌ

There were cops all over the place, in the corridor, in the living room, in the bedroom and bathroom. They'd torn the place apart. The cushions from the couch were on the floor and the rugs had been pulled every which way. The kitchen was a shambles, the refrigerator door wide open and its contents spread on the counter next to the sink. She saw all this in a split second, didn't know what to make of it, and stood with her mouth open until a large black man in a tight dark blue suit came over to her and said, "Who are you?"

She didn't say anything, looked at the black man and into the apartment again.

He asked, "Did you know Herbie?"

She caught the word "did." Not "do." "Did."

She dropped her purse, opened her mouth in a tall oval O, covered it with her hand.

Thirst

The black man slumped a little, his body relaxed. He took her elbow and gently guided her back into the hallway. There was a bench next to the elevator and he sat her down. Her knees were trembling; she thought they might actually knock together.

"Did you know Herbie?"

Her throat tightened, closed. She coughed, swallowed, and coughed again. She felt the cushion sag as the man joined her on the bench. She looked at his face, saw nothing there she could identify save a mild curiosity maybe tinged with sadness. She said, "Herbie's…"

The man nodded. He took a small notepad and a pen from his breast pocket. "I'm Detective Robinson. With the Metro police. Homicide. I'm sorry."

The words hung in the air above her. She took a deep breath, ran both hands through her hair, sat silent. After a while, Robinson said, "You obviously knew him. Any ideas?"

She shook her head no, found her voice. "You're sure? I mean, sure it's him? Herbie?"

"Pretty sure. He had his wallet on him. And he wasn't exactly a stranger, you know?"

Not a stranger? That didn't make much sense. Josie squinched her eyes shut. She hadn't known anyone dead before and an image of Herbie in a coffin flew past her. She shuddered.

"You okay?"

She nodded, sat up straight. "Yeah, I guess. God." She felt her entire body begin to shake, kept from trembling through an effort of will. She stole a glance through the apartment door. "I guess he was telling the truth, saying there were some people who didn't like him."

That struck Robinson as interesting. He made a '1' on his notebook, circled it.

"People who didn't like him?"

Thierry Sagnier

Josie's mouth was dry; she licked her lips, reached for her purse, foraged in it. She found the stick of balm, ran it around her mouth, and was struck by how silly it must look. She quickly capped it.

Robinson repeated, "People who didn't like him? Did he mention any names?"

Now she was shaking, couldn't control it anymore. There was a pounding between her ears like road construction. She made a conscious effort to pull herself together.

Had he? Josie couldn't think. Probably not, and if he had it wasn't the kind of thing she would remember. She forgot the names of people she saw every day, people who shared at the meetings, identified themselves, and clearly remembered *her*. It was embarrassing, one of the reasons she didn't like to hang around with the others after meetings. She looked down at her shoes, sighed, and shook her head.

"No. No names. Just people, he said. He only mentioned it once or twice, that there were some dudes who'd be happy to see him gone, that's all, I thought he was being, you know, like, dramatic or something, trying to impress me."

Detective Robinson nodded, looked sympathetic. She started speaking faster, and he let her ramble. Then, when she was drained, he encouraged her. They talked generalities, what Herbie was like, how long she'd known him, what they did when they were together. Did Herbie like movies, restaurants, nightclubs? Which ones? Did she know his friends well? How well?

Afterwards, he took her name down again and asked a lot of other questions, but she didn't have much to say, which made her realize how little she knew Herbie, even though they'd been together kind of a while. Then he inquired in a roundabout way whether she knew what Herbie did for a living. Josie said she didn't, though she had suspected it right from the start. The cop said, "He dealt drugs. You do drugs?"

Thirst

She'd wondered when the question was going to come. She shook her head, said "No," but there was no conviction to her voice.

She wasn't stupid, had figured out right from the start that Herbie wasn't in real estate like he claimed; he didn't know the difference between a rambler and a Victorian, and his friends were hardly the investor type. Herbie wasn't into anything taxable; he was too easy with money, always sprang and bought her little gifts on a whim. He had two cellular phones, a Blackberry, and a Platinum Amex. Secretly, she found it kind of exciting that he might be involved with drugs; she liked flirting with the dark but she'd never, not once, asked him to set her up. And Herbie, to his credit, had never used in front of her, though a couple of times at clubs he'd gone to the men's room and come back with glazed eyes. She said, "I do NA. You know. Narcotics Anonymous."

Detective Robinson opened his eyes a little wider. "Yeah? How long?"

"Almost a year."

He nodded again. "A year? Well, good. Good for you." He paused, closed his notebook, and placed it back in his pocket. "Got a brother in NA, but he never has managed more than four, five weeks. Did you do a rehab?"

She looked at him. The expression on his face had changed. Now it mirrored real interest, concern.

"Three times."

"Three? Last one took, I guess." He paused, smiled. "Well, good. Good for you," he said again. Then he sighed. His voice turned flat, sad. "My brother tried it. Ran away the second day."

Josie was tired. Her anger had vanished. There were things she hadn't said to Herbie yet, stuff they were supposed to talk about and laugh over and now he was dead. She closed her eyes, rubbed them with her thumb and index finger, trying to change the colors in there. "Yeah. That happens all the time. There was a girl who did that the last go-round. Ran away, I mean. Went straight to the Safeway, bought a gallon of burgundy and some Nyquil…"

He stood, reached out a hand for her. "I'm sorry about all this. I might have to call you, get more information. You sure you gave me the right number? I'm trusting you, now."

Josie took the hand, pulled on it to stand up. "What happened to Herbie, was it, you know, gross?"

The cop avoided her eyes and looked somewhere over her left shoulder. After a moment, he said, "Yeah. Yeah, it was."

"But it was, like, quick?"

She could tell by the way he hunched his shoulders and shuffled his feet for a moment or two that whatever he'd answer would be a lie.

He said, "Yeah. I think so. I think it was quick."

Josie expected to be taken to the station, that was how they did it on cop shows, but Detective Robinson didn't suggest it. Instead she rode the elevator down, found herself in the lobby of the building with people looking at her as if she'd done something. All the residents were there; word had spread quick that somebody'd been killed and the old lady retirees and stay-at-home wives, the janitor, guards, and doorman, the Chinese take-out driver and mailman, the delivery guy from the diaper service, all of them were talking in hushed tones, darting glances at her when they thought she wasn't looking. She was close to tears, had to get out of there.

She left the building, eyes straight ahead, not willing to give the biddies satisfaction. Out on the sidewalk, she searched through her purse for the emergency fifty she kept in the secret flap, but it wasn't there. She remembered Herbie had taken it a week before, saying he'd pay it back the very next day, but she hadn't seen him until three days later and by that time they'd both forgotten. So all she had was a couple of bucks, some change, and an ATM card, but there wasn't a bank in sight. She felt a tear slide down her cheek and wiped it away.

Thirst

Truth was, she'd gone to the apartment to break up with Herbie. She wasn't willing to admit it but that was it. She was going to bail, and now he had bailed first, most terminally, and it made her feel both cheated and sad.

She remembered an incident when she was a kid, when this woman neighbor who was mean and smelled like a musty closet had yelled at her for stepping on some flowers, and she'd wished right there and then for the old lady to die. And that night, the old lady did. Like Josie had willed it or something. And that was the way she felt right now, that perhaps in some weird strange way Herbie had been killed because she'd been so pissed off she almost *wanted* him dead.

That same night, back when she was a kid, she'd woken up yelling that it hadn't been her fault about the old lady, and her mother had come and held her for a long time, her breath all booze and minty cough drops. Her mother had told her to always be careful about wishing for things—they might come true. She hadn't thought about that for years.

&

The Zulu didn't like what he was hearing. It was his birthday. It should have been a good day. He had now lived forty-one years, as long as the most famous man ever to come out of Natal, and the two fools he was turning his back to were ruining it.

He closed his eyes, tried to focus on the voice of his great great grandfather. Sometimes the ancestor spoke with certain wisdom; most times his advice might have been good but was rendered useless by modern practicalities. This time the old warrior was silent.

Akim and Comfort were silent as well. They knew better than to plead their case, knew also that the Zulu's anger would quickly dissipate. They were family, kind of, and he was all in all a fair employer who on occasion would tolerate errors. They hoped this would be one of the occasions.

The Zulu said, "The van hit a bump?" He still had his back turned, refused to look at them.

The younger Nigerian nodded. "Yes, Dingane. The roads are very bad in Washington. Worse than in Lagos. It's a very poorly run city and…"

"And because it's a poorly run city," the Zulu interrupted, "the thief was killed, and he did not tell you what I needed to know." He paused. "I shall have to tell the mayor. I will tell His Honor that the roads he does not fix have cost me a million dollars. I'm sure he will understand and hasten to reimburse me. Tell me, Akim, do you think he will reimburse me?"

Akim, the younger man, did not respond. Any minute now, Dingane would say, "My great great grandfather…" And things would be all right.

The Zulu said, "My great great grandfather, who was a warrior under Shaka, would find this hard to believe. He would have you killed. Both of you. No ceremony. Or perhaps tortured you first."

The Zulu was a short man with a round head on which fit round features. He wore glasses and was partial to three-piece suits, one of which he had on tonight. He had unusually small feet, owned forty-two pairs of expensive shoes and a single piece of jewelry, a platinum and gold diamond ring on his right index finger. He was a full-fledged Zulu, and his great great grandfather had indeed been one of Shaka's lieutenants.

He was an educated man whose own father had believed a proper gentleman spoke the King's English and Molière's French, so as a child and adolescent the Zulu had been sent both to Paris and London to polish his language skills. In London, he had fallen in with some gamblers and in two nights lost his year's allowance. A

Thirst

week later he had discovered the cocaine trade and a month after that he was supplying students and gambling friends with the substance.

The money involved astounded him. The violence he dealt with quickly and with finality. He had killed four people to establish himself in London and had not enjoyed it. It was messy, dirty work and it soiled his clothes. But soon, the money he made allowed him to hire others to do the killing and he discovered to his surprise that Nigerians were generally efficient and cheap. Also superstitious, a trait he played upon by making them swear a "holy" oath that involved rituals of minor bloodletting. The ceremony made them brothers, he said, and he was the supreme brother, personally linked to the greatest African who had ever lived.

Once, in order to manifest his superiority, he had gathered his acolytes and, before their very eyes, slit the throat of a street dealer who had argued with him. The impact had been immediate; the Nigerians had fallen to their knees and sworn obedience. But the dying dealer had had the bad grace of showering great gouts of blood upon the Zulu's shirt, which the Zulu found disgusting.

He had been in the United States ten years now, five of them in Washington, where the demand was high and the police virtually powerless. He liked the city and enjoyed the museums and took art appreciation courses at Georgetown and George Washington Universities. He had made friends at the World Bank and International Monetary Fund. He had a couple of customers who worked there too. He still traded in cocaine brought back from Bolivia and Columbia by travelers bearing UN *laissez passers*, which were better than passports since they entitled the bearers to semi-diplomatic immunity. And he had discovered heroin was making a comeback. Herbie had been the go-between, the liaison. The Zulu had never, in his wildest dreams, imagined being robbed by someone like Herbie, but there it was. It wasn't even the money that mattered, he could afford a million or two, but the sheer gall of the dealer outraged him.

He turned to face the Nigerians. They both stood a bit straighter and pulled in their stomachs.

"So," he said, "now I have to think of something else, something the two of you will be able to do without bungling." He pulled down a short spear from a display on the wall, traced its point with a finger, and smiled.

"This is just like the weapon my great great grandfather employed. Isn't it a pretty thing?" He held up the *assegai* for the two men to see. The younger one leaned forward to admire it. The Zulu thrust once, wrenched up and sideways. The room was suddenly filled with a noxious smell. The Zulu held the spear at a forty-five degree angle—he was quite strong for his size—and watched as the eyes of the impaled man lost their glow. The older Nigerian reared back, made a moaning sound, the white around his own eyes like dinner plates. The Zulu gently lowered his trophy to the floor, inspected his shoes, and noted with satisfaction that this time the slaying had been cleanly done.

༄

When Josie came home she swept by her mother, but not quickly enough. Catherine saw her daughter's puffy face, red-rimmed eyes, and wasted mascara. She put a hand on Josie's shoulder but the girl shrugged it off, less in anger than in weariness. She said, "Oh, mom!" Catherine saw whirlpools of sadness in her daughter's eyes. She held on to the moment as long as she could but it was gone, she couldn't tell what was there now. Then Josie shook her head, mumbled, "It's not important. See you tomorrow." And went straight up the stairs and locked herself in her bedroom.

Chapter Two

Two days later there was a massive storm and three picnickers were swept away and drowned in Rock Creek, the generally timid stream that bisects Washington's northwest section. Trees planted up and down the major avenues snapped, sewers overflowed, and power lines fell. Colin Marsh's apartment was one of thousands in the Virginia suburbs darkened by a blackout. He was watching sheet lightning flare across the horizon when his phone rang. It was Orin G.

"Lights are out but the phones are still working. Is this a great country or what? Listen, I'm bored. TV's down and Martha's taking a nap. The woman could sleep through a carpet bombing. I haven't seen you for a while and generally when you don't want to see me, it means you should 'cause you got something on your mind. So come on over. Oh, and stop by Giant and get me some salami—thin-sliced Genoa."

Colin drove through the rain to his AA sponsor's house. The occasional one-on-ones were something Orin G had insisted upon before taking Colin on, and Colin seldom looked forward to them. Orin was not a friend, probably never would be; he'd been sponsoring Colin more than five years now and still their encounters were punctuated with long silences that made Colin uncomfortable, though Orin never seemed to mind. He just sat, overflowing his wheelchair, an ever-present glass of two-percent milk by his side.

Once Orin had stood more than six feet tall, but not anymore. His left leg had been amputated after a motorcycle accident when he was sixteen. His right leg had been taken off just above the knee fifteen years later when gangrene had set in after a month spent shooting speedballs in his inner thigh and between his toes with bad needles. After that, Orin started drinking. Eight years later on a bright Sunday afternoon he hit his personal bottom and wheeled his chair with himself in it onto the middle island of the Beltway just north of the Tyson's exit. Police cars surrounded him within minutes. He had a gun, a chrome plated Smith & Wesson with which he threatened the cops. A young officer shot him twice in the chest. Orin had shown Colin the scars, two hard, puckered nodes, one below each clavicle.

After he came out of the hospital he was charged with more offenses than the county judge had ever seen applied against one man at one time, and this had impressed the magistrate so much that he proposed a deal. Orin would go into a rehab for as long as necessary. After that he would live in a sober halfway house for an indeterminate amount of time, and he would go to at least one AA or NA meeting daily. He would personally see the judge each month at the judge's home. He would get counseling, learn to read and write properly, pass his high school equivalency, get a trade. Orin did all that and on the fifth anniversary of his sobriety, he married the judge's daughter.

Now he and Martha had three kids, and he spent most of his time on the front porch of the rancher they'd bought and equipped with hand rails and ramps.

THIRST

For all his accomplishments he was not a nice man. Colin found him loud, offensive, short-tempered, and rude to waiters. At restaurants, Orin didn't eat his food, he fought it. He was not above calling the shaky newcomers to AA assholes, and he had little tolerance for fools of any stripe or color. Political correctness did not exist at Orin's house.

The first thing he did after Colin got there was take the plastic bag of salami, open it, and roll two slices into his mouth. Then he asked, "You still fucking that rich lady?"

Colin ignored him. This was how Orin generally started their conversations.

"Guess you are, uh?" Orin nodded, looked smug. "Well, none of my business, I suppose, but when your dick falls off, don't bother bringing it here."

"Course," he thought it over, looked down at where his lap should have been, "considering my personal state of affairs, and the number of things that have dropped off *me*, I probably shouldn't be the one to talk…"

Every time they met, Colin had quickly noticed, Orin G. brought it up, as if maybe Colin hadn't noticed that Orin was legless.

Colin smiled. "You said it. I didn't."

"And you'd fuckin' better not either," Orin showed a mean smile. "You haven't earned the right.

"So," his face changed, became more tolerant. "Joe the Cop still your pigeon?"

"Saw him a couple of days ago. He's doing okay. Said I should paint my apartment. Putting the plug in the jug hasn't changed him."

Orin laughed, a dry brittle sound. "Joe's okay. Got the right idea, for a cop that is. He's been straight how long now?"

Colin thought for a moment, "Two years, a bit more."

"You working on anything now?"

Thierry Sagnier

Colin looked up, nodded. "Research for a writer who's doing a book on Washington in the twenties."

"Pay well?"

"Standard. Twenty-two an hour."

Orin made a sucking noise with his lips. "Not bad for staring at a screen and hanging around the library. How did the last book you worked on do?"

"Pretty well. The writer called me and said they were going into a second printing, then paperback."

Orin nodded again. "One of these days, I'll have to read some of that stuff." He'd been promising that for years.

This was Colin's work now, research. He was good at it, had learned his trade in the newsroom and writing The Book. It allowed him to do things at his own speed and by himself. He knew how to ferret out the snippets of information that changed a story from mundane to interesting. Ten steady writers wouldn't work without him, and his expertise over the years had become far-ranging. Cocteau, Haile Selassie, St. Exupery. The mating rites of gorillas. Silk weaving in Karnataka, the architecture of cyclotrons. Colin's name was in the acknowledgment section of a dozen books. He was on a first-name basis with every librarian in a twenty-square-mile area, a frequent visitor to the Archives, and privy to the secrets of the Library of Congress. He knew the National Zoo inside out and held a Smithsonian Associate card. On the whole, the work pleased him and paid adequately, though sometimes it was feast or famine. He enjoyed being self-employed, had toyed with the idea of setting up a small firm with two or three similarly bent individuals, then quickly given up the notion when he realized somebody would have to manage the work flow, and that the somebody would probably be him.

"That married woman you're seeing, she's got a daughter in the program?"

Thirst

Colin lowered himself onto the rocking chair Martha usually occupied. "Yeah, she does. Never seen her though. That's something Cat, Catherine and me, we agreed on. Her family doesn't get involved with this."

"And you're happy with that set up?"

Colin shrugged. "It works."

Orin went, "Hmmm." He reached into a bag strapped to the side of his wheelchair, withdrew a battered pipe and a pouch of Carter Hall tobacco. He filled the pipe with great deliberation, tamped the tobacco down with a dirty index finger, then lit it with a kitchen match and spewed out a great cloud of gray smoke.

"The reason I'm asking all this, Colin, is that you've gotten kinda isolated, lately. Stuff like that always worries me. You're out of sorts and I start wondering if maybe you're thinkin' about goin' out, doing a little more research out there? Your cross addiction workin' on you?"

Colin said, "No."

"You're mumbling."

Colin said "No" again, this time louder.

Orin nodded. "Well. I'm glad to hear that." He paused, puffed on his pipe. "So what's eatin' at you?"

It took a moment for Colin to answer. "Boredom, I think."

Orin laughed, puffed. "Like, you don't lead an interesting life? Like that?"

Colin stood, paced the porch. "I don't know. Sometimes it's like a closed circle, you know? Meetings. People at meetings. It's always the same stuff. 'I want to do this. I want to do that.' Drunks are amazingly boring, Orin. A lot of them don't have much of a life outside AA. I get tired of hearing about their hassles, about their relationships, about them wanting to drink or smoke or snort. I even get tired of hearing how happy they are that they're not drunks anymore. I don't care if their lives have gotten better. It never changes. Different people, same crappy stories." He paused, rubbed his face with his hands. "And then suddenly you realize it's a different generation at meetings. Whole bunch of kids, and it starts all over again. It gets tiring..."

Orin thought that over but not too strenuously. "You're obviously not going to the same meetings I'm going to. Or not talking to the same people. Most of the ones I see, they've got some hope back, they think they're better off now. Mind you, that shit is just as boring as the tales of woe and tragedy, but at least they've got kind of a happy ending. Why're you hearing only the crappy stuff, Colin? Last time you felt like this, you ended up getting into some really deep shit. Remember?"

Colin did.

"Correct me if I'm wrong," Orin continued. "I remember we had this little talk, oh, about six, seven months ago, and I told you to start going to more meetings and doing service work. Answer phones, drive people around, make coffee, whatever. And instead, you got involved with Stan and DD. And the only reason you've still got both your balls was that DD didn't know it was a starter pistol. If she'd had the real thing, we'd be calling you Lefty."

Colin held up a hand. "It wasn't like that. Stan asked."

"Oh bullshit." Orin looked disgusted, sucked hard on his pipe, stuck out his tongue, and spat a small piece of tobacco.

"You didn't have any business being involved in any of that mess. Everyone knows DD's a slut, including Stan. And Stan! Fifty-two year old man thinking he found the fountain of youth, screwing a nineteen—year-old bimbo who's not even sober a month..."

Colin sat down again. In the kitchen, he could hear Martha humming a tune, something from the sixties by Judy Collins. He said, "They were married three weeks, she files for divorce, tries to take his house and car away from him. That's fair?"

THIRST

Orin gave Colin a pig-eyed stare. "Fair ain't got squat to do with this, Colin. You ain't a divorce investigator! Sneaking around in the middle of the night trying to catch that little slut with Billy O. She *should* have shot you in the balls, would have gotten what you deserved. Lucky thing Billy O's a fool and he bought that pistol thinking it was the real thing. Cause if DD had...oh, never mind."

The screen door opened and Martha came out bearing a plate of sandwiches on a tray and a bottle of Shasta ginger ale.

She smiled at Colin. "You getting Orin all excited about something?"

She was a tall, sparse woman whose sharp features belied her kindness. Colin had rarely seen her without a smile, but when she didn't have one he was reminded of an American Gothic farmwife. "Don't get his blood pressure up, now. He's mean enough as is."

"We were talking about Stan and DD," Orin said.

Martha's face narrowed in distaste. "Oh. Them." She set the plate of sandwiches down, looked at Colin, "They deserved each other, those two. DD, I wouldn't credit her with much sense. But Stan? I thought he was smarter than that." Her lip curled. "Men."

Later Orin wanted to go out and eat some spaghetti. "Sometimes," he said, "I feel like Martha's a warden. 'Watch your blood pressure. Don't get excited, it's bad for you.' Once, we were screwing, she says, 'Take it easy, you'll hurt yourself.' Jesus. Woman says something like that, it ain't inspiring Melts your hard-on, believe me."

A perfect reason to have spaghetti.

Colin drove the ramp-equipped van, a $65,000 custom job with hand controls. Orin hated the thing and never drove it. It reminded him of his handicap. "You know what else really pisses me off? Sometimes, when she's talking to some of her friends on the phone and she thinks I can't hear, she says I'm 'physically challenged.' Fuck. There ain't no *challenge* for Chrissake. I don't have any legs? What the fuck is challenging about that?"

Thierry Sagnier

At the restaurant Orin had the special, fought the food battle and won, emptied his third cup of coffee. Colin admired the hundred little spots the tomato sauce made on Orin's shirt. He thought it looked like a star map. Orin belched, wiped his lips, said, "I really wish you weren't screwing that woman, Colin. I'm being serious now. I've known you a real long time. She's gonna get you into a shitload of trouble. Don't ask me how I know, but I know."

CHAPTER THREE

Johnny D. did what he was told. It had to do with his lifestyle, which he liked and wanted to maintain. Yes, he had given up booze. Yes, he had given up doping. Yes, he had every intention of staying straight. But that didn't mean he wanted to give up all the other things he enjoyed, like hanging out late at clubs and getting up at noon, like his car, like not working a nine-to-five like the schmoes and getting paid peanuts. So when the Zulu called and asked for a favor, Johnny D. said, "Yeah, sure. No problem."

And it wasn't, not really. He knew the girl, and if the Zulu wanted him to bring her over, he would. On the drive to her house, while zipping through the white Northern Virginia neighborhoods, he managed to persuade himself that the Zulu wouldn't harm her, and this made him feel a little less guilty. She was a nice white girl, cute, trying really hard to stay clean, and that was good. The $500 the Zulu promised was even better.

Thierry Sagnier

⁂

The eight-thirty meeting was crowded. Of the thirty or so people around the room, Colin recognized only one person, a gaunt woman with ruined eyes. The guest speaker's topic was sponsorship. Asked to share, Colin said, "What gets me, pisses me off more often than I'm willing to admit, is that my sponsor is right a lot of times. Like he has a crystal ball and my immediate future is transparent to him. I can't bullshit him and that upsets me. That's what I do as an alcoholic, bullshit. It's what I've always done. And the worst part is I don't even really *like* my sponsor."

He noticed that the gaunt woman smiled slightly. She knew Orin. After the meeting ended she approached Colin and said, "I know where you're at. I can't *stand* my sponsor. She's a Goddamned Nazi. But that's not the issue. Keep that in mind." As she walked away, she turned around, added, "But Orin, yeah, he's a particularly nasty sonofabitch."

⁂

Catherine thought she heard the front door slam, but wasn't entirely sure. It was either very late at night or very early in the morning, she didn't pay much attention to it; sleep had been hard to come by and harder to give up. She'd been to two women's meetings that day, and the intensity of the second one had left her exhausted. There were horrible things happening to women out there, events crowded in such emotional and physical violence that the stuff on her mind was inconsequential in comparison. One woman was just out of the hospital, and her husband—a small brutish man with a heroin habit—had beaten her with the mean end of a hammer, broken her nose, split her upper lip. Catherine herself had never faced such a

Thirst

thing—all Lars did was ignore her; pretty benign behavior, really, more infuriating than anything else.

When Josie didn't come down, Catherine thought nothing of it. The girl often left early, her movements largely unaccounted for. When she didn't hear from Josie and the girl didn't come home that night, Catherine began to get seriously worried. They had a deal. Josie had to sleep at home no matter what. The agreement had been forced on her daughter and signed and witnessed at the end of the last rehab by a counselor. Josie had bitched, moaned, and once or twice tested the limits by returning at the break of dawn, but she'd never, not once during the last year, spent the whole night out.

At noon, Catherine called Lars at his office and got nothing from him but an irate reminder that she wasn't supposed to disturb him there.

In Josie's room she found an address book and methodically started dialing numbers. A lot of them were bad, disconnected, no answer. A few had voicemail. Most entries were first name only and the people she managed to reach had very young voices and weren't overly interested in her daughter's whereabouts, though they promised to pass the message if they ran into her. A few didn't even know her daughter, or pretended not to. She left several messages asking for callbacks.

By five that afternoon Catherine was frantic.

Nothing meaningful was gone from Josie's room; the small possessions the girl would never willingly part with were still there: the stuffed turtle and one-eyed plush rabbit that had accompanied Josie to rehab, the Chinese jade necklace she seldom wore but treasured, the not-so-secret sixty-dollar stash in her left cowboy boot.

Catherine sat in the kitchen, picked up the phone, dialed 911, and hung up before anyone could answer. She couldn't call the police. What if Josie was dealing again? What if she'd gotten herself in trouble? She was nineteen now, an adult. She might be sentenced, taken away from Catherine, and imprisoned. They'd make an example of her. Nice white girl, see? Just to prove to you that everyone is treated equal under the law, we're going to nail her.

Catherine wouldn't be able to tolerate that. Three times Josie had gone away to treatment centers and three times Catherine had died a little, wondering who would be returning, her daughter or some stranger living in Josie's skin, sleeping in Josie's bed.

She dialed her husband's office number again, heard the phone ring three times, heard, "Hi, I can't come to the phone right now, but if you'll leave a message…" She didn't, hung up. Lars would tell her she was being dramatic, reading catastrophes where none existed. Then he would get angry, sermonize, justify his reactions, and hang up.

She poured a glass of ginger ale, added ice, sipped without tasting. She wanted her daughter back. Safe, sheltered, in her arms. She wanted to tuck Josie into bed and read her a story. She wanted time to reverse itself or at least to stop. She stared out the window, seeing blurry trees and blurry grass. She prayed with a fervor that almost frightened her, willing her thoughts into God's ear. She glanced at the clock. Time hadn't stopped.

Chapter Four

Colin let the phone ring. He was awash in sweat, the veins on his arms reliefed like summer vines. Sitting, his back pressed hard against the vinyl of the bench, he counted a slow three seconds up, pause, then three seconds down. The air hissed through his nose, gushed out of his mouth, the dumbbell rising in a methodical 180 degree arc that ended just short of the shoulder.

The work-out gloves he wore had once been white but now were almost black with use, the wrist straps gray; he never washed them, it was an article of faith. When he finished fifteen reps on each arm, he dropped the fifty-pounders, picked up the thirties, and started over. It hurt, a kind of welcome and friendly ache, a warm pain.

The phone chimed again and stopped after three rings. He adjusted the bench, lay on his back, held the thirty-pounders straight out, and let them sink to the floor. His arms extended, up and up, meeting over his forehead with a dull clink. Twenty minutes later when the phone broke his concentration for the third time, he dropped the weights and said, "Shit!" then answered it.

"It's Catherine. I'm downstairs. Can I come up?"

Thierry Sagnier

※

She said, "I was afraid maybe you had a woman up here. That would have been embarrassing."

He motioned her in, shut the door. "Slim chance of that. I don't think watching a man push large weights around would be particularly stimulating."

She smiled very briefly, nodded once, said, "Josie's gone."

"As in Josie-your-daughter?"

A look of annoyance shimmered across her face. Colin saw it, added, "I've never met her or seen her, Cat, and you don't mention her that often."

She shrugged. "Yeah. That's true. Sorry." She gathered herself, looked around the apartment briefly. "She's gone. Didn't come home last night, and that's something she hasn't done since rehab. She didn't take anything with her. She's just…gone."

Colin saw she had more to say. "And?"

"And I'm really worried. I didn't know who to talk to."

"What about Lars?"

She shot him a dry look. "Lars?"

"Never mind."

There was an awkward silence. "You're going to make me beg, Colin?"

He turned from her, walked to the kitchen, busied himself there. She followed him.

"I know you've done things for people before, Colin. Program people. Everybody knows that. With DD and Stan…"

"That wasn't quite the same, Cat."

She nodded. "I know that. But still. Colin, I don't know what to do…" Her face fell apart. He moved to her, felt her shoulders

Thirst

shaking beneath his hands, led her to the couch. "Start from the beginning, Cat. How do you know she's really missing?"

Catherine fished a Kleenex from her purse, blew her nose noisily and wiped her eyes. "I *know*. I just know." She balled the tissue in her hand, looked for a place to dispose it. Colin took it from her.

"When she was a little kid, maybe three years old, I took her to a shopping center and one moment she was there, and the next she *wasn't*. I knew in the pit of my stomach that something terrible would happen if I didn't find her fast. Mother's intuition, whatever. So I had the security guards help me, and it took maybe fifteen minutes but it felt like a lifetime; they didn't believe me, kept saying she must have wandered away, but I knew she hadn't. She'd been *taken*, Colin. I can't explain how I was certain of that." She paused, blew her nose again.

"And I was *right*! You know where they found her? Some deranged woman had just taken her by the hand when I wasn't looking for less than a second and locked her in her car in the back of the parking lot. And you know what this crazy woman said? She said she'd gone shopping, wanted to buy some English muffins—I'll never forget that—and when she saw Josie she just thought she'd take her home too. But then when she got to her car, she realized she'd forgotten the muffins! So she had to go back because that's why she went shopping in the first place—for the muffins. That's the only reason I got Josie back, because this crazy woman forgot her Goddamned *muffins*."

She shook her head. "I swear a part of me died that day, Colin. And sometimes I still wonder if maybe deep down Josie remembers that, thinks maybe I was trying to give her away or something. And maybe that's why she's the way she is, addicted I mean. Because she thought I didn't care enough to not let her be taken by a crazy woman."

Thierry Sagnier

She stopped, took a long breath. "So that's how I *know*. I'm feeling exactly the same thing now as I did then. Something bad has happened to her, Colin, and I wouldn't be here if I had any other option, believe me. Really. I wouldn't involve you if there was another way."

"You could call the cops, tell them she's missing."

She shook her head. "No. I can't. I…" She fluttered her hands nervously.

"They're used to stuff like that, finding people."

She shook her head again, this time more emphatically. "No. You don't understand. *I don't know what she's been doing!*"

Colin nodded. "Sorry. I wasn't thinking."

"She's been busted before. She's a grown-up now. They won't just send her to rehab. They'll take her away if she's been…involved with drugs again." Catherine paced the room, short choppy steps. "I want to trust her; I want to think she'd never get in trouble again. She's my daughter, for God's sake! But above everything she's an addict, Colin, and addicts lie and steal and do stuff…you know all about that. We all do. I call the police, they find her, maybe she *is* dealing. What happens then? I couldn't bear that, Colin, I simply couldn't."

"What about Lars?"

"Forget Lars. He won't help. He disowned us a long time ago."

Colin turned to the leg machine, started to remove the forty-five pound plates, made three careful stacks, said, "Okay."

Catherine bowed her head, nodded. "Thank you. I knew you would."

She fished in her purse, removed an envelope, took a photo from it and handed it to him. "That's her high school yearbook picture. She was in the tenth—no, eleventh—grade."

Long blonde hair, green eyes, Catherine's mouth. The girl was staring frankly at the camera, the corners of her lips raised just short of a smile, as if she found the event vaguely amusing. She wore a white blouse buttoned to the neck.

"She looks familiar."

Catherine canted her head. "Really? She doesn't go to your meetings, at least I don't think so."

"I probably would have remembered her if it were that. No. Maybe I saw her at a store or something. Anyway. That's the most recent photo?"

Catherine's forehead wrinkled. "That's the one I like best. She looks, you know, innocent. And yes, as far as I know. We haven't taken many pictures lately. There hasn't been that many festive occasions in our family recently."

Colin peered at the picture. "It's strange. I'm sure I know her, maybe even spoke with her, but I can't place it. Can I keep it? I'll call Joe."

"Joe the Cop? I told you—"

"Joe will do it discreetly, nothing official, just ask around the station, see if anyone's heard anything. If he has, we'll take it from there. One step at a time, Cat. Just like everything else."

෨

Joe the Cop said of course he'd help, he liked that kind of thing and was good at it. He'd met Catherine once at Colin's apartment, had found her an interesting lady and asked Colin if she was single. She wasn't, so his curiosity had faded somewhat but not entirely.

Yes, he would keep his inquiries discreet. A lot of people— mostly cops but also a fair amount of street scum—owed him, and he'd put the word out as quietly as possible about the missing girl.

Thierry Sagnier

%%

At the Zulu's house, things were not going well. Comfort Okwuike thought the Zulu had over-reacted. A warning would have sufficed; there'd been no call for that great bloody display of power and vengeance. The Zulu was a sick man.

True, Akim had not been very smart, but then Akim had *never* been very smart, even as a small boy in the village he had never shown the least propensity for anything original or unusual. Comfort remembered Akim's mother, his sister's husband's first cousin, holding the boy in her lap, pointing at his head and shaking her own. "This one, I don't know about," she'd said. "Monkey ears, thin lips. Bad signs."

Now Akim was dead, split open like a goat before the Ramadan feast. He hadn't suffered, or at least not much. Comfort had seen a lot of death in his time, babies and children and women and men, many of whom had died very slowly, life refusing to relinquish its hold, so he thought Akim was lucky, sort of. Comfort's job had been to divide Akim's body into several pieces, which he packaged in Saran Wrap and plain brown shopping bags and placed carefully in twelve dumpsters. Akim's head had been remarkably heavy, which made Comfort wonder about the relationship between weight and intelligence.

Comfort had cleaned out Akim's room in the basement of the Zulu's house. Akim's collection of pornographic magazines showing large black males with tiny white women had made Comfort uncomfortable. He had also discovered several vibrating phalluses in Akim's closet—some were huge, beyond human comprehension or tolerance—and that had worried him most of all. What if the young woman had found them? He'd thrown the nasty things away, saving the batteries.

Thirst

The girl was now in Akim's former room. Comfort checked on her every fifteen-or-so minutes, though there was no real reason to. She was nodding out, her eyes glazed, unseeing. It made her much less pretty than she'd been just hours ago when she was first brought in. The Zulu had personally lit the pipe, slapped her three times sharply on the stomach to force her to inhale, and that was that. The girl struggled but not that much, not like she really meant it, sucked on the pipe a few more times and when the drug connected, her muscles went flat.

Comfort didn't like crack, wrinkled his nose whenever the sharp tang of the burning crystals reached him. He was perplexed by the whys and the whos of the substance. There was something disconcerting about so many once-young people willing and eager to perform indescribably evil things simply to get enough of the substance for a day, for an hour. The way it transformed its users amazed him; there had certainly never been anything like that during his own childhood. People drank ginger beer or stronger beverages if they could afford them. They got drunk. They sang. They shouted. They smoked *khat*. They fell asleep. and occasionally they fought. But they seldom became slack-jawed. They didn't drool. They didn't become old in months.

Sitting in his room in the Zulu's basement, Comfort thought about all this and it made him vaguely unhappy. He liked to live up to his name. He stood, kneeled next to his bed, squirreled a hand beneath the mattress, retrieved the small black book hidden there, and opened it. The coded numbers reassured him. $57,327 in the bank of Ibadan, soon almost twenty times that in other accounts across Europe. A fortune, a legacy. In a short time there would be servants and a young wife. There would be a small house with a red roof and three or four or five children bearing his name and resemblance. There would be a vegetable patch in the backyard where he would grow yams and carrots. When he closed his eyes he could see his face in such a setting, smell his contentment. He could picture his smile and almost feel the weight of a first-born boy on his lap. The Zulu had promised that Comfort could return home in a few months, had hinted at a sizable going-away bonus. Not that the Zulu's generosity mattered much anymore. Comfort would call his house Sunrise. He had seen the name on a retirement home outside Washington and liked it. In a few months he would return to sanity and never again leave it behind.

ℰ

When she came out of it she did so slowly. She knew immediately what had happened. She'd done crack before just to see what it was like, and of course she hadn't gotten hooked. That was a suburban bullshit belief that one time got you addicted. But it had felt the same, a great lightness suffusing her body, an absence of anxiety, a feeling that things were as they should be everywhere but especially within herself. Except that the roof of her mouth was so dry she thought it would peel off, and her eyes felt gritty. That was the same too.

Josie looked around, not so much frightened as curious. A windowless room, cheap fake pine paneling on the walls, dim light above. She was in a beanbag chair, black, not leather, maybe plastic or the stuff they made car seat covers from. She wondered why Johnny D. had left in such a hurry. Why had he taken her to this place? He was gay, so it wouldn't be a sex thing. There had to be another reason. She didn't know what time it was.

Johnny D. had called and told her he needed to see her. She knew him from the meetings; he'd given her rides home before. In retrospect, he'd sounded kind of weird but with someone like Johnny D., weird was just a word; the guy was off the scale dawn to dusk.

Thirst

In the car he was hyper, more so than usual, grinning like an idiot, not at all cool, but she hadn't paid much attention to it. The fact that Herbie was truly, truly gone was finally edging into her reality. She'd never known anyone who'd been killed, not if you didn't count a couple of druggies and a friend in the fifth grade who had died with her parents in a car accident. She wasn't paying much attention to where Johnny D. was driving, either, but it took a long time and after a while they were in a part of town she'd never seen, on a wide, dirty avenue with boarded up storefronts. She asked, "Where are we?"

Johnny D. kept his eyes on the road. Whenever they were about to hit a red light, he slowed the car a long time before the intersection so he never had to come to a full stop.

"Anacostia," he said. "Man, I don't like it here. Not at all. Look at this," he pointed to the side. "Can't even fix the Goddamned streetlights, and then they wonder about crime and shit." The street was dark and almost shadowless. "Bunch of assholes…"

She nodded. She wasn't focusing; life had thrown her one bad curve. Herbie'd been offed. That's how they said it in the police novels. Offed.

She was half-listening to an old reggae tune on the car radio, UB-40 or someone like that, when Johnny D. came to a full stop, jumped out, opened her door, and hurried her up the front steps of a clapboard house. She had no idea where she was. The notion flashed by that maybe he'd taken her to a party to raise her spirits, but that went away fast when she saw two black guys step out of the house. Johnny said, "Here she is," accepted a bunch of bills, and turned and sprinted back to the car. The tires screamed in his hurry to get away.

She got scared, pee-in-your-pants scared. The two black guys didn't look threatening, but they weren't friendly either. She clutched at her purse, fingers nervously working the clasp.

Thierry Sagnier

There was a tall one and a round one; the tall one was older and had kinder eyes. Together they reminded her of early morning Laurel and Hardy cartoons, except the cartoon guys were white and these guys weren't.

The round one nodded to the tall one. The tall one nodded to her and opened the door to the house. "Come in. Please. You won't be harmed."

Not much choice there. The living room was dingy, with lots of leather, which she immediately thought as tacky. Not that long ago but before Herbie, Josie had spent a single night with a man who had a leather couch. She thought he was kind of cool until she saw his furniture, but by then it was too late to back out. It would maybe have created problems; the guy was pretty insistent. They'd screwed on the leather couch. It had been mercifully quick, but her back and butt had stuck there and made her feel all clammy. And then the guy had complained that she'd left stains on the leather, and that was just about all she remembered about that particular gomer, his sticky couch.

She sensed this wouldn't be about screwing, and it made her more nervous. Screwing she could handle, had been doing so since she was fifteen.

She hesitated a second and the round black guy said, "Comfort never lies, Miss Stilwell. Please do come in. You'll be quite safe."

So she did. The round black guy said, "I would have invited your friend Johnny to join us, but he was in a hurry. Have you noticed gay people are always in a hurry? As if their perversions leave them no time? No?" He was both pleased by his own observation and disappointed in her lack of response.

"At any rate, I'm glad we have a mutual friend. It makes things much easier. Now"—he gestured her toward the couch—"all I need is a bit of information from you, and then Comfort will see you home. Door-to-door service, I promise."

Thirst

Josie looked at the couch and sat on it with misgivings. The round man had a British accent, so she knew he wasn't a local. She said, "This is about Herbie, isn't it?" Her voice came out squeaky, not at all as she wanted it to. She cleared her throat and tried again. "Herbie's dead, you know."

She noticed that the tall black man was staring at his shoes. The round black man nodded. "Sadly, I do know. A tragedy, but not an uncommon one for men in his line of work." He moved to sit next to her. She squirmed to one end of the couch. He looked slightly offended.

"You, on the other hand, are alive, Miss Stilwell. For which I'm eternally thankful, I might add." He smiled. Josie noticed he had very white teeth. She saw his eyes weren't smiling, as if the man's face was made up of two entirely different parts that only matched haphazardly. She said, "I really don't know anything about that."

The man's smile remained fixed. "Of course you do, Miss Stilwell. The detective you spoke to, Mr. Robinson, isn't it? He told you what the unfortunate Herbie did for a living. Or maybe he didn't offer the necessary details. Herbie, you see, worked for me."

☙

Josie looked at the men. It was important to keep things together, in perspective, as her mom would say. In rehab, particularly the inner city one she'd hated and sat through mostly silent, she'd learned never to back down in front of a black guy. A black guy himself had told her that. "They see you flinch, you be meat." A simple piece of advice, but she'd abided by it since.

She sat up straight, said, "And who might you be?" God, that sounded ridiculous, probably real nervy coming from a white chick with no visible means of escape, but there it was, out of her mouth almost before she realized it. The round black guy pointed to the other man and said, "That is Comfort. He works for me as well. My name is Dingane. Perhaps Herbie mentioned me?"

Josie shook her head.

"Or perhaps he mentioned the Zulu? A lot of my associates refer to me by that name."

That rang a vague bell, but Josie couldn't tell where. There was a movie, one of those things shown late in the night, bunch of black guys wearing animal skins charging down a hill and mostly getting killed. She'd seen it some months ago, hadn't found it particularly interesting. She shrugged. "Sorry." There was a little quaver in her voice.

The round black guy must have picked it up. "Don't be frightened, please. I suppose that in spite of his many faults, our late friend Herbie at least knew how to keep his mouth shut. Which all in all is a good thing." He shrugged, withdrew a small rectangular box from a pocket, took out a cigarette, lit it with a gold lighter that looked heavy. Josie watched him do it, wanted to stand silent but blurted out, "Did you kill him?" And knew immediately it was the wrong thing to say.

The round black guy sucked in his gut, tried to sit a bit taller. "I certainly did not. There was no need to resort to violence, absolutely none. Violence is a tool only fools abuse."

But the other black guy, the taller one, got an evasive look in his eyes, grew smaller under the Zulu's gaze. Josie wondered why. She shrugged. "Whatever."

There was a pause, a silence, then the Zulu said, "Well, let's get down to business, Miss Stilwell. Where are my drugs?"

Josie thought he said "rugs" but wasn't sure. The Zulu did have a funny accent, kind of British but not really. She said, "Your what?"

He repeated. "Drugs. As in heroin. China White, to be exact. As in, a lot of heroin that your late boyfriend, Herbie, stole from me,

Thirst

which accounted for his unfortunate accident, though I am not to blame. Where is it?"

She said, "I don't know what you're talking about. Really."

The Zulu's face turned sad. He said, "Oh my." Then he walked into an adjoining room and returned with a wooden box, a cigar box, Josie thought. He opened it, withdrew a glass object that was all too familiar. She'd seen people in the street stroke such pipes, scrape them clean for residue, wrap them in small squares of felt or chamois. She'd seen people cry and plead and, in one instance, fight with insane determination over such pipes. She even had one stashed at home, had bought it just to be cool, which looking back was pretty silly. She should have gotten rid of it but it was well hidden; if she ever got home she'd trash it.

The Zulu uncorked a tiny vial, carefully placed a crystal into the pipe's bowl, lit it without inhaling, and thrust it at Josie's face. She turned her head. At a nod from the Zulu, the tall black guy took Josie's head in two large hands, held it still, and squeezed beneath her cheekbones. Her jaw popped open. The Zulu stuck the stem of the pipe in and slapped her sharply just above her stomach. She gasped and took it in. Then did it again. Then did it a third time.

∞

When she came down fully from the sweetness and light—it may have been hours but perhaps only minutes—the jarring suddenness of the need hit her, and she first felt the crawling in her stomach. She remembered something she'd been told after a meeting, a phrase that hadn't made much sense at the time. It had been an old guy, in his sixties at least, a former jazz sax player who still had an eye for young blondes, so she hadn't paid much attention. He'd sucked hard on his Tareyton, exhaled, breathed, and said, "While you're trying to live a normal life, your addiction is in the next room doing pushups."

And a counselor in her first rehab had said, "Your disease picks up where it left off."

And countless people who'd relapsed had told her, "It took me years to build my habit the first time; it only took days the second time around."

Now it made sense. She felt a gnawing in her gut, like something trying to chew its way out. She remembered the sensation, dreaded what she knew was coming. Her innards twisted. The tips of her fingers twitched, felt numb. Her lungs were raw. She sat cross-legged on the floor, Indian-style, very still, eyes closed. Her forehead started sweating. She tried to recite program mantras but the words took flight. With the tip of her tongue she could feel the warm smoothness of the glass pipe's stem. She bit her tongue. The pain brought a moment of clarity but no more. Her mouth went dry and she gathered enough saliva to swallow just once. She gagged, coughed, felt like throwing up, and mustered every gram of willpower not to do so. Then the cycle started again. After a nauseating eternity, the Zulu came into the room, smiled, said, "Can we talk?"

Chapter Five

He had come into the room—what? Three, four times? Each time he fed her the pipe. Once, he said, "Do you like this? It's a new compound, somewhat experimental but very potent, they tell me. Apparently, the effects are immediate but rather short-lived, as such things go. Unfortunate for the users, of course, but quite lucrative to everyone else. Now," he smiled. "Have you remembered anything? Anything at all?"

Truly, she hadn't. Herbie, his death, stolen drugs. To the depths of her being she didn't know what the black man wanted from her. It was terribly important that she somehow communicate that very basic fact to the Zulu. It was essential. It was life.

In the darkness between the Zulu's visits, she filtered thoughts, impressions, memories. She reviewed every instant spent with Herbie, every moment she could recall. Time became liquid.

The taller black guy—Comfort, what a wonderful name—brought her food, an Italian sub that she picked the onions and pickles out of. She didn't want to eat, wasn't hungry at all, but Comfort stood by until she did.

The beanbag chair became home. Once, she threw up on it. Comfort must have been just outside the door and heard the retching sounds she made; he came with a bucket and some rags, cleaned the mess up, and took her to a bathroom. She peed, stripped, and cleaned herself as best she could in the sink. Comfort took her soiled clothes away so she wrapped herself in the damp towel she'd used and returned to the beanbag chair.

She wondered how her mom was reacting to her disappearance, felt guilty over the panic she was causing. And her father? Was he concerned, worried? Probably not. She could visualize his face, his hands, his frown, downturned lips shaping disgust and disbelief. She wondered if her mom had ever used crack.

No. They'd talked about drugs and alcohol many times and there were few secrets there, though many in other areas of both their lives. Her mom had dabbled with the stuff people took in the seventies and eighties, dope of course, hash, acid. Coke a time or two, but it had scared her. Josie remembered the conversation well. Her mom had said, "It felt *too* good. You understand what I'm saying? Anything that felt that good had to demand a heavy price. It couldn't possibly come free and that scared me, the idea that somewhere down the line I'd have to pay up."

Crack hadn't even been invented then, had it?

Josie wondered if her parents had called the police, decided they probably hadn't. Had her Dad ever tried drugs? Had that ever tempted him? She'd seen him slightly drunk a number of times, a jolly smiling man too quick with the embraces, a man who got very red in the face after a third martini. Drugs and he were unlikely. Still, she'd been in the program long enough to realize that the straightest-looking, most normal people often rode their addictions to the meanest bottoms. It was the pale, bookish types who had the worst stories, the ones full of violence and theft and betrayal.

Thirst

Her thoughts meandered back to Herbie. Dead Herbie, whom the Zulu claimed had told her things she couldn't remember but eventually would.

It struck her in an idle way that she would probably be dead very soon too. If the Zulu found out what he wanted to know, that would be that, he wouldn't keep her around, certainly wouldn't release her. And if she didn't know, couldn't tell him anything, the result would be the same. The thought had a certain appeal. In her mind she'd seen her own death hundreds of times, had created endless scenarios. During her rehabs, it had helped while away the silent hours and come to term with things, this vision and understanding of death. How would they do it? She hoped for an overdose. That would be best, too much of a good thing. After a while the cravings returned and she thought of nothing else.

Sunlight didn't penetrate the basement. She might have been down there maybe a day, maybe two, but it could have been less or more.

The Zulu knew when to appear with a fresh dose. He would sit across from her on a footstool and play with the crack vials, tapping two against each other so they made a glassine sound, like muted wind chimes. He'd hand her the pipe and light it, she'd suck at it greedily. He'd ask the same questions over and over again. He had patience, never raised his voice, never threatened her. He would stay a few moments and then stand, straighten the crease in his trousers, and walk away.

∞

"What if she has nothing to tell us?" Comfort asked.

The Zulu thought about it for a moment, smiled. "She does. She perhaps doesn't know it, but she does." He paused, scratched his head, smiled again. "Because the late Herbie was not a stupid man. I know this. I hired him and, with few exceptions," he gave Comfort a sidelong look, "I have not been known to hire fools.

"With that amount of money, Herbie would have, what do they call it with computers? A back door? Yes. A back door, someone he could trust to get the money for him should he be unable to. Herbie had no family. Few friends. No one he could really trust, save of course Miss Stilwell. And he would want to boast. But Herbie was a paranoid man. All good drug dealers are, so his trust would only go so far. He would tell her, but without telling her. It's really very simple, if you think about it." The Zulu looked quite pleased with himself. Comfort less so.

৯

She thought it odd, interesting, somehow right that it would end this way. For so many years drugs had been her life, her joy and nemesis. Fighting their pull had been the hardest thing she'd ever done, and she'd never actually won, not really. She hardly remembered life before drugs. She'd been victorious in a few battles but had lost the war, no sense pretending otherwise, and what was occurring now was truly beyond her control. She hadn't wanted this, hadn't looked for it; it had just happened, an evil, wasted miracle. She spent minutes or hours wondering if, left on her own, she would have stayed away. In Greek mythology class she'd read about the sirens' call, and this was truly hers; it was her karma. Kind of like a Buddhist thing. She'd read about that too.

They'd left her purse after searching it, and when she became bored she took everything out and lined it up on the floor. Not much to show for a life: some spare change, a tube of lipstick, some

THIRST

Clearasil. Eight bucks, three singles, and a five in her wallet. A credit card, driver's license, ATM card.

In the bottom of the purse she found the charm bracelet Herbie had given her when they'd visited Baltimore Harbor. They'd taken pictures. Herbie had a new digital camera he wanted to try out, a tiny Nikon that fit in the palm of her hand. The bracelet wasn't an expensive thing, plain silver links with a clasp and a single charm, silver as well, a tiny ship he'd bought her with the bracelet.

She stared at it. Used her teeth to separate the ship from the bracelet. Squeezed it between the palms of her hands until it hurt. She peered at it, saw it wasn't really that well made. There was a visible line the long way down the middle, and she supposed that had happened when they stamped the piece in Korea or wherever it came from.

She stuck it in her mouth, bit down, felt the slightest give. Now there was the imprint of her molars on the hull. She wished she were on a ship, somewhere on a bright clean sea where the wind would whip at her skin and leave it feeling tight and good. At the harbor in Baltimore where Herbie had bought the bracelet, there'd been a big ship, one of those boats that circled the world and stopped at interesting tropical places where friendly natives sold trinkets to the tourists and smiled a lot. Herbie had hired a limo to drive them to Baltimore that day. He didn't have a license, said he hated driving, and the black chauffeur had taken a photo of them with the new camera, she sitting on the hood of the car, Herbie next to her, the tourist ship visible in the distance. She had few mementos, didn't believe in the past very much, but Herbie had had a print enlarged and framed and given it to her so she'd kept it. It had been an almost perfect day, but now it belonged to a different lifetime and a different person.

Chapter Six

"We have a small problem," said the captain's mistress to the captain.

Captain Roderick Stuart looked up. As always, he was charmed by the sight of her. She was deeply tanned, but the sun had not ravaged her skin. He knew from having watched her that she adhered to a nightly discipline of applying three different moisturizers, skin scrubs, and a thick coat of mud from the Dead Sea where the scrolls had been discovered. Her hair was thick and auburn, tied back at the nape of her neck with a bow. Captain Stuart smiled, pulled her down so she was sitting on his lap. "And what would that be?"

"A couple of hookers."

"Again?" Lately it seemed every single cruise was beset by them. Captain Stuart remembered earlier days when this was not so.

"I already called the home office," said his mistress. "They did some checking and just got back to me." She waved a sheet of fax paper in front of him. "I wouldn't have bothered you with it but you are, after all, the captain."

It pleased him to hear this. At home, he wasn't much of anything, as his wife liked to remind him. At sea, he was God.

Thirst

He dislodged her gently from his lap and stood. "So what do we have?"

His mistress handed him the fax, took the chair he had just vacated.

"Jennifer Jamieson and Clare Drake. Two school teachers, ostensibly from the Middleburg Middle School in Virginia. According to the form, the cruise was awarded to them by grateful parents. Very hoity-toity place, attended by children of the horse country set. The problem is when the home office called the school, the school had never heard of these two." Captain Stuart said, "Hm." The home office, he knew, retained the services of private investigators throughout the world and was on quite friendly terms with Interpol as well as the police forces of numerous nations. It was the price of being a successful cruise line that catered to the wealthy. The home office had long ago learned that where the wealthy went, so did predators of all kinds. It sought to protect its clients and did not shrink from using its web of informants to avoid the slightest whiff of scandal.

"They're in cabin 5-18," said the mistress. "They've been discreet, actually, but they apparently aroused the suspicion of Mrs. Worthington, of the Ontario Worthingtons, who saw her husband conversing with both of them and then caught him cashing in a handful of traveler's checks. The poor man was not up to his wife's onslaught and confessed. These ladies do not come cheap. Mr. Worthington had more than $4,000. That is apparently their fee for an afternoon's pleasure."

"$4,000 for both?"

The captain's mistress gave him a sidelong glance. "Yes, for both. Do I detect a note of interest?"

Captain Stuart made a great show of denying any such thing. "No, no. I was just wondering. That's quite a lot of money. What could they possibly have to offer for such a sum?"

The captain's mistress ran her hands around his waist and down, cupped him gently through his trousers. "Well," she said, "I can't be sure. But if you offer me $4,000 for an afternoon's work, I'm sure I could invent an interesting thing or two."

∞

"I hate doing this. Really, I do." Catherine and Colin were in Josie's room. The place was torn apart, Catherine's doing. "If Josie ever finds out, she'll never talk to me again. We had a long, long argument about stuff like that—privacy, me going through her things."

They'd moved the mattress off the box spring. Josie's clothes were spread all around the room; Colin was on all fours, his hands under the bed.

"Nothing there. Jewel box," he opened it, peered inside, closed it. "You're sure you've gone through all the drawers, all the books?"

Catherine had. She nodded.

"See if the carpet's been lifted, look in the corners. That's the easiest place to start."

Catherine paced around the room, bent down, tugged at the rug. "No. Shit. Shit shit shit!"

Colin turned, touched her shoulder. "Okay. Let's stop a second. Maybe there's nothing here. Someplace else in the house? Try to think, Cat. Maybe when she was a little kid, did she hide stuff in the garage? In the yard?"

He looked around the room, tried to find an area they hadn't thought of. His eyes came to rest on the grill covering the heat vent. It wasn't quite flush with the wall. He rotated the two screws holding it in, pulled. The unit came out with a small puff of dust. He reached into the duct. "Bingo."

Thirst

It was a small box no larger than three decks of cards stacked on top of one another. Across the top, scribbled in childlike letters was the word "Emergency." Four blue rubber bands held it all together. Colin handed it to Catherine, who looked at it for a moment, then shook it.

"Open it, Cat."

She looked torn. "It just feels like such an invasion of…"

"Just open it!"

She shot him a hurt glance, rolled the rubber bands off.

Josie had lined the bottom with cheap red velveteen. The glass crack pipe glowed against the fabric. The pipe was clear; either it hadn't been used or Josie had cleaned it thoroughly. The box dropped from Catherine's hand and the pipe rolled out.

"Oh jeez, oh, Colin, shit, how could she? After everything that's happened, all the promises and talk and, shit…Goddamit! How could the stupid little bitch *do* that!"

Colin bent down, retrieved the box, stepped on the pipe, and felt the stem crack in two pieces beneath his foot.

"When I first got out of rehab, Cat, I kept a bottle, just one. Johnny Walker Red. It was in a paper bag closed at the top with duct tape, in a gym bag in a bigger bag in a suitcase in the back of the closet. I never opened it, but knowing it was there made me feel safer."

Catherine was shaking her head, tears running down her face. Her hands were balled fists, knuckles white. She brought up a foot, smashed it on the floor. The pipe's bowl vanished beneath her heel and shattered with a small crinkling sound. She stomped it again and again, ground it into the carpet. Then she did the same to the stem.

Colin reached into the duct again. "There's something else there." He pulled out a folded manila envelope, opened it. "There's some papers, letters, a picture."

The letter was only two lines long, written in a hasty scrawl. Colin scanned it, gave it to Catherine.

Dear J:

*You exhausted me. Let's do it again.
Sunday. My place.*

*On the floor. In the kitchen. In the tub.
Can't wait.*

H

The poem was eight lines of undying love and promises in Josie's handwriting. It rhymed poorly and the meter was bad. The photo showed Josie and a man, she smiling, he squinting into the sun. She was sitting on the hood of a long black car; he was standing next to her with one hand draped across her shoulder.

"Do you know the guy?"

Catherine shook her head no. The hand holding the letter was trembling.

"Baltimore Harbor," Colin said. "That's where the picture was taken. I recognize it. That's the aquarium in the background. I had to do some research there a month ago. On sharks."

He peered at the photo, held it closer. "Oh shit." The shot had been developed in May. Colin felt the breath hiss out of him. He looked at the photo again, muttered, "Can't be."

Catherine said, "Can't be what?"

He paused a moment, shook his head. "Nothing, Cat. Thought I saw something. My mistake."

But Catherine caught the look of astonishment, saw bewilderment cross his eyes.

Thirst

"Colin?"

He glanced at the photo a last time, gave it back to her. "Nothing, Cat. Really."

She didn't press him, said, "You can just make out a couple of letters on the license plate. See? AFR, and then Josie's feet are in the way, and then 1. Do you think your cop friend, Joe, can do something with that license plate? Colin? You're looking kind of weird. Are you okay?"

Colin wasn't really listening, nodded anyway. The face of the young woman was etched in his mind. It looked nothing like the earlier photo Catherine had shown him. Now the resemblance between her and Catherine was obvious. Mother, daughter. Couldn't be, he thought, yet knew it was.

To Catherine, he said, "I'll check with him and call you later."

ಜ

On his way back to the apartment he stopped by Orin's. The man in the wheelchair at first looked at him incredulously, then roared in genuine and vast amusement.

"You mean you did the daughter too? You did the mother *and* the daughter and didn't even know it? Oh Jeez, Colin, you'll never ever cease to amaze me. That's the most hilarious thing I've heard in weeks!"

Orin took two deep breaths. "The doctor told me I shouldn't get over-excited. Bad for the heart." He pulled a large handkerchief from his shirt pocket, cleared his throat, mopped his forehead.

"So what're you asking me, Colin? What do you want me to do with that little tidbit? Course you got to tell her. That's a no-brainer. Is that all you wanted to know?"

He wheezed, coughed, and cleared his throat again. "You know, that reminds me of when I was a kid, and I finally got this girl, Amy, I think her name was, into the sack after weeks and weeks, and then her sister, I forget her name, started to come on to me really strong. So—"

Colin could hear Martha bustling inside the house. In a moment she was at the screen door. "What're you trying to do to my husband, Colin, make him laugh to death?"

Orin cleared his throat a third time. "But that's another story."

Colin went home.

※

It took Joe the Cop less than three minutes to find the name of the owner of the limo bearing the license plate Africa 1.

"Kind of an interesting guy, Colin, into lots of stuff, apparently, in for questioning a few times but never charged with anything. Caters to the African diplomatic corps and some of the higher-class dealers. His name is Dioh, Mamadou Dioh. Owns the Africorps Limo Service, five cars, family business. He's from Africa, Senegal or something, naturalized a couple of years ago. If you want, I can probably get more information."

Colin thanked him, said no, he wouldn't need anything else, and hung up the phone, the photo still dancing behind his eyes.

Chapter Seven

Mamadou Dioh didn't dislikes whites. They were an alien species, even though he believed they'd done some beautiful things, though not so much recently. Offenbach, Rimbaud, Saint Exupery. Whites. Balzac, Cocteau, Delacroix. Whites. Ravel, Poulenc. Whites. Mamadou had a particular admiration for Charles de Gaulle, one of the ugliest men ever to walk the earth (a white giant), was fascinated by Napoleon as well (a short white emperor). The fact that most notable men he admired were white and French was not lost on him. He was Senegalese, and the decades his country had spent under French rule had forever skewed its people and culture.

Still and all, they were different, whites were, occasionally downright bizarre. History has a tendency to gloss over the eccentricities of the greats, and it was his considered opinion that whiteness had contributed to strangeness, which in turn had permitted the ones he so admired to become historical figures in the first place.

And Mamadou was no fool. He knew if he himself had been white, life would have been very, very different.

Thierry Sagnier

For one thing, most of the tragic events that had befallen him since his arrival in the United States probably would not have happened. Had he been white, he was certain, he would not have had to spend the first few years in his new country as an illegal immigrant. His first home most assuredly would not have been a damp and stinking basement shared with eight other illegals from four continents. He would not have lost his sister.

On the other hand, were he white he would never have been a policeman in Dakar, probably never would have migrated to the West in the first person, and would not now be the owner of the Africorps Limousine Service.

Mamadou Dioh thought events had a way of evening life out.

He double-parked the limo near the corner of M Street and Wisconsin, adjusted his chauffeur's cap, walked into Georgetown Pipe and Tobacco, and bought three packs of Gauloises Disque Bleu. Back on the sidewalk he opened a pack, pulled one of the thick cigarettes out, lit it with a gold Dupont lighter, and watched with interest as traffic flowed around his illegally parked automobile. No one gave the car a second glance. This was Washington, where limos were as ubiquitous as Toyotas. Drivers in the nation's capital were used to circumnavigating the obstacles caused by the rich and powerful. The trappings of the wealthy gave Washingtonians a particular vanity they could revile in public and embrace in private.

He took a deep puff and exhaled blue smoke through his nose.

He smiled at two black women waiting for a bus, was gratified to see one of them grin back. For a while he watched the pedestrians, shoppers, tourists.

Wisconsin Avenue and M street, once the hub of Washington's entertainment district, had changed, become seedy. The streets were dirtier and unswept, victims of the capital's drastic budget cuts. A sex shop was cater-corner to the Farmer and Mechanics' Bank, whose gold cupola still dominated the corner but now looked in

Thirst

sore need of regilding. The panhandlers were out in force, squatting on thin haunches at every street corner and brandishing Styrofoam cups. Some had been there years, taking home more than a hundred dollars daily in change and singles. There were more tourists; too many Arabs, many Nordics and Germans, fewer Japanese; non-English speakers outnumbered the locals at least three to one.

He dropped the cigarette, ground it underfoot, dusted imaginary lint from the shoulders of his black suit, and returned to the car.

Life was good. He was wealthy by most standards and eventually, when all the business he needed to take care of was finished, he'd go back to Senegal, buy a small house near the sea, and life would be even better.

He eased the car back into traffic, whistled tunelessly. Tonight a party of twenty had rented his four cars. They were, like him, Africans, not Senegalese but from some impoverished nation that had recently changed its name for the third time in hope of erasing its debt, sad past, and even bleaker future. The Minister of Finance and his entourage were in Washington to celebrate the signing of a World Bank loan that would line their pockets and, with luck, build a few schools and health stations back home. Mamadou had never seen that particular minister but could describe him perfectly, probably knew by sight the expensive women rented for the night.

Mamadou shrugged, took his chauffeur's cap off, and carefully placed it on the seat next to him.

The minister would no doubt be generous. The imminent windfall provided by the World Bank would make His Excellency drink perhaps a bit too much and indulge in other vices not approved by any religion. Mamadou anticipated a good tip, a couple hundred dollars— more if the hired girls were particularly adept. The girls would be white, he was sure of that. And blonde.

Mamadou could even anticipate the exact proceedings for the coming night. First there would be a reception at the Embassy. The minister and his minions would show up late, dressed in flowing national garb. They would be very serious, the minister wearing glasses purchased in Paris to make him look professorial, and there would be a speech followed by much talk about development, about poverty alleviation, about the necessity for macroeconomic reform and how to encourage the nation's private sector. The hired ladies would not be present.

After the reception the group would eat at one of the better restaurants—Mamadou made a small bet with himself that it would be the La Ruche or Citronelle—and drink a few bottles of good wine. The minister would ask to be taken back to his hotel so they could all change to Western wear. After that, Mamadou would drive them up Massachusetts Avenue to an elegant apartment building near American University, where they would pick up the ladies.

In the beginning, it would be all good manners, social graces, and exaggerated politeness. The minister would take his glasses off. The party would hit a club or two, after-hour places, drink more, dance, get much friendlier with the ladies, who would of course respond in kind. In the end it would be a free-for-all. The minister and his friends would complain about having to wear condoms, offer blandishments and bribes. The girls would refuse. The Africans would be adamant at first, vocal and loud in their protest, but in the end they would comply and spend a night long remembered and certainly often retold.

None of this would happen in the limo, however. That was the rule even the most illiterate visitor from whatever godforsaken nation knew. Discreet touching, that was all the owner of Africorps allowed in his vehicles. Mamadou Dioh, a strict and moral man, had spent years cultivating two divergent clienteles. One was the African diplomatic corps in Washington. He knew all the *attachés*, all the secretaries, the entire level of lesser embassy employees who made

Thirst

reservations, set up appointments, were hired to see that things ran smoothly. All these people knew his rules.

The other clientele was largely drug dealers.

⁂

The offices of Africorps were shabby; Mamadou recognized this and didn't much care. The company's business was done over the phone or, increasingly, by email and fax. No need for a fancy storefront; in this Northeast neighborhood, vandals would smash it nightly for the sheer thrill of it.

The limos were housed in a converted garage. There was a small sitting room to the side with one desk, a phone with three lines, the fax machine, a stained and rarely used coffee-maker, a ratty leather chair Mamadou had found at an Abby Rents auction of discarded furniture, and an aging Apple computer. No windows, no water cooler, and a restroom the drivers avoided except in the direst emergencies. At night, a moonlighting city cop provided security. The man didn't have to do much save make sure the two Dobermans he had trained and now handled were properly fed. There hadn't been a break-in since a year earlier when two young men, recently arrived from Missouri and unaware of the place's canine threat, had jimmied open the front door and, in the deep gloom, heard the growling of monsters from hell followed by the *kachunka* sound of a shotgun being loaded. That had proved to be enough for the visitors. The cop later told Mamadou he wished the boys had come in, it would have added a bit of excitement to an otherwise boring night.

Mamadou clicked the remote, waited for the overhead door to rise, and eased his limo in. He would vacuum and wash it before the night's assignment, spray the insides with Nu Car, polish the chrome, and make sure oil, transmission fluid, and water were topped off. He was getting out of the car when he noticed the man sitting in the chair usually reserved for the guard. He was a large man who filled the chair, his shoulders somehow overflowing it. And he was white. That, more than anything, piqued Mamadou's interest.

He nodded at the man, said, "I'll be with you in a moment," reached under the seat of the limo where he kept the pistol. It was an inexpensive weapon he'd bought on the street a year before when a serial killer was roaming Washington streets and murdering cabdrivers. With his back to the man, Mamadou slipped the gun into his waistband, pulled his jacket to cover it.

Now the man was standing. He was shorter than Mamadou expected; he'd somehow looked more imposing sitting. Mamadou asked, "What can I do for you?"

The man reached into a pocket and Mamadou's heart skipped. He moved his hand, wrapped his fingers around the gun's butt, had it halfway out when he saw the stranger raise both hands. "Please, Mr. Dioh. I'm not armed."

Mamadou loosened his grip. "Sorry. Nature of the trade." He motioned for the man to relax. "I am at a disadvantage here. You obviously know who I am, while I have no idea who you are, or how you got in here."

"Colin Marsh, Mr. Dioh, and one of your drivers let me in. I told him it was important that I speak to you personally."

Mamadou nodded, turned back to the limo. "You have my undivided attention. Well, not quite undivided. I have to get this car ready. What can I do for you?"

Marsh handed him a photo. Mamadou glanced at it, handed it back. "Handsome couple."

"Customers?"

Mamadou sprayed the inside of the vehicle with NuCar, did it carefully. Then he wiped the dashboard with a cloth, ran it around the steering wheel.

Thirst

"Are you a policeman, Mr. Marsh?"

The man shook his head no.

"I didn't think so. I was a policeman in my country of origin, and policemen all over the world recognize each other. And you don't look like a private detective. So you're an acquaintance of one of the people in the photo, am I right?"

He didn't wait for an answer. "And I doubt your acquaintance is with the man portrayed. Call it a hunch, as you say in America. So it must be the young woman." He paused long enough to flick the rag, fold it into a neat square. "I have excellent powers of deduction, which is why I was an excellent, if unappreciated, law enforcement officer in my native country. How did you get my name?"

"A friend. A policeman."

Mamadou nodded. "I see. That should not have been particularly difficult, I expect. A phone call or two, at best. Or a computer. They do everything with computers nowadays."

Marsh said, "The young woman in the photo. She's missing."

Mamadou Dioh thought that over for a moment. "Young women vanish all the time, Mr. Marsh. It's a very hostile world out there, as I'm sure you know. Perhaps she ran away with the young man. How do you say, eloped?"

Marsh shook his head. "No. Something's happened to her."

"Well, that is unfortunate." Mamadou unfolded the rag, wiped the limo's radio antenna, squatted, rubbed away at a smudge on one of the wheel covers. "But I still don't see how I can help you, Mr. Marsh." The smudge was resistant. Mamadou spit on the cloth, applied more pressure.

The calm West African voice angered Colin. He drew two steps closer until he was standing over him. The Senegalese looked up at him calmly. "You're standing in my light."

He saw Colin Marsh's fists clench. They were large, backed by overly developed forearms and biceps.

Dio's arm sliced in a blur, connected with an ankle. Marsh yelled, fell to the floor. In one fluid motion the African grabbed a wrist, twisted it.

"I really do not like it when people move in a threatening manner, Mr. Marsh. Not one bit. It is impolite and it scares me. We are not well enough acquainted for me to permit you such familiarities." He rose to his feet slowly, keeping the pressure on. Marsh tried to dance away, couldn't.

"Now. Mr. Marsh, it's obvious that you're immensely strong, and this is a very silly situation for two grown men to be in. And given time, I'm sure you would overpower me. But you would get seriously hurt before you did so." He walked Marsh back to the chair. "When I was a policeman in Dakar, I was called upon to move immensely strong men from one cell to another. It's not difficult at all if you know how." He squeezed Marsh's wrist. Marsh grunted, stood on tip-toes to relieve the pressure.

Mamadou Dioh said, "I'll strike a bargain. No more threatening moves and we'll try to resolve whatever is troubling you as civilized men should. Please sit down. May I rely on your word?"

Marsh nodded. "I wasn't going to attack you."

"Good. Then I apologize, Mr. Marsh. But you looked quite fearsome for a moment, and the best defense is a good offense. Isn't that the saying?"

Mamadou eased the pressure on Marsh's wrist, allowed the large man to sit. Marsh looked up. "Aikido?"

Mamadou nodded, pleased. "A West African version. Less stylish than the Oriental schools but more effective."

Marsh rubbed his wrist, rolled his shoulder.

"But you see?" Mamadou Dioh smiled. "Now we're talking like well-bred people. Isn't this much better?" He turned his back, entered the small office. "Coffee, Mr. Marsh? Instant is all I have, I'm afraid." He returned in a moment bearing two stained mugs.

Thirst

"So I should help you because you suspect I know people who traffic in drugs, and since the young woman was, is, a recovering addict, perhaps it'll assuage my conscience." Mamadou Dioh shook his head. "That's quite un-American, Mr. Marsh, declaring a man guilty, basing it on assumptions and hearsay. Are you sure you're not French? You appear to abide by the Napoleonic code."

"In America, Mr. Dioh, we say that if it walks like a duck and quacks like a duck...."

Colin's wrist still hurt. Whatever anger he'd felt had been replaced by grudging admiration. He had told the Senegalese most of the story and the black man had listened impassively, asking questions now and again. When Colin was through talking, Dioh had refilled both their mugs.

Now he smiled slightly. "Please. I am neither a duck nor a drug dealer. I'm a simple immigrant. I make my money quite legally, pay all my taxes and licensing fees."

He stood, walked Colin to the door. "Let me think about all this, Mr. Marsh. I'll call you tomorrow. We'll talk again."

Chapter Eight

That evening the job with the minister and his party went as Mamadou had expected, with one slight hitch. The girls wanted to be paid in advance; the minister balked and as the argument between the two parties grew more heated, the scent of the minister's cologne in the closed confines of the limo almost overwhelmed Mamadou.

The girls had been stiffed a few weeks earlier by a party of Ugandans and the minister's protest that *he* was *not* from that disreputable country had fallen on deaf ears. To the women, African was African. They wanted their money now or no partying, period. Mamadou finally interceded, something he rarely did. But the evening was well on its way to a disastrous ending. No party for the minister. No tip for the driver, and the likelihood of losing customers in the future.

So Mamadou said, "Your Excellency, you should not allow such a successful day to end this way. And arguing with ladies of the evening is far below your dignity and that of the office you hold. May I suggest that you pay three-quarters of the agreed upon fee

Thirst

now and the remainder later? This will give your escorts an incentive to be particularly inventive and attentive to your wishes."

The minister thought about it for a moment, conferred with two of his minions, and grudgingly accepted the deal. Later in the evening, when he and his countrymen were very drunk and happy, he suggested Mamadou's skills were wasted as a chauffeur; he should come to his country and work in the Ministry of Finance. Then he gave Mamadou $200. Later, as Mamadou dropped his passengers off so they could continue their evening in more private surroundings, one of the girls had shoved a fifty in his hand and whispered, "We're gonna fleece these assholes..." Which they undoubtedly had done.

It was three in the morning by the time Mamadou got home. His apartment near the Washington Marina overlooked the Potomac, and for a few long moments he focused on the moon's reflection playing on the water. The streets were empty and the only sound that reached him was the clinking of halyards against masts. He took off his shoes, jacket, and shirt, went to the kitchen, poured himself a liberal amount of Wild Turkey over a few ice cubes, returned to the living room, and collapsed in his favorite chair. He missed his nation, his African continent, his family.

Moustapha, brother number two, was a chef in New Orleans. Macodou owned a flower shop in San Diego. Fatimatou, his middle sister, had married a wealthy entrepreneur from Togo and lived in splendor in Montreal. Micheline, the eldest, taught French to privileged girls in a private school in Connecticut. And Amelie was...dead.

Mamadou swallowed the last of the Wild Turkey, wiped his lips with the back of his hand, went to the kitchen, and fixed a second, larger drink.

He had managed to avoid thinking about Amelie for a few days, though that wasn't precisely true. He *always* thought of her; she occupied a permanent crevice in his mind. Her death had been a soul-numbing tragedy, the greatest catastrophe of his life. Still, to this day, he could not comprehend how such a thing had happened, how he could have allowed it to happen, because she had been his responsibility and he had failed her, had let her first be subverted, then ravaged, then destroyed. Sometimes he dreamed he'd actually been the one who had snuffed out her life.

Now there was an opportunity to atone—he remembered learning the word and the concept as a child from the Christian nuns who had set up a makeshift school in his district. Atonement had seemed absurd at first until he realized it was a form of vengeance, almost the same thing in a more positive way.

The alcohol slipped through his body, loosened his thoughts.

The boy who'd come to see Amelie that night had brought flowers. Mamadou remembered that distinctly because the colors and shapes of the blossoms reminded him of the gardens back home. Amelie's friend was an outwardly pleasant young man, soft-spoken, somewhat glib, but that was typical of youth. He dressed strangely, in overly large clothes, gaudy jewelry, and sunglasses indoors. Mamadou was careful not to be too inquisitive; there'd been a row with Amelie a week earlier when she accused him of scaring her friends away with his questions and forbidding looks.

So he'd hidden his misgivings and watched the baby of the family, the child entrusted to him, flounce away in a too-tight dress with a young man Mamadou did not entirely trust. Mamadou had waited until their return, which had displeased Amelie greatly. The young man hadn't been very happy either.

Three days later Amelie had been out when he came home from work, and this was unusual. Amelie was the family's cook; supper was normally ready to be served by the time Mamadou returned. His brothers didn't know where she was, remembered only that the same young man had appeared at their door—flowerless this time—and whisked her away. Moustapha cooked the meal that evening and

THIRST

commented slyly that, had *he* been the eldest, he would not have allowed Amelie to go out wearing the minimal wardrobe she'd had on.

When Amelie came back that night she was drunk and disheveled. Mamadou was tired, exhausted from an extra shift at the restaurant where he washed dishes. He'd lost his patience and slapped her—he had never done that before and the blow had shocked him more than hurt her. He forced her fully dressed—what there was of a dress, which had been scanty at best—into the shower. She had screamed, wept, and cursed using words Mamadou had only heard on the streets. She was sullen the next day and the day after that and though Mamadou tried to apologize to her, he knew his anger had wounded something important and precious. In the two-bedroom apartment already crowded by the five of them, resentment became a sixth occupant that took up too much space.

And then Amelie was gone. No explanation, no note, no telephone call. Mamadou contacted the police, who said they couldn't be involved until a crime was committed and it was too early to file a missing person report. No hospital had admitted anyone fitting her description. Her friends, the few Mamadou had met, provided no help. Mamadou took to driving the streets at night but that proved fruitless as well.

Ten days later she returned accompanied by the same young man who drew a gun from his waistband and aimed it at the family, telling them not to move. Amelie's eyes were vacant. She went and retrieved her clothes and shoes from the bedroom closet, taking as well some items belonging to her sisters. Then she demanded that the brothers give her their watches, chains, rings. The brothers did so, speechless, astounded more than frightened. The young man with the gun nodded, pocketed the jewelry. He followed Amelie out, slammed the door as he left.

Moustapha's legs buckled and he sat down hard on the floor, muttering in Wolof and French. Macodou crossed himself. Mamadou rushed to the window just in time to see the young man's car vanish around a corner.

Three days after that Amelie came home for the last time. Mamadou found her in the dingy lobby of the building where they all lived, and she was very close to dead. Her breathing was shallow, the pupils of her eyes like great black holes. She died on the way to the hospital where an uninterested white intern told Mamadou she'd overdosed on a lethal combination of cocaine and heroin, something called a speedball. The mixture had been injected directly into the veins in her neck and it had killed her. The intern said that was happening a lot recently, there'd been three other cases just like Amelie; it had something to do with a new supply of high octane junk recently brought into the neighborhoods. He said he was sorry and hurried away to a more survivable emergency. Mamadou went home to explain the inconceivable to his brothers.

※

Finding Amelie's young man had been the hard part; killing him had been remarkably easy and largely unsatisfying. Mamadou had killed three people when he was a policeman in Dakar, and each time he'd felt an overwhelming sense of remorse. Never mind that in all three instances his own life had been on the line and that he still bore the scars inflicted by a huge drunkard with a machete. The killings had left him shaking and horrified, as if they'd been the work of a separate, darker self. It was inconceivable to him that he'd ended a life, inconceivable that divine retribution hadn't struck him down on the spot. But it hadn't, his existence had continued unchanged save

Thirst

that he was decorated for the first and third killings and that younger policemen grew to be in awe of him.

Ridding the world of the young man who'd encouraged Amelie's destruction, on the other hand, was a public service. He remembered feeling greater pain when, as a boy, he'd used a home-made sling to down a pigeon. The mass of gray and white feathers that still fluttered as he gathered the fallen bird in his hands was so small, so weightless and unthreatening that he'd run to the church and babbled his confession to the local priest. The cleric had reprimanded and calmed the boy, then ordered him to sweep the church for a month as penance. Mamadou gladly did so.

Running the murderer to ground had proved tricky until Mamadou realized it would be far easier to let the boy find *him* than vice versa. During his years with the Dakar police, Mamadou had learned a universal truism: money talks. He put out the word on the street, virtually shouted it. A large reward, very large, for the whereabouts of the young man. He was purposefully indiscreet, had an artist friend create a handbill bearing the boy's likeness, and posted it on every telephone pole. In less than twenty-four hours the entire ward knew the man from Senegal had cash to burn.

Then George, the elderly black gentleman who called himself a friend of Aunt Mim's, showed up one morning, impeccably dressed in an old-fashioned three-piece suit only slightly faded at the elbows. Mamadou had no idea who Aunt Mim was, and the old man, sitting primly with his knees tightly together had explained. "In your country, Monsieur Dioh, the lady in question might be called a *grande dame*, a person who because of her influence and knowledge has earned the deep respect of her community. At any rate," the old man stood, tugged at his sleeves so the cuffs of his shirt showed just so, "she would like to help you. Are you amenable? If you are, I believe you'll soon encounter the young man you're seeking."

Thierry Sagnier

The next day Mamadou sent Moustapha, Micheline, Macodou, and Fatimatou to New York to stay with distant cousins. They'd always wanted to go there but had never had the opportunity. He filled the apartment's refrigerator with food, mostly fruits and vegetables. He went to Home Depot and returned with several gallons of paint, brushes, rollers, spackling compound, and sandpaper. Then he took the Orange Line metro and a bus to a shopping mall in Virginia, found a sporting supply store, and purchased two shotguns, a Remington 870 and a Mossberg 500. He bought seven-shot mag extensions for both, barrel shrouds, front and rear assault grips and folding stocks, and five boxes of shells. He returned home, disassembled the weapons, and put them back together with the custom parts.

The old man had not lied. The boy came three days later accompanied by two friends, gangly youths with loud voices and baseball caps worn sideways. They shouted at him through the door, challenged him to come out. He didn't. A day earlier, Mamadou had put up a makeshift barricade of end tables, sofas, and mattresses. The boy and his friends broke down the door. Mamadou saw at a glance that they were not well armed. He had expected better weapons, but the three had gone for size rather than effectiveness. The boy had a massive Magnum that dwarfed his hands and wrists; the others each held a Walther 9mm at a jaunty angle. Mamadou let the boy have the first shot—which went far wide and blasted a hole in the living room wall—then downed the three of them with two blasts each from the Mossberg and Remington. He was reloading when he saw a fourth man, face black, round, impassive. The man vanished before Mamadou could react.

The police came, marveled at the damage, and shook their heads, but Mamadou could see there was a measure of admiration in their eyes. He knew cops; they were the same everywhere. When he told them he himself had been a policeman, they nodded in understanding. A detective confiscated his weapons. He followed the

Thirst

detective to the station, returned two hours later without having been charged. It was clearly a case of home invasion and self-defense, and the three boys in the morgue were known to the police as minor but dangerous dealers who were suspected of a dozen violent crimes.

Mamadou spent the next day and better part of the night repairing the damage to the apartment. He used up the spackling compound but was left with a gallon of Home Depot paint. Aunt Mim's friend, the elderly gentleman named George, came to help him, and together they worked silently through most of the afternoon. When they were finished, he took Mamadou to meet Aunt Mim and suggested he buy a box of chocolates for her. The shoot-out made the back page of the next day's paper. He never told the police about the fourth man.

※

Mamadou rose from the chair heavily. His head swam; he knew he was well on his way to being very drunk. He glanced at the clock on the kitchen range. Past two in the morning. He found the slip of paper with Marsh's number, dialed. When Marsh answered, Mamadou said, "I'll try to help you, Mr. Marsh. Come by tomorrow, around three. But there are no guarantees. There never are." He hung up before the man could respond. He staggered to bed, didn't bother with the sheets or blanket. He drifted off to uneasy sleep with the words 'unfinished business' circling in his head.

Chapter Nine

Captain Roderick Stuart was not an unworldly man. He had wandered the planet as chief of a ship no single human could ever dream of owning, and he had seen firsthand the frailties and strength of humankind. He knew men were weak, knew their lust had no bounds, and knew, if for this very reason alone, that prostitutes would be drawn to the *Isadora* as, well, bees to honey.

In his heart of hearts, Captain Stuart knew such people were necessary to the functioning of a well-ordered society. He believed, though he never would dream of admitting it to anyone, that all relationships had a basis in some form of prostitution. It was, after all, the oldest profession for a good reason.

So he wasn't shocked to hear that two such ladies were plying their trade on his ship. What he resented was that they had been caught, which showed a certain lack of intelligence, and that their prey had been one of the ship's venerated clients. The Worthingtons of Ontario were on the A-list. They booked at least three cruises a year, sometimes four. They always stayed in first class and, though hugely wealthy, were content to play shuffleboard in the morning, bridge in the afternoon, and canasta at night. Mr. Worthington drank a bit too much on occasion, but that was forgivable, considering his spouse. Mrs. Worthington had a tendency to be short with the crew—she had once called a steward a dunderhead—and her no salt, no fat, gluten-free, low carbohydrate, and high fiber diet was a constant challenge to the chef.

Jennifer Jamieson and Clare Drake. Cabin 5-18. The captain checked his watch. In half-an-hour's time, dinner would be served. The two would probably be in their cabin, getting ready. He drafted a quick note on the *Isadora*'s letterhead paper, sealed it in an envelope. He asked one of the men to deliver it immediately to cabin 5-18.

ଛ

The two young women *were* attractive. Very much so. Captain Roderick Stuart was surprised that he had not noticed them before. Certainly, they stood out. One blonde, one brunette; they could have been sisters. Captain Steward estimated their age at between twenty-two and twenty-five. They were poised, and very angry.

The blonde one, Jennifer, was speaking for them both. "Fuck you."

The brunette nodded her head.

Their language left a bit to be desired.

The brunette said, "We'll sue."

The captain smiled. "Then you'll do so from shore. We shall ask you to leave at the next port."

"You can't—"

"Yes, I most assuredly *can*. This is my ship. I can do almost anything here. Putting you ashore will be a minor inconvenience, believe me."

Both women wore petulant, offended looks. The brunette broke first. "Oh shit," she said.

The blonde smiled. "Can't we work something out?"

The captain stood silent for a long moment. It was important the two women think his decision was the product of much deliberation. It wasn't. The handbook distributed to all ship officers by the *Isadora*'s mother company stated that dumping clients—any clients—was a last resort.

"Perhaps we can," said the captain.

In fact, the problem was easily solved. The captain knew how quickly gossip traveled among both the crew and the passengers. He had no intention of fostering a *cause célèbre*. Clare Drake and Jennifer Jamieson would therefore be allowed to enjoy almost all the pleasures the ship had to offer but they would not practice their profession. If they did, they would spend the remainder of the cruise in the brig and be delivered to the local police at the next port of call.

The blonde shrugged her beautiful shoulders. "Okay."

The brunette mimicked her.

Captain Roderick Stuart bowed very slightly at the waist to show there were no hard feelings.

℘

In the morning Colin remembered the black man's deep voice, recalled that it was rounded about the edges, as if Mamadou had been drinking. Catherine answered on the first ring.

"No news?"

She sounded tired. "Nothing. Not a word, I'm worried sick, Colin. Lars decided *he* wasn't going to worry so I'm doing it for both of us."

"I think I have some good news. I found the limo driver. He said he'd help. That's a step in the right direction, anyway."

"Did he know anything, have any ideas? Maybe he…"

Thirst

"I don't know, Cat. I saw him yesterday and he called me last night. I can't tell you anything yet, save that he's an ex-cop from Africa…"

"Africa?" Catherine laughed but it was empty. "Jesus. That's all we need, some corrupt Third World cop. I've been to Africa. Thanks but no thanks."

"Actually, I think he's in the States because he *wasn't* corrupt, so his career ended. And he came here."

Catherine sounded resigned. "Sounds like a far reach, Colin. What do you expect from him?"

"Got to start somewhere."

Catherine's voice was instantly chastened. "Jeez, Colin. I'm sorry. I don't know what's got into me. Nerves, I guess. Or Lars's attitude. I don't mean to sound so negative. You know I'm grateful."

"It's tough, Cat. Going to a meeting later?"

"No. Yes. I mean, I need one, but I'm afraid to get too far from the house. In case she comes back."

Colin glanced at his watch. "Come to the club. There's a meeting in an hour-and-a-half. We'll get something to eat afterwards, and I'll tell you about my encounter with Mr. Dioh, the limo guy. We'll try to work something out, a plan of some sort."

He hung up. He didn't expect much from Catherine, but left home alone she'd become a loose cannon. He turned on his computer, Googled "Mamadou Dioh." Nothing local. He typed in the *Washington Post* online address, entered his signup name and password, then headed for the Post's archives. He punched in a couple of commands, typed in "Mamadou Dioh," and pressed the Enter key. He waited and watched the screen as the central computer at the Post digested his request, sorting through the millions of references on file. There were only two entries under the Senegalese's name. He printed both.

Thierry Sagnier

☙

The meeting was small; Colin counted fourteen people, eight men and six women. Catherine was late, came during the *How it Works* reading after the door had closed. Colin pointed to the empty chair next to him and she slid in, sat, smiled at the others in apology. She whispered, "There was a call just as I was leaving. I thought it might be Josie. It wasn't. It was Lars, asking what I making for dinner tonight. I really lost it, with him, I mean. Yelled at him. He hung up."

The speaker introduced himself, spoke for five minutes, and threw the meeting open. Colin listened to the litanies, tried hard to remember Orin G's admonitions, failed. He passed as the sharing went around the room, unwilling to divulge the origins of his unease or identify them for himself. Then, glancing at Catherine, he remembered the gist of the conversation with his sponsor. He muttered, "Oh shit." The man seated on his other side looked at him briefly, raised an eyebrow.

Catherine raised her hand, identified herself, and went into details about Lars's behavior, but Colin noticed she didn't mention Josie. When the meeting ended, he took her by the arm and said, "Listen, I've got to talk to you about something."

Catherine canted her head, a quizzical look. They walked through the parking lot to her car Catherine said, "So talk…"

Colin nodded. "I don't know how to go about this. You're really going to get pissed. So first I'm going to apologize and say I had no way of knowing. Because I'd never met her, you know? She said her name was Jane, and of course I had no idea how old she was. She looked like maybe mid-twenties…"

Catherine wore a half-smile. "Colin, what are you trying to say? I've got no idea what you're talking about."

Thirst

Colin focused his gaze on something far away, avoided looking at Catherine's face.

"What happened is, I recognized her from the picture you found, the one taken in Baltimore. It was a while back, during a low period. And I wasn't very rational, I wasn't thinking, I just wanted somebody to be close to, just for the night, a body thing. It just happened."

"What happened, Colin?"

"I slept with Josie."

Catherine's eyes became very round and bugged out a little, and her jaw dropped. It was just like in the cartoons when Bugs did something outlandish to Elmer Fudd, and it stayed there. Her mouth was open. Colin could see the inside of her lower lip, her tongue, her even teeth, the tiny veins in the whites of her eyes, the eyebrows shaped like horizontal parentheses.

Catherine quaked once from head to toe. "You *what??*"

"I didn't know, Cat, couldn't have known…"

"*You* slept with *my* daughter? With my *Josie?*"

Colin tried to move her into the car, guided her elbow. She stiffened, resisted, angrily batted his hand away.

"You're joking." She looked at him, drew her face close to his, tried to see past his eyes. "No. You're not. My God. You're serious." She squinched her eyes shut like a kid making a desperate wish. "No, you can't be."

She moved away as if repulsed, and then her arm came in a long fast arc and she struck him on the right side of the head with her closed fist. She drew back her other hand and struck him again, then closed her eyes. Her body went soft, lost its strength. She whimpered, turned from him, first walked and then ran away. Colin started to go after her but she stopped, spun around. "Don't come near me. Don't fucking come *anywhere* near me."

People in the parking lot were watching. Colin saw heads come together, heard vague whispers. Catherine strode to the curb with great deliberation, waved a hand in the air. A Yellow cab veered in from the far left lane and she got in amid a chorus of horns, then closed the door softly. Colin watched the cab pull away.

"She all right?" It was one of the women who'd been at the meeting. "Something wrong?"

Colin shook his head. "No. It's okay. Just a misunderstanding. She just had to get home. She's fine."

He looked down the street but the taxi was gone.

⁂

In the cab Catherine held her breath. Her body was convinced something terrible would happen if she exhaled so she didn't for as long as possible, then did so with small quiet gasps, a little at a time. The cabdriver glanced at her through the rearview mirror. He didn't want a fare getting sick in his back seat; stuff like that happened with regularity and it was disgusting, cleaning up afterwards. But this fare appeared all right, pale and maybe a bit shaky but definitely under control.

Catherine gave her home address, saw the driver nod his head, and leaned back. She wondered whether she'd overreacted, decided she hadn't, tried to persuade herself that Colin must have made a mistake. Must have.

She had few illusions about Josie and sex; the remaining ones had disappeared when her daughter had blithely announced she was pregnant. But Catherine had always thought that the men were boys, that Josie's sexual experimentations had been hapless fumblings quickly consummated in the dark. She had kept count of Josie's boyfriends, had thought two, maybe three had been serious, had led to sex, but Colin? *Her* Colin?

Thirst

Wrong. The man was not *her* anything. At very most, he was fucking her. No. *She* was fucking *him*. The notion made her uncomfortable. What an ugly word, she thought. And then she had an image of Colin's overlarge torso pressed hard against her daughter's pale breasts. She gagged and the cabdriver turned to shoot her a worried look.

She pushed the picture from her mind, tried to focus on something else. The cabby was driving fast and shifting from lane to lane. He was a swarthy man with a bull neck and from the back she could see overlarge hands spanning the steering wheel. The image of Colin and Josie pulled at her. She rubbed her eyes, tried a smile, asked, "Where are you from?"

The man answered, "Georgia." He had a strange accent; the r's weren't right and she wondered what town in Georgia until she realized he meant Georgia in Eastern Europe. She explored what she knew about the former Soviet country and it gave her five seconds of freedom before Colin and Josie resurfaced, clearer now; she could almost picture the muscles defined in Colin's back. She balled her fist, hit her knee hard, cursed. She had struck him with that same fist and he hadn't reacted though she'd put everything in the blow.

The cabby jammed on his brakes, punched his horn, and yelled something incomprehensible. She was thrown against the rear of the front seat, bounced back, saw her purse hit the car's floor, the contents strewn across the entire width of the car. She scrambled to pick them up, grabbed the lipstick before it could roll under the seat, and cut the top of her index finger on something sharp. The pain made her sit up. It was a small cut, a slice just above the fingernail. A drop of blood was forming there. She stuck the finger in her mouth and, very quietly so the driver wouldn't notice, started crying.

Thierry Sagnier

❀

By eleven that night Colin had done everything he could think of in the apartment short of painting it. He'd laundered, folded, cleaned, scrubbed, and washed, and the place was as neat as it could get without major renovations. He'd pushed and pulled at the weights too, but the weariness in his arms and legs had failed to make him feel better. In retrospect he thought he'd handled the situation badly; it was foolish and shortsighted to have said anything at all to Catherine.

Stupid to think it wouldn't harm her, stupid to believe the burden of guilt would go away. Confession was *not* always good for the soul. Colin shook his head, thought, *so many years of sobriety and I'm still an asshole, I still can't trust my judgment.*

When the phone rang he grabbed it thinking it was Catherine but it wasn't. He heard the voice of Mamadou Dioh. "Are you free Mr. Marsh? I have the night off. It's one of the perquisites of being the boss. Can we meet? I think I learned some things that could be of interest."

❀

"This is one of my favorite establishments," the Senegalese said, spinning a fork in his spaghetti. Colin knew the restaurant well. It was a favorite of the AA crowd; they all came to Angelo's after the meetings and mostly drank coffee and sodas. Colin had never understood why the place was popular—the coffee was weak and the food mostly microwaved. Neither could he fathom Angelo's hospitality toward a bunch of people who talked loud and rarely spent more than five dollars apiece.

Thirst

"It's not that the food is good," the Senegalese continued. "Because it isn't. I guess the fact that it's open all night is a major advantage. I often come here after a job at three, four in the morning, and even if there's not a single other customer, they carry the full menu and I get good service." He forked the spaghetti into his mouth, chewed contemplatively. "You're sure you don't want anything other than pie? I'm buying. My nickel, as you Americans say."

Colin shook his head. He toyed with the wedge of pie, separating the apple quarters from the dough. It looked like a Mrs. Something-or-Other from the freezer section at Food Lion, and not quite baked enough.

Mamadou tore a bit of garlic bread in half. "The photo you showed me? I took that. You may have deduced that by now. Incidentally, is that how you found me? The license plate?"

Colin nodded.

"I thought so," Mamadou said. "The young man in the photo, of course I know him. He is—was, I should say—a fairly steady customer. Whenever he met a new lady I could count on his patronage. He liked to impress them, you see, and a limo is far cheaper than a Cartier watch or, for that fact, two nights at the Four Seasons or even a good suit. He was a dealer, a fairly minor player, two steps up from the street corner."

He paused, popped the bread in his mouth. "You know, of course, that he's dead?"

"No. I didn't."

"Oh yes. Very dead. Not an important loss to society, but I'll miss him as a client. He tipped well, never misbehaved in my cars."

"Recently?"

"Day before yesterday, I think. Found near Klingle Road, in Northwest. Stabbed. Shot."

Colin nodded, remembering an item in the *Post*. "It was in the papers, but they didn't identify him."

"Correct," said Mamadou. "But they don't have to as far as the street is concerned. The people there know instantly."

Angelo's lobster-shift waitress was sitting at a nearby booth watching the science fiction channel on cable TV. A giant slug was sliming its way down the major avenues of what could have been Tokyo. Mamadou waved his hand in the air until he got her attention and ordered a piece of baklava and coffee. Colin nodded yes as she hovered the pot over his cup.

"His name was Herbie French. He was thirty-two, went to law school at Georgetown for a couple of semesters, then decided there were too many lawyers already, so he opted to go into business for himself."

Colin sipped at his coffee. It was lukewarm. "How do you know all this?"

Mamadou looked up, slightly annoyed. "I'm not deaf, Mr. Marsh. I drive people around all day and often all night. They talk. They don't pay much attention to me. I listen."

"Sorry."

Mamadou picked up where he had left off. "So he went into business for himself. Small transactions to start with, peddling amphetamines and such to his former classmates. Big profits during exam time. Students stay up all night to study, and they need help; Herbie is there. One of his friends, a fellow student, turned out to be the son of a Colombian gentleman with connections. Herbie starts dealing cocaine. Very lucrative as I'm sure you know. In no time at all Herbie is making a lot of money. He uses my limo service with increasing frequency, gets to be quite a man about town. For a while, as a matter of fact, he hires my limos as rolling offices. Quite safe, you see. I have an excellent reputation about town. I cater to the diplomats, and more than one discreet meeting between representatives of nations that are not supposed to be on speaking terms has taken place in the back seat of my cars. The limos are

Thirst

swept for bugs before every new assignment, that's one of the services we offer." Mamadou Dioh tore another piece of bread in half, mopped up the sauce in his plate.

"So Herbie is moving up in the world. But he's a smart young man, he realizes the higher he goes, the more visibility he acquires, the bigger the target he becomes. The drug business is dog eat dog. Herbie made sure he kept a low profile, didn't handle *too* much business. In effect, he became a large, small dealer. I suspect he came to realize there's only so much money one individual can spend. After that, money becomes moot and what you're dealing with is power. Herbie, I think, was never really interested in power.

"As such things happen, the Colombian and his son, the people Herbie was now working for full time, meet with an unfortunate accident. You may have read about it, it made the papers some time back, a really ruthless set of murders. Father and son were literally eviscerated, left to bleed to death with their entrails draped about them. The media did not carry the full story but shortly thereafter photos of the corpses, official pictures from the medical examiner's office, started appearing in the street, a message to advise dealers and suppliers that the father and son team had somehow offended another organization in town, one that didn't shrink from acts of violence."

The Senegalese belched discreetly, covering his mouth. "All this talking has made me thirsty, Mr. Marsh. There's a tavern down the street. Let's go there and continue our conversation." He signaled for the check, paid it with two twenty dollar bills.

In the bar, a place called Palmer's, Mamadou ordered a scotch on the rocks, Colin asked for a ginger ale.

"You don't drink, Mr. Marsh?"

"I'm allergic to alcohol."

The Senegalese made a face. "How unfortunate. What happens?"

Colin smiled without amusement. "I get drunk."

The Senegalese stared for a moment, burst out laughing. "What an excellent response! Consider me admonished, Mr. Marsh. Whether you drink or not is none of my business. I was only trying to make conversation."

Colin nodded. "No offense taken. I've actually wanted to use that line for quite a while." This time, his smile was genuine.

"Well." Mamadou took a long sip of his drink, sighed contentedly. "Back to our friend Herbie. You're not bored, I trust?"

Colin shook his head.

"Good. So Herbie is left without a supplier. To make a long story short, he finds gainful employment with the very people whom the police suspect deprived him of an employer."

"Isn't that a bit unusual?"

Mamadou sipped again. "Perhaps. But smart as well, if you think about it. Herbie was an experienced dealer with an established clientele, a ready-made market. When the new partnership was established, Herbie knew what could happen to him if he was tempted to stray. As I mentioned, the photos were circulating…"

Colin emptied his glass, walked to the bar to get a refill, returned and sat down. "You got all this by listening to conversations in your car?"

The Senegalese frowned. "Please Mr. Marsh, you make me sound like a common eavesdropper. No, of course I didn't. But I have many, many clients, from all walks of life. Almost all of them talk. Like any other professionals, whether they're deacons or drug dealers, they like to share the latest gossip. And I have quite a few contacts on the street, including some with the police. On one or two occasions, I've offered the authorities very discreet help. They've shown their appreciation by sharing information with me."

"And you obviously have a good memory."

"No," Mamadou said. "I have an *excellent* memory. And very strong powers of deduction, which is what made me a superior

THIRST

police officer in my native country. But mostly, Mr. Marsh, it's due to the fact that Washington is a very small town. And when you start dealing with the moneyed folks, the people who routinely rent a limo for a night, the fact of the matter is, all these people know each other. Perhaps not directly, I'm not suggesting that the President of United First Bank is a personal friend of criminals, but I can guarantee you that somewhere, somehow, there's a link. Money knows money."

He sat back, rattled the remaining ice in his drink.

Colin said, "And the girl, Josie. What were she and Herbie talking about that night, the time they were both in your car?"

Mamadou shrugged. "I have no idea. There was no reason for me to notice." He looked inside his glass as if to make sure it was empty. "Perhaps I haven't made myself entirely clear, Colin—may I call you Colin? Good. Herbie never bragged about his employment, particularly to the women he was with. To them he was a successful real estate entrepreneur, or a lawyer, or merely a young man with inherited wealth. I wouldn't be in the least surprised if your young lady had no inkling of what he actually did for a living. As a matter of fact, I'd wager she was unaware. He was handsome, he had money, he showed her a good time. She probably had no idea."

It made sense. Colin glanced at the bar, took note of two teenagers who were too young to be drinking. They wore baseball caps on backwards, slammed Budweiser from long-necked bottles.

He asked, "Why?"

Mamadou looked up. "Why what?"

Colin took the *Post* printouts from his pocket, slid them across the table. The Senegalese found a pair of thin reading glasses in a pocket, put them on. He scanned the pages, smiled.

"Well, I'm honored. You've done your research." He refolded the sheets, slid them back to Colin. "The story's essentially accurate. Some gunmen attacked me in my home. I defended it. I believe that's one of the express rights I have in this country."

"Just like that? Attacked you."

"Absolutely. Burst into my living room. I had no choice."

"Lucky you had weapons to defend yourself."

Mamadou smiled. "Lucky indeed. I'm a former policeman, Colin. I was trained to handle weapons of all sorts, and in this violent nation of yours, it's a right I exercised."

Both men fell silent. The two teenagers left. Mamadou laughed briefly. "That's such a strange fashion, the baseball caps. It always makes me think their heads are facing the wrong way."

Colin smiled. The image would stick. "So where do we go from here?"

Mamadou raised an eyebrow. "We? I don't know about *we*. What I'll do is ask around. There're bound to be rumors. Everyone knows about Herbie's fate by now. Maybe someone knows about his girlfriend's as well."

∞

Colin declined Mamadou's offer of a ride and walked home. The bar was less than a mile from his apartment building and it was a pleasant night; a full moon bathed the trees and the temperature had become bearable. He hoped Catherine would call, was uneasy about becoming too closely involved with the Senegalese.

He wondered whether Dioh himself was a dealer; the man claimed to know the workings of the street and drug cultures, but if that was the case, why volunteer to help? No, Colin thought. That didn't feel right. There was something else going on, something more complex.

Why had Dioh been so willing to talk? Colin replayed the conversation. It had been full of suppositions and inferences, without much concrete information. With enough time, anyone

Thirst

could have gathered that knowledge. And yet through the disquiet he felt, Colin also felt a measure of admiration. Policeman or not, it had taken nerve and audacity to face down the gang members. And the Senegalese had voiced no regrets.

By the time Colin reached his building it was nearly midnight. As he opened the door he saw Joe the Cop dozing on a bench in the vestibule, a copy of that morning's *Post* on his lap.

"Hey, there you are! I was gonna give it five more minutes." He folded the paper, put it his jacket pocket.

Joe the Cop wore a rumpled gray suit over a light blue shirt with a wide brown tie pulled loose at the neck. He had on thin white socks and cordovan wingtips. One of his shoes was unlaced.

"I had the late shift. I just dropped by, hope you don't mind."

Colin shook his head. "No. You doing all right?"

They headed for the elevator, waited. Joe said, "Couldn't be better. No screaming desires. No drinking dreams anymore. I'm still doing it a day at a time and I have to admit it's getting easier. This is something else. I thought you might want to know about it."

The elevator stopped at Colin's floor. Joe waited for Colin to unlock the door, made a beeline for the kitchen. Colin could hear him open the fridge, pour something in a glass, close the fridge again.

Joe asked, "Want anything?"

"No thanks."

"Good, cause there's not much in there and I just finished the last of your orange juice."

He came into the living room, dropped his weight on the couch, noticed his untied lace. He took a moment to do it properly, pulled his tie off and stuffed it in a pocket, opened the two top buttons of his shirt. Then he glanced at his shoes, shook his head, and toed them off. "Damn, that feels good." He wiggled his feet, scratched an ankle.

"Better. Anyway. This is about your missing friend. I was at a meeting earlier—I'm trying to do one a day whenever I can—and afterwards I was hanging around the parking lot for a minute to see if there was anyone I know who wanted to go for coffee. Got nothing better to do, and sometimes I don't want to be at home. You know. I'm alone, sometimes I start thinking stuff I shouldn't be thinking." He looked up at Colin to make sure he understood. Colin nodded, rubbed his eyes. When Joe started talking, it was always a long haul. He allowed himself to sink into the chair.

"So I'm sitting there but turns out I don't know anybody by name but I see these two girls, young women, early twenties, max. I've seen them around at a meeting or two. They're always together, one sponsors the other, I guess. I think maybe I've talked to them, you know? Standard meeting-after-the-meeting shit. I catch the eye of one of them and she smiles, so I go over there and we start talking, nothing special, just shooting the breeze. And I think, 'Well, what the hell. Why not,' and I ask about your friend, Josie. You know how it is, AA's always a small town. Everybody knows everybody else or if they don't, they know someone who does. That's why they call it a fellowship, I guess."

"They knew her?"

"Hang on, okay? Yeah, they do, but lemme tell the story, all right?" Joe paused, waited for Colin's nod.

"Well at first they're a little bit wary, you know? But that's normal, young girls like that. There's always some old fart trying to get close to 'em after the meeting, impart his wisdom, that kinda shit. So I'm not offended. I mean, I think it's pitiful how some of these guys hit on women like they do; if I were a chick, I sure wouldn't want anything to do with 'em. But me, I look trustworthy. People always tell me that. I go on the crime scene, and people tell me stuff. I say to the captain, 'It's a blessing.' He should give me a raise."

Colin closed his eyes. This was going to take some time. "Josie?"

Thirst

Joe nodded. "Yeah yeah…so anyway, they know her. They tell me about this women's meeting they go to, a church basement. Turns out it's Josie's meeting, she's been chairing it for three, four months now, and she's really good about it, makes sure the speakers are on time, coffee's made, helps straighten the place out afterwards, that kinda thing. And she wasn't there yesterday, a first, one of the girls says.

"Well, I tell 'em I know Josie a little—okay, it's not true, but it's not a big lie, either. I *kinda* know her, you could say. So we keep talking and I get the feeling that maybe they're not all that nuts about her after all. And I'm right, they're not, they think your Josie's kind of a control freak, as far as the meetings go. Apparently, conscientious as she is, she really runs that meeting like she owns it; nobody likes that shit, and these other two, they've been straight a lot longer, and they don't really care for that. Matter of fact, in spite of Josie doing such a good job, there's people who wanna see about turning the meeting over to someone else. You know how AA politics are… come to think of it, I guess they're no different from anyplace else." Joe got up. "Be back in a minute." He went into the bathroom and closed the door. Colin took the opportunity to check his voice mail for messages. Nothing.

Joe reappeared holding a glass of water and sat back down.

"So, to make a long story short, we do go for coffee. And like always it turns out we got a lot of people in common, you know? 'Have you heard from so and so?' and 'Whatever happened to whosits,' and 'It's so sad whatshisname went out again, but I knew he would, he never really worked the program,' that sort of stuff. I told them I was a cop and that didn't faze 'em. They asked about that guy who turned out to be the prostitute killer, you remember, the one who dumped their bodies next to the Dulles access road, and I was a little involved in that case. Anyway, the conversation drifts back to Josie, and they ask me whether I know the pigeon she's sponsoring, someone new in the program who apparently looked like hell the first day she came in. Well of course I don't, so we start talking about sponsors and incidentally, your name came up, Colin; one of them knows you by sight. Called you 'that huge guy.'" Joe the Cop smirked. "Course, I didn't ask 'em what part of you they found huge. Okay, so what it comes down to is that Josie was sponsoring someone new, a real young girl name of Mollie who came in maybe seven or eight weeks ago. This girl, she looks like she could suck-start a Harley—one of the women said that, I didn't. Anyway, she made a big fuss during a recent meeting, started cussing and stuff, really took the group to task for being a bunch of snobs and not being friendly at all. She accuses them of not treating her right because she's a dancer and a heroin addict.

"Well Josie got her to quiet down, asked her to share her story so the other people can get to know her better, and she did. She dances in this DC club, Pete's Place. You might have heard about it, it's right in the business district, next to MCI, a couple of blocks from the White House. These legit businesses tried to prevent it from opening and couldn't, and they've been trying to close it down and can't. I think it's mob owned. Not a good place, bikers and a lot of druggies in there, but students and some high-paid city bureaucrats too. Rough sometimes, gets the emergency squad at least once a week, but it's near George Washington University Hospital. Kind of a tough job, being a dancer there, I'd guess. You know, you're working on your recovery, it's kinda like trying to maintain a diet in a bakery, but the tips are good, which is why she's there—working in that bar, I mean."

Joe drained the glass of water. "You don't happen to have a Coke or something?"

Colin shook his head. "Sorry."

Joe shrugged, continued. "So the two girls I'm talking to have to leave after a while, and I've got nothing to do so I go back to

Thirst

the station and hit the computer because I remember Pete's Place was busted not too long ago. I think a couple of German tourists got stabbed right around there and the police finally had to do something. They don't want another Miami in the Nation's Capital. Place has a bad enough rep as is, and lo and behold, there's a Mollie Catfish—no shit, that's her name—she was nabbed in the sweep. And I figure that's got to be her. She gave a bogus address on the forms, by the way, and no phone number but nobody cared because she was clean. But she sure made an impression on a couple of the boys. Gary Smelk, this DC cop I play poker with sometimes—he's in the program too, got six, seven years—he was part of the action that went into Pete's and he just couldn't stop talking about this girl. Tits out to there, he says, and a mouth on her like you wouldn't believe. He said he'd give a week's pay for an hour's rack time with her."

Colin said, "Hang on a second, Joe. Let me make a couple of notes."

Joe waited until Colin found a pen and some paper, then continued, "Thing is, I don't know where this Mollie lives, DC or Virginia, maybe even Maryland. She's not in any of the phone books, maybe she just moved here, but I thought it might be helpful."

He took a deep breath and added, "You know, I got a couple of days off coming up, so if you want, I could maybe kind of talk to her, find out whatever she knows if you like." Joe looked at Colin expectantly. The prospect of talking to a woman with tits out to there had him interested.

Colin laughed. "I'd guess her recent experiences with the police might make you unwelcome. Save your days off, Joe. I'll go look her up." He paused. "That's really her name, Mollie Catfish?"

Joe the Cop shrugged away his disappointment, then nodded. "Yes indeed. North Carolina driver's license. Probably a fake, it says she's twenty-one. Mollie Catfish. Isn't that a hell of a thing? Imagine being her daddy and hanging a name like that on your daughter. Should be against the law."

※

The next day Colin waited until eleven, then called Pete's Place. A woman answered and he asked if Mollie was dancing there today. The woman said, "Hold a sec," let the phone drop, returned in a moment. "No Mollie here but come on down anyway, all the girls are real good dancers. You want a reservation? You need one for lunch."

Colin made sure the woman could hear his disappointment. "Just my luck. I must have gotten her name wrong last week. Thought she said Mollie Catfish? She told me she'd be there."

"You mean MC? Why didn't you say so? Yeah, lemme see. She'll be here at two. Gets the tail end of the lunch trade. C'mon over. I'm sure she'll be glad to see you."

※

Pete's Place was a pale brick three-story brownstone that had once been a home, then a rooming house, then a hardware store, and finally a series of restaurants. There was an awning over a window painted flat white and a Budweiser banner announcing a karaoke contest. The building was wedged between a Chinese take-out restaurant and a PMI parking lot full of pickup trucks, new and expensive foreign imports, and older American cars. A half-dozen Harleys were lined up with military precision in front.

It was just after two when he got there and paid the five dollars to get in. He let his eyes adjust to the dim light. Inside, tiny Bose speakers hung from the ceiling and poured out music so loud it went into and through him, vibrating his bones. It amazed him that such a

Thirst

place could thrive even during the day; he wondered how the people who worked there could stand it, and then noticed that the bouncer wore bright yellow ear plugs.

There was a small dance floor ringed by diminutive tables. Colin found an empty one and sat. The blue-jeaned waitress had ear plugs too. She stared at his lips when he ordered a Coke and a cup of coffee, nodded, ran a hand through lank blonde hair. "You gonna eat?" Her voice somehow reached under the music. Colin shook his head. The waitress shrugged. "One Coke, one coffee. Seven dollars." He handed her a ten. "Change?" Colin mouthed, "No." She took the ten, smiled briefly.

The owners had tried for a show of style, brass accents and a long polished bar on the farthest side, green plants that may have been real. There were three large rooms painted different colors. Against a wall in each area was a raised dais backed with a mirror and a fireman's pole running from floor to ceiling. On each dais was a dancer. The three women, two brunettes and a blonde, were totally nude save for one garter. The brunettes had their pubic hair shaved. All had surgically enhanced breasts attached to hard, thin bodies.

The dancer nearest Colin, a brunette with a wealth of permed hair that cascaded to her hips, flashed him a bright smile and blew him a kiss. When he didn't react, her eyes snaked past him to another patron seated two tables away. The man wore a well-fed look on a pink face that deepened to florid in places. His hair was combed carefully over his bald spot, but the heat of the moment had caused a few strands to slip and expose flaking scalp. Colin saw that as soon as the man looked up, the girl began dancing more suggestively, coiling long legs around the pole, pelvis thrusting to the beat of the music. Then she spun around, bent over and, head turned so as not to lose eye contact with the customer, did a split. Colin blinked. The bureaucrat made an O with his mouth and clapped; his tongue ran pink all the way around his lips. He took a five dollar bill from his wallet, held it up for the girl to see, spun an index finger in the air. Do it again. The girl repeated the movement, letting her legs splay wide with agonizing slowness. Colin, like the other customer, was mesmerized. The girl noticed, shot him another smile. He tried to focus on her face but his eyes had a will of their own, resting first on her breasts and then lower. The girl rammed her hips in his direction and winked.

The music ended and the dancer's movement slowed and stopped like a clock winding down. She pulled a translucent camisole over her head and jumped from the dais to the floor. Colin found a five dollar bill and handed it to her as she walked past his table. She glanced at the money, took it from his hand, and put the bill in her garter belt and gave him the briefest of grins, then moved on to the other customer, who now held up two tens. He stood as she neared and pulled a chair out but she shook her head. No socializing with the customers. Colin saw the man fumble for his wallet and hand her a card. The girl smiled, palmed it, and walked toward a door that said Employees Only.

Five minutes later the waitress reappeared. "Refill, hon?"

Colin nodded. While the waitress poured the coffee, he asked, "Has MC been around?"

She gave him an odd look, reached into her apron and dropped two white containers of Half and Half in his saucer.

"You know her?"

Colin shook his head. "No. Friend of a friend."

The waitress lost interest. "Well, you just missed her." She pointed her chin toward the dais. "Anything else you want? My shift's ending."

Colin found two tens. "Keep it."

The waitress understood. "Want me to see if she's still here? They do forty on, twenty off." The money made her talkative. "But I think you're wasting your time. MC dances. That's all she does,

THIRST

nothing more. She's a nice girl." She rearranged the salt and pepper shakers, moved the French's Mustard an inch to the left. "You want something else, talk to Marylin or Sandrah," her eyes moved to the second dais where a tall redhead with perfect teeth was gyrating. "Cat doesn't date the customers."

Colin wondered if that was true, said, "Can you just ask if she can come by?"

The waitress shrugged. "Sure thing. But I wouldn't expect much if I were you."

She walked to the Employees Only door, was gone less than a minute. "She's changing. Wants to know who the friend is."

Colin made another ten appear. "Josie. Tell her I'm a friend of Josie's."

The waitress sighed, tired of playing messenger, took the money. "It's your nickel."

When she reappeared the second time, she said, "MC'll be out in a minute." She glanced at her wristwatch, took her apron off, balled it up. "I'm outta here. Have a nice day."

Colin sipped his Coke. The ice had melted and the drink had almost no flavor left. He thought about who he knew in AA, tried to recall another nude dancer. He couldn't remember one, though in meetings the strangest people kept cropping up. The sword swallower who'd showed up drunk for a show and had the tools of her trade confiscated by an angry nightclub owner was about as exotic as he could remember.

"You seen Josie?"

She was standing behind him; he hadn't heard her coming.

"Mollie, right? Or MC?"

"Either one, I don't really care. MC's the name I use here. You know Josie?"

Colin turned to face the woman. Off the dais she looked smaller. She was wearing silver sandals and a Hawaiian print shift that hid her figure. Her face was pocked by childhood chickenpox, and up close Colin could see her hair wasn't her own.

As if reading his thought, she said, "We look a lot less glamorous without the music." She glanced around the room, "Look, I don't have a lot of time. This is when I go home and I'd like to get off my feet. What about Josie?"

Colin said, "I'm a friend of Bill's." Bill W., the founder of AA.

The woman's expression didn't change. "Good for you. I'm duly impressed. But Bill has about a zillion friends so you're not exactly special." For a moment she looked thoughtful, and her eyes narrowed. "Are you a cop? Has something happened to Josie? Is that why you're here?" She took a step back, drew away. "Cause I haven't seen her in a couple of weeks. So if this is some sort of bullshit cop stuff, gimme a break, OK? I really don't need this kinda crap, you know? You guys tried to bust my ass a month ago, and enough's enough."

Her voice rose, hovered between anger and fright. "Look. I'm telling you the truth, I haven't seen her, and I'm going now."

Colin held up a hand. "I'm not a cop. Really."

The bouncer had moved from the door, was eying them. "Can we go someplace to talk? Please. It's important. Josie's missing. I'm trying to find her."

She thought about it. The bouncer was ten feet away and coming closer. He moved on his toes like a boxer. "MC? You being bothered?"

She glanced down at Colin, who was still sitting, and made up her mind. "It's okay, Benny. It's cool."

The bouncer stopped. "You sure?"

She nodded. "Yeah, Benny. Thanks. Just a little misunderstanding."

The bouncer retreated to his station by the door. She said, "Benny's a friend of Bill's too. Takes all kinds, doesn't it."

Thirst

Colin stood and was about to give the dancer a bill when he thought better of it. The music had started again and a different girl was on the dais. He said, "There's a coffee place on the corner. Can we meet there?"

She thought about that too. "Yeah. Okay. You go there, I'll meet you in fifteen minutes. I've gotta clean up, and I don't want anybody to see me leaving with a customer. They'll get the wrong idea." She turned to leave. "You sure you're not a cop? Cause if you are, I'm gonna really be pissed off."

※

Outside it was bright; Colin felt like he was coming out of a cave. He walked to the Quartermaine, ordered a double espresso. The kid behind the bar called out, "One dopey O!" to a slightly older colleague who echoed the command. The big chrome machine hissed and sputtered. The kid handed Colin a tiny cup.

Colin looked into it. "That's it?"

"It's quality, not quantity. You want another shot? That's an extra buck. As is, two seventy -five."

Colin handed him three singles. "Keep the change."

The kid said, "Thanks," rang up the sale, and dropped the solitary quarter into a mug by the cash register. "Just so you know, we split the tips at night among all the staff."

Colin said, "That's nice," dropped two packs of Equal into the cup, stirred it with a wooden stick, and remembered reading about tropical deforestation that was caused by the Japanese demand for disposable chopsticks. He took a seat by the window, stuck the stirrer in his mouth, and watched the traffic rumble by.

He noticed traffic cops at both ends of the street and remembered the closing of Pennsylvania Avenue in front of the White House for security reasons. The Reagan years. The resulting rerouting of some 16,000 cars, trucks, and buses daily had immediately rendered obsolete all the traffic signals in a six-square-block area. Cops had been pulled off street patrol to handle the horde of tourists and commuters who poured into and out of the city and used the avenue as a thoroughfare. As a safety measure, the closure hadn't been particularly effective. The day after the avenue was blocked off, a man with a concealed kitchen knife climbed the fence to pay the President an impromptu visit.

Colin drank his espresso in one swallow and looked at his watch. The girl was already late, and he wondered whether she'd agreed to meet him to get him out of the club. He ordered a second double, left another quarter tip, and resumed his seat on the stool by the window.

He didn't recognize the woman who came into the shop, walked past him, and ordered a decaf. The dancer had taken off her hair, stripped her makeup, and was now wearing jeans, bright green leather sandals, and a University of Maryland Terrapins sweatshirt. She looked like a student, perhaps a tourist. Only her breasts were out of place.

She took the stool next to his. "Show me your chip."

It took a moment to register.

She said, "Your chip. You're in AA, your chip is your most prized possession. Lemme see it."

Colin stood, reached into the bottom of his right pants pocket, dropped it on the counter. It made a coppery sound. She picked it up, scrutinized it.

"Ten years?"

She sounded disappointed, and for some reason he felt he had to apologize.

"Would have been fourteen. I blew it once."

"Slip or relapse?"

Thirst

"Full-fledged relapse. I was out seven months. Came back in, went out again a week later. Did that three times. Fourth time around it took, but only because I spent three days in the tank. After that, the county put me in detox, then I rehabbed."

She pondered that. "I'm still brand new. It's going to be four months next week if I don't fuck up. See?" She wore her chip on a gold chain around her neck, allowed him to look at it for a second, then dropped it back down into her sweatshirt.

"So," she said. "Now we've gotten over the formalities. Let's get down to the serious stuff, like who are you, what you want. Like I said, I haven't seen Josie, not in a couple of weeks."

"She's your sponsor?"

The woman put her coffee cup down. "Look, before we get all personal and buddy-buddy, I don't know you from some asshole that comes into the bar and just wants to get laid, pardon my French. Which is okay, getting laid, I mean, but not with me 'cause I stopped doing that about the same time I stopped drinking. Which means I make a lot less tip money, which means in turn that I have another job, and I have to be there in about an hour. The only reason I came is that you had the good manners *not* to shove some money at me back there in the bar, because if you had, then I would have been sure you were an asshole and I would have asked Benny to kick your ass out. And he would have, too, because he likes me and he thinks I'm crazy to work in there while trying to stay straight. I tell him if I'm crazy, he's crazy too, but he thinks he's justified, 'cause he's been drinking only fruit juice for twelve years, but I personally think it's a bunch of macho crap. Okay, now you know my life story, and I still don't know who the hell you are."

Colin smiled. Her speech had made her likable. He said, "I'm Colin Marsh. I'm not a cop. That doesn't mean I'm not an asshole, sometimes—make that often—but I came in there looking for you because I thought you could help." He stuck his hand out. She shook it. He was surprised to feel the firmness of her grasp. There were calluses in her palm.

She flexed her fingers. "You get those from gripping the pole and swinging around. What about Josie?"

He swished the coffee in the cup. "I don't know Josie personally, or at least not well. But her mother and I are friends, and she thinks something bad may have happened to her. She hasn't been home in a couple of days. I asked around, and someone told me she was your sponsor. That's all there is."

The woman reached into her purse, drew out a cigarette and a lighter. "There's a table free outside. I can't smoke in here. Which is pretty stupid, a coffee place where they don't allow you to smoke, but I lit up here once, thinking of something else, and the two faggots back there almost had conniptions." She stood up, straightened her jeans.

Once outside and seated, she said, "Yeah. Josie is, was, my sponsor, kind of. It's not official cause she doesn't have a year yet; we're supposed to meet twice a week but she missed the last four meetings. I thought maybe she'd run away with Herbie, you know Herbie, her boyfriend?"

"She's not with Herbie. Herbie's dead."

The woman nodded. "Yeah, well, I'm not shocked. Not really sorry, either, Herbie was an asshole too. I met him once for five minutes and as soon as Josie had her back turned he started hitting on me. When I told her about it later she just kind of shrugged, but I could tell it bothered her. What happened?"

"Police says he was beaten up, stabbed, and shot. His body was found near Rock Creek Park. They think he was dealing."

That made her grimace. "They *think*? Christ. He practically shoved a coke spoon up my nose, one of those horrible tiny gold numbers like people used to have hanging from a chain around their neck, except he kept his in this little leather bag in his pocket. Had this greasy smile on and said there was plenty more if we got to be friends. Used those very words."

"Was Josie using, Mollie?"

The woman looked him in the eyes for the very first time. "Actually, I *do* prefer 'MC.' I've always hated 'Mollie.' That was my first foster parents' idea. They named me after a cocker spaniel they had when they were newlyweds."

"Mollie Catfish."

"Yeah. Shit, can you imagine anyone having 'Catfish' as a family name? But it's right there on my birth certificate. I've been meaning for years to have it changed; never get around to it."

She puffed on the cigarette without inhaling. "But it's kinda distinctive, you know? Stands out. I took a lot of shit about it when I was a kid, but you get over it. Makes you tougher, that's what my stepfather used to say."

She dropped the cigarette on the sidewalk, crushed it. "So Herbie's dead..." She let the sentence hang.

"What can you tell me about Josie that could help me find her?"

She pushed back her chair, extended her legs. Colin could see the muscles in her calf through the denim, the red polish on her toe nails. "I really don't know her that well, and not that long. I went to a women's meeting maybe ten, twelve weeks ago, and they announced that there were temporary sponsors, and I saw her standing next to the coffee pot and introduced myself. I didn't have a sponsor; it was time to get one but you know how it is, it's the kinda thing you keep delaying. We exchanged phone numbers and of course I didn't call her like she asked me to. There's always an excuse, too busy, don't need it, ashamed, embarrassed, whatever. The 1000-pound telephone. So a couple of days later she called me; I was kinda surprised. We met and had coffee, talked about stuff, nothing very meaningful. I told her right away what I did and it didn't faze her. I thought that was cool. She didn't tell me to quit my job, and that was cool too, because that's all I hear, get another job, don't hang around slippery places." She laughed but there was distaste there.

"It's like, what do these people expect? In a good week, I make a grand, sometimes more, and that's just in tips. It's a pretty clean place. No blowjobs in the booths, excuse my French. Owners don't allow it, though they let the girls go out on their own time with the customers. What am I supposed to do, work at Burger King? Six bucks an hour and mop the place down after it closes?

"Anyway, Josie didn't comment on that. Just asked if I thought I could stay straight there, with all the booze and, yeah, there's drugs too. I said it's a lot better than where I worked before. Real redneck joint in Bladensburg where if you *didn't* give blowjobs you were out on your ass. Simple as that."

She threw Colin a glance, tried to read his face. He kept it impassive. She asked, "Am I shocking you?"

"Are you trying to?"

She laughed. This time her eyes were in it. "Yeah, I suppose a little. That's how I gauge people; they have a problem with what I do, then fuck 'em if they can't take a joke, you know? I don't have the time. Anyhow, Josie didn't give me a lot of grief. I think she found it kinda exciting. The second time we saw each other, all she had was questions. How'd I get started? How'd I deal with the assholes? How much I got paid. Then we got into girl stuff. It was silly. She tried on some of the outfits I wear and I showed her a few steps, simple stuff. Time after that I took her to the gym with me, wore her out. I thought maybe she was gonna be a friend."

Colin asked, "What did she talk about?"

Mollie Catfish shrugged. "Her addictions. How it was for her. Rehab. AA and NA. Herbie, when I got to know her a little. Her parents. Her father and how he's a dick. You know her parents?"

Colin hesitated. "I know her mother. I've only met her father once or twice."

Thirst

"I went to her house once and he looked right through me, like I wasn't there. She introduced me and I stuck my hand out. He looked at it like it was a dead animal by the side of the road or something. Just kinda nodded and walked away. Josie told me not to get upset about it. He treats everybody like that. I mean, you're talking about a real dork.

"Her mother was pretty nice, though, I liked her. Josie just said I was a friend, not that she was my sponsor or anything. She wanted to keep that to herself, I think, like it was our secret. I didn't mind. Anyway, her mother talked to me a couple of minutes, and then she went away too. I think Josie feels sorry for her mother, having an asshole husband and all, but she kinda blames her too. Like her mother should have done better for herself somehow. What it comes down to is, I think Josie's pretty confused." She stirred another pack of Equal into her coffee. "So that day I went to her house, we just sat around the back yard and that's when she talked about Herbie."

Colin asked, "You never answered my first question, Cat. Was she using, you think?"

The woman looked up. "You mean because she was hanging with Herbie? No. No, she was clean. She didn't *know* he was dealing, or if she did, she just blocked it out. She really liked him, at least at the start. And I guess he was okay at the beginning, I suppose."

"But you didn't like him."

Mollie Catfish considered the statement before answering. "Not so much that I didn't like him. It's just that he came on to me, you know? And that's what men do all the time at the club, they shove a couple of bucks at me and half the time there's a phone number there, like they expect me to call, right? In the beginning it pissed me off and then I got used to it. It's just part of the business, and some of the girls do call, and it's always like a quickie at some cheesy motel. I mean, they make a lot of bucks that way; some of these guys are really desperate. So when Herbie came on, it just made him *un*special, you know, just another asshole after a quick bang while his wife—or in this case girlfriend—has her back turned. I mean, Josie could do a lot better than Herbie. She's pretty and she's smart, to me it was like she just settled for…what do they call it? The lowest common denominator."

"Why do you think that is?"

She considered that too. "Why? Jeez, I'm no shrink. But I read a lot of self-help books, you know? Positive thinking, stuff like that. So off the top of my head, what I'd say is she's got real low self-esteem. She shouldn't. There's no reason for it, but she does. Lots of people like that in AA, but you've been there longer than me, so I don't have to tell you that. And like I said, I'm no expert. That's just me thinking out loud."

Colin changed subjects. "You said you have a second job?"

She looked at her watch, nodded. "Just a minute more. Yeah, I do. Actually I'm in training. It's just a couple of hours a day. The brother of this girl I know has a little travel agency. Mostly he books cruises. He said he'd teach me how to use the computer to actually make the reservations and then eventually I could become a travel agent. Good pay, free trips. Sounds like the good life, huh?"

She looked at her watch again.

Colin asked, "Nothing else you can tell me?"

She stood. "Gotta go. Nope. Nothing I can think of."

Colin scribbled his name and phone number on a napkin and handed it to her. "Give me a call if you think of anything, or if you just want to talk."

She looked at the napkin doubtfully and stuffed it in her purse. "Sure thing." She walked off, turned around, added without a smile, "As long as it's just talk."

Thirst

☯

Colin drove home over the Roosevelt Bridge and cut over to 66. The ashtray in the old Porsche 924's console had three butts in it, and the entire car smelled like McDonald's. He turned the radio on. A Latino station came in loud and strong, which meant the parking lot attendant had taken his lunch break in the Porsche and hadn't appreciated Colin's taste in music. Another good reason not to come into DC.

In his apartment he checked his voice mail and retrieved two messages. The first one was from Catherine. He heard, "I'm still angry, and I'm disgusted. I don't have to tell you that this completely changes the way you and I are going to be. There's still no word from Josie. Please call me."

The second message was from Joe the Cop and it was longer. "Colin, there was a body and I thought it might be the girl. The description fit so I went to the morgue, except the description was wrong. It turned out to be a guy wearing a dress, a wig, and fake fingernails. Apparently nobody noticed she was a he. I guess that's good news since it's not the girl, but it doesn't say much for the quality of police work around here. If you change your mind and want me to check out the dancer, call and leave a message. Bye."

Colin picked up the phone, dialed Catherine's number, hung up. He hadn't really learned anything substantial from Mollie Catfish. The dancer knew Josie, but only slightly, and the information she'd provided on Josie's boyfriend was conjecture at best, which meant that any conversation with Cat would focus on his brief liaison with her daughter. And what was there to say about that?

Thierry Sagnier

He hadn't really noticed the girl. It was late, chilly; the grounds around the Serenity Club still bore patches of ice from the winter's final snowfall. The last of the parking lot people had either gone home or retreated to the IHOP a block away for one final cup of coffee.

Colin's newest pigeon hadn't shown up at the meeting. He was a young man, less than a month sober, and they were to meet there after the boy got off work pounding dough at the nearby Pizza Hut. Except that the boy never came. Colin hadn't been surprised, though he was annoyed at having to wait in the cold. He didn't particularly want to be a sponsor; Orin G. has pushed him to it and the pigeon had been both shaky and defiant, barely out of detox, full of anger and wary of the program. Colin would give it five more minutes and go home.

The girl, though he didn't know it was a girl at the time, leaned against a wall some twenty feet away and seemed to be waiting as well, chain-smoking and rubbing her gloved hands together. She wore jeans, a heavy parka, and a ski cap and every few seconds glanced at her watch, straightened, took a few steps, scanned the parking lot. Once, when the headlights of a car pushed through the gloom she picked up her knapsack and walked quickly in that direction but the car swept past her.

A few minutes after that she threw her cigarette down, stepped on it angrily, slung the knapsack over her shoulder, and disappeared around a corner. Five seconds later Colin heard the sound of a scuffle and a woman's voice yell, "Lay off, motherfucker!" A man's voice, muffled, followed. "Hey! Hey! C'mon, babe. Quiet, now! Nothin's gonna happen, c'mon." Then there was the sound of fabric ripping and the woman's voice rose in pitch. "Get *away* from me, asshole!"

THIRST

Later Colin would decide once again that there are no coincidences in life, that everything and every moment has its own reason for being and that the links between moments were there for a purpose. He moved quickly, saw two indistinct shapes of different sizes grappling. He grabbed the bigger shape, yanked back sharply. The shape said, "What the fuck?" and swung wildly. Colin ducked. It wasn't a very good blow and its momentum turned the man around. Colin took a step, braced himself, and threw one short, very hard punch that hit the man just below the solar plexus and lifted him inches off the ground. He fell with a dull thud, coughed, retched, and threw up on himself. The night air was suddenly suffused with the stink of warm booze and digestive fluids.

Colin moved to the woman. Her ski cap had been knocked off and the front of her parka was torn. The flap of her knapsack was open, her belongings spilled in a puddle. Without looking at him she dropped to both knees and started picking them up. A few feet away the man crawled off, rose to his feet, fell again, mumbled, "I wasn't gonna hurt her. I jus' wanted to fuck her…"

Colin knelt beside the girl, saw close-cropped blonde hair kept in place by a yellow headband. Her eyes were brown or green and very round. There was a small cut on her right cheekbone and a drop of blood was bright red against her pale skin. Her breathing came in short gasps. He said, "You all right?" She nodded her head, but he knew she wasn't.

He helped her gather a bottle of Advil, a hairbrush, and a pocket edition of the Big Book. She grasped his hand and rose to her feet. He felt a thin arm quiver, caught her as her knees buckled. He said, "Do you want me to call someone? Get the police…"

She shook her head. "No. No."

She leaned against him and there wasn't much weight there. She brought a gloved hand to her face, touched the cut, and in a very small voice said, "Shit. I'm bleeding."

Colin said. "It's a scratch. You're okay. Are you sure you don't want me to call…"

She shook her head. "Fine. I'm fine. Gotta lie down for a second, that's all."

So he did as she asked, took her to his apartment. During the ride there she didn't say anything but her fingers touched the cut repeatedly, wiped at the blood so it made a small dark circle like the exaggerated makeup of a mime.

In the building's elevator she leaned against him and in the apartment she headed straight for the bathroom, shedding parka, headband, sweater, bra. She closed the bathroom door and Colin heard the shower run. He busied himself in the kitchen, boiled water for tea, found a Band Aid in the junk drawer.

She was in the bathroom a long time. He heard the toilet flush twice, then the whine of the hair dryer he never used. Steam billowed out when she opened the door.

She was wrapped in two towels, one from the shoulders to the knees, one around her head. His toothbrush was sticking out of her mouth. He handed her a cup of tea and she took it, nodded. Then she said, "I'm gonna lie down. You mind?"

She was tall and very slender and he couldn't tell her age; he thought she might be in her twenties, though her walk was older. He followed her to the bedroom, holding the Band Aid and feeling silly. She dropped the bottom towel, lifted the cover from the bed, crawled in. "You coming?"

He thought maybe she just wanted to be held, he really thought that, it was a common reaction to physical stress, and for minutes that's all he did until her trembling subsided. He asked her name and she said, "Jane. Now shush," and pressed against him. He still had all his clothes on.

After a while he thought she was asleep but then felt her lips against his neck. She whispered, "Thank you."

THIRST

Then she moved so his hips and hers were in line and there was a subtle tension, a barely rhythmic pressure. She was breathing evenly now and her face was turned half against the pillow. Her arm snaked out, found the switch to the bed lamp. She got up, pushed the door shut. Now the room was in complete darkness save for a strip of light filtering through a gap in the doorway. She undid the buttons of his shirt, slid it off, unbuckled his belt, kept removing clothing silently.

He said, "You don't have to…"

"I know." She took his hand, moved his thumb to her lips. "See? I'm smiling."

When he was entirely naked she kissed his Adam's apple and moved down, lingered on his nipples, traveled to his navel, then lower. She took him in her mouth and he held her head lightly in both hands as it moved insistently. When he was hard she sat up and straddled him, moved two fingers to her mouth and made herself wet. She let him enter her very slowly though without hesitation and only when he was fully in did she allow her weight to rest on him. She stayed there without moving for a while, then leaned down, placed her hands on his chest, and began a slow purposeful thrust that was more horizontal than anything else. He matched her, heard her gasp slightly. She shifted her body so she was leaning back, slight breasts thrust to the ceiling, hips still moving forward and back with measured regularity.

Then she swung off, got on her hands and knees beside him. "This way."

She guided him and he entered her from behind, pushing at him and squashing her cheeks. He took her slim hips in both hands and pulled her against him, and she grunted softly, said, "Yeah, like that," so he did it again and again, felt himself surge. She reached down and back between her legs, held him between her thumb and forefinger. Her touch there was the trigger he needed but didn't really want yet. He tried to hold back, couldn't, and stopped trying. The bed trembled beneath them and he heard her smile.

A little while later he tried to talk again but she held her palm against his mouth. She said, "It doesn't matter." Then she got up.

"Gotta go."

He moved to stand up but she pushed him back. "Stay there. I'm going to call a cab, and I don't want you to come with me, okay?"

He started to argue but she said, "Please? I know what I'm doing. Really." She pulled her jeans on. "Just say yes."

So he did. She walked to the bedroom door, closed it behind her. He heard her dial the phone, stood, and had the door half opened when she said, "Please don't come out. It'll ruin everything." So he didn't. She finished dressing in the living room and after a while there was the faint click of the latch thrown, the door opened and softly closed.

In the morning it was more like a dream, less like a fantasy. The bed still held the girl's smell, a faint mélange of sweat, soap, and shampoo. He found a couple of blonde hairs on his pillow. Her teacup was still full and cold on the night table.

☙

Catherine said, "I talked to my sponsor."

Her voice was calm and dry on the phone. "I'm still furious, but I don't want to kill you anymore. That's what I felt like, Colin, killing you. But then I thought that out of this bizarre situation, there's something good coming. And that's that I was beginning to care too much about you, and now I don't. Now I'm just angry, and sad, and repulsed."

Colin listened, phone cradled against a shoulder.

Thirst

"And I don't want any explanations from you. Really, I don't, it wouldn't help; it would make things worse. And when we find Josie, I won't ask her about it because that won't help either."

Colin heard the "we." He said, "You still want me to help?"

Catherine hesitated. "Yeah. I don't feel good about it, and if I could think of another way, I would. But I don't have much choice in the matter. So you can call it your atonement, for lack of a better word."

"Cat…"

"No. I'm serious, Colin. There's no winning here. It's not a game. Whatever you have to say about it, it's going to be wrong."

She took a deep breath that hissed over the phone. "If you just fucked her—God, I hate that word, ugliness in four letters—if you just fucked her then I can't forgive that. I picture you and her and my stomach knots. It's an image from hell. And if there was something else, something more…serious, then it's just as bad." Her voice broke and she reached deep inside to control it. "Because then, what am I supposed to do then, Colin? What am I supposed to ask? Whether Josie was better than me? My own daughter?"

Colin stayed silent. The seconds stretched until he heard Catherine take a deep breath. "God. Do you see what I mean, Colin? Do you understand?"

He closed his eyes, nodded. "Yes."

"Just help me find her."

There wasn't much of anything more to say. "I'll do all I can."

"I hope so."

There was a miserable silence. Colin's palms felt clammy. Eventually, he said, "I've got some information, nothing solid, but it's a start."

Chapter Ten

When Catherine came over her eyes were cold. She had jeans on that might have been a half-size too small, a T-shirt with 'Put the fun back in dysfunctional' across the front, and a pair of high-heeled cowboy boots. She stood framed in the doorway, and Colin was afraid of getting too close and invading her space.

She refused his offer of coffee, took a sixteen-ouncer from a Seven-Eleven bag, and spent extra time stirring in creamer and Splenda. Finally, she said, "I suppose we can try to get over this and still be acquaintances, but I'm not sure it's worth it. So for the time being, let's just stick to the subject at hand. Where do we go from here?"

The night before on the phone he had told her almost everything, had described his meetings both with Mollie Catfish and with Mamadou, explained the existence and death of the late Herbie. Catherine's fears and frustrations had grown even as he spoke, and he'd tried without success to reassure her. He hadn't told her about Joe the Cop's encounter with the dead drag queen.

"So the upshot of all this is that we still don't know anything, not really. We don't know whether she's dead or alive, or run away,

THIRST

or kidnapped. Am I right? So she could be on the street and using again." There had been the faintest note of hysteria in her voice.

Today she was better, though her face showed another sleepless night. Once inside the door her first words were, "You know, I've always hated your apartment. Always."

She dropped her handbag to the floor, foraged in a pocket of her jacket, found a cigarette, and lit it with a Bic.

"Started again last night. After four years, isn't that a bitch? Found this pack of stale Winstons in a drawer. Somebody who came over once forgot it, how long ago I don't want to know. They taste pretty rotten."

"I'm sorry."

She shook her head. "Don't pride yourself, Colin. I didn't start again because of you; I did it because last night I really desperately wanted a drink. I got Lars's stupid bottle of vodka out of the fridge and I had a glass all ready with ice cubes. That's how close I came. I watched myself doing it, knowing it was completely insane but I was going to do it anyway, it didn't matter. Then I poured it down the drain. So lighting up was the lesser of two evils."

Colin stood silent. She took the apartment in with one glance, gestured at the furniture. "Where do you *find* this stuff, anyway? How can you stand to live in here? It looks like college dorm. Worse, actually."

She walked to the open bedroom door. "Is this where it happened?" She pointed her chin to the futon, made a disgusted sound. "I still can't believe it. I can't even believe I'm here. You and Josie. Jesus Christ. Is there a club for people like you? The Mother and Daughter Fuck Club, or something? Jesus." Then lower. "This really hurts."

Colin took three steps, wrapped his arms around her, squeezed. He felt her entire body tighten momentarily, the resistance like a current phasing through her. Her arms hung by her side. She let her head drop on his shoulder; it stayed there a moment and then she drew back.

"Okay. Sorry. Enough of that, it won't solve or improve anything."

They were standing on a small rug that Colin had meant to throw away a long time ago; it always slipped when he stepped on it. She nudged the rug with her toe, bent down to pick it up, held it up to the light, and said, "This is really filthy." She walked to the kitchen and folded the rug carefully into the trash can.

Then she moved the big easy chair Colin read in from one side of the room to the other, dragged the coffee table next to it.

She reached under the couch, tried to lift one end, and grunted. "Help me with this. Move this end over there. It'll open up the room, make it less claustrophobic." It did, though Colin noticed that where the couch had been, the carpet was a different shade of brown. She noticed it too. "Sunlight. That'll fade in a week or two."

They worked without speaking for half-an-hour. She asked for a hammer and nails and made him rehang the four prints he had haphazardly stapled to his walls. She found a rag and a bottle of Windex in the hall closet and started spraying windows. She said, "You got a vacuum cleaner? Get it. Do something, don't just stand there."

He pushed the machine around the room, glad for the noise that prevented conversation. When he was through with that, she said, "Do the ceilings and the baseboards. There's cobwebs all over the place, see? Use that brush attachment but put a new bag in first."

So he did that too. He could feel her darting glances whenever his head was turned. Then she stood back, evaluated her work. She dropped the spray bottle, let the rag fall to the floor, and looked around the room, hands on her hips. "I'm not sure what that was all about, but I feel better, at least a little. Maybe I just wanted to alter the scene of the crime. Does that make sense?"

Thirst

He nodded. Her lips turned down. "Jesus. Look who I'm asking…"

"Thanks."

Catherine had made the meager furnishings somehow fit better in the available space but it wasn't *right*, it had lost the feel of familiarity. The chair where he read would no longer get light from the window. The weights were in the wrong place. He looked around again, said, "I think you'd better get over this."

Catherine's face immediately went hard. "Get *over* it?"

He nodded, went to the chair, pulled it back to its original place in the room. "It's not helping anything. It's certainly not helping Josie. You're acting as if I committed some sin and I didn't. I already told you. I didn't know she was your daughter. If I had…"

Catherine cut him off. "I can't believe I'm hearing this."

Colin tugged the coffee table so it was next to the chair. "Who are you angry at, anyway? Me or her? If it's me, and you still want me to help find her, then put your anger away for now, okay? And if it's Josie, take it up with her when she's back."

Catherine swung at him. It was a better blow than the one in the parking lot. He caught her hand in his, enveloped her fist. "You already did that once. It didn't help either, so just stop."

Catherine's face was white, the cheeks drained of blood. She let her arm drop.

Colin said, "I think it's time you meet Mamadou."

⁂

On Tuesdays and Fridays the Zulu took care of his legitimate businesses. There was a three-store barbecue franchise that specialized in family meals. One was in the Fort Belvoir community, the second in affluent McLean, and the third on Georgia Avenue near the 16th Street Gold Coast in Washington. Next to that restaurant was an adult books and video store featuring mostly interracial porn. Restaurant returns were down a bit, and he attributed this to a variety of reasons. People spent more time outdoors in the summer and the restaurant trade was down everywhere. The Zulu also believed that pornography was a seasonal thing, that his customers' baser instincts were closer to the surface during the winter months when night fell at five in the afternoon and more layers of clothing were worn, making disrobing—and therefore sex—increasingly tempting.

The Zulu also owned a small production company that produced eight- to fifteen-minute pornographic clips destined for predominantly Muslim nations. The grainy color footage invariably showed bearded men with Arabic features doing things forbidden by the Koran to women whose Nordic good looks would bear little scrutiny. A Jewish producer created the clips and his work, considering an almost non-existent budget, was imaginative. The Zulu thought the late Herbie's girlfriend might be a good subject for the clips since a dozen could be shot in a single day. The girl had not yet acquired the wasted look of the prostitutes and addicts often used in these productions, and there was no sense letting the young woman's potential go to waste—a fresh young face was always welcome in the porn market. He liked the idea of getting some returns on the troublesome investment she represented.

Other financial initiatives included loans at heretical—but legal—interest rates to Ethiopian and Somali hot-dog vendors who needed cash to buy their carts and operating stock; partial interest in three downtown nightclubs; a used car dealership; two very tidy eight-unit apartment buildings in Northeast; and a liquor store in Oakton, Virginia, some twenty miles from Washington. The liquor store was next door to a topless place called The Eleventh Hour. The Zulu owned that establishment as well.

Thirst

On all these investments the Zulu paid federal, state, and local taxes. His returns were always on time and correct to the penny. He had never been audited. He employed a full-time certified public accountant who kept straight books.

The Zulu's investments served a twofold purpose. They masked the income he made from the sale of drugs, and, since he encouraged the local mob to launder its cash through his establishments, the stores, dealerships, and clubs allowed him to operate relatively free of the Washington-based organized crime family that could, in a moment, have shut him down. His name had more than once been linked to the capital's thriving drug trade but there was simply no proof. The Zulu operated quietly—if sometimes with great violence—and did not espouse the trappings of vulgar wealth. He was simply a black businessman, a naturalized U.S. citizen, an acquaintance and occasional guest of local politicians including the Councilmen of several mostly black wards. The true source of his original wealth was unknown to all but a handful of people. When faced with someone so indiscreet as to openly question his background, the Zulu shrugged and hinted at the vast—if discrete—wealth of his tribe. People assumed he was a prince, and he met this assumption with a shy but knowing smile.

The Zulu turned his attention to the important matter of finding temporary manpower to replace the late and unlamented Akim. The boy had been promising, and the Zulu was disappointed in how things had turned out but didn't dwell on it. He liked to think of himself as a man who created opportunities from setbacks. Akim and Comfort had made a good pair but that was no more; Comfort alone might have his uses but what the Zulu really needed was a two-man team capable of doing great harm to others as needed.

Thierry Sagnier

He had heard good things about a pair of disgraced former cops whose last employer had attempted to renege on an agreement. The ex-officers had drowned him in the Tidal Basin, but the employer's death was ruled accidental by a grand jury. The two were looking for work.

CHAPTER ELEVEN

Mollie Catfish's conception began with a lie, and the pattern of her life was fixed from that day on.

When Billy Raoul (Boy) Custis and Tammy Coe were clotheless from feet to waist near Skag Lake, Missouri, and Boy was in and on top of Tammy, he said, "I won't come in you. I promise." But he lied, and he did. Later, he'd say he couldn't help himself so it wasn't really his fault. Even later, he'd add that the baby wasn't his because Custis men *always* fathered boys, which, since Tammy's baby was a girl, was all the justification Boy needed to leave Skagville and Tammy behind.

Tammy knew the child was his, but since she had no desire to marry Boy, she felt a certain relief when he left town. She would raise the baby herself with the help of family and church and everything would work out fine, except that it didn't. The child was taken in by the state on the eve of her first birthday when Tammy eloped with Billy Raoul Custis' younger brother Joe. Joe was willing to take Tammy with him to California but he didn't want children. Children would get in the way, cramp their style. After a few minutes' consideration, Tammy agreed. Motherhood had not been as fun as she'd expected, in fact it hadn't been fun at all, and everyone is entitled to a second chance. So Joe and Tammie left the infant on the steps of the Skagville Baptist Church in a pink plastic laundry basket Tammy had bought for the occasion at K-Mart.

The baby was adopted by a childless couple from the northern part of the state and quickly handed back to the authorities. She was colicky, whiny, and rarely slept at night, and the young couple gave up after a month. She was in six foster homes in four years but things never worked out. The little girl played with matches and set things on fire; she ruined her clothing on purpose; she liked to run around the neighborhood without a stitch on. By the time she was six years old the authorities seldom bothered to show potential parents her file and she was relegated to a series of state-run schools where she read voraciously, got A's in English, and failed every other subject.

When she was twelve she seduced the school's janitor in a broom closet that smelled of Pine-Sol and Windex. She persuaded the young, slow-witted man to drive her across the state line to Jolieville and to give her his life savings of $272.27 as well as a change of clothes he stole from his sister. The jeans fit, though the T-shirt was tight across her top which enabled her to lie about her age and get a job in a roadhouse serving beer and boilermakers to good old boys who drove trucks interstate. One of the drivers took a fancy to her and for six weeks she crisscrossed Mississippi, Georgia, Louisiana, South and North Carolina, Virginia, and Tennessee. She charged forty dollars a day plus meals and would do pretty much anything the man wanted whether the truck was moving or not. The driver thought this was a fair deal, considering the girl didn't eat much, kept quiet, and had a knack for tuning in good country stations. She got close to $2,000 in twenties and fifties when she stole his wallet.

Thirst

~

When Mollie met Herbie she immediately saw him for what and who he was. Never mind that he grabbed for her ass five minutes after being introduced to her by his girlfriend; never mind that when he did it Josie was standing not five feet away, feeding quarters into the jukebox. Mollie was used to people grabbing at her; she had all sorts of snappy rejoinders for people with Roman hands. What she found interesting was that Herbie was a scam artist, that they were kindred spirits, and that there might be something there for her if she played it right.

When she and Herbie were on the couch in his apartment later that night after Josie had gone home, Mollie felt the faintest trace of disgust with herself—here we go again, she thought—but it wasn't enough to stop what was happening, which was Herbie unzipping her jeans, lowering her panties, then pausing to get a beer from the kitchen. *That* was when she became sure about Herbie.

Herbie did a couple of lines, offered her some, drank his beer, and offered her some of that too. She refused both. Mollie was serious about the AA stuff. The last time she'd done coke, her nose had rained blood. It hadn't hurt but she'd gotten scared. At the public clinic the next day the young doctor who volunteered there said the insides of her nostrils were seriously abraded and that the membranes in there had become paper thin. One more line would lead to surgery, putting in a plastic plug to replace the damaged cartilage. And then he'd added, "And incidentally, those little broken veins on your cheeks? The ones under the makeup? They're going to get bigger. How old are you? Seventeen, eighteen? Kind of early to start dying. So you might want to think about giving up drinking too." Then he'd looked at her arms, seen the tracks there, and shook his head. "Forget it. You're already dead. You just don't know it yet."

That had scared her, a total stranger being able to say that just by looking at her.

So she turned down the booze and the dope at Herbie's, endured his thrusting and humping, made all the necessary ooh and aaah sounds. It was a pretty good performance on her part and it fooled Herbie, who kept losing his hard-on and trying to get it back with more and more blow. He kept lubricating himself with spit, rubbing himself until he was half-hard, which Mollie had always found disgusting. God knows what he'd had for lunch. Nothing worked, least of all the coke, but it made him increasingly talkative.

It was something Mollie had noticed in the past, that scammers needed to talk, to boast, to expose themselves and confess their sins with a mixed measure of pride and humility, though often not much of the latter. Maybe it was a perverted form of trust, a weird kind of sharing; maybe it was simply that they had no one else to talk to, couldn't reveal their genius to the straight people they scammed, so they did so to their peers. Prostitutes talked about their johns and pimps, muggers described to each other the shocked faces of their victims, junkies crowed about their latest scores. Mollie had discovered this early in life and learned to exploit it, listening carefully and filing the tidbits of information. You could learn a lot that way. She had.

Herbie talked and talked and talked, stayed up all night flapping his mouth, and Mollie listened, smiled, made approving sounds in spite of the fact that she was dying to go to sleep. Her eyes wanted to rest and only sheer force of will kept them open. He told her about his parents, about his sainted grandmother, his first drunk, his first drug deals with the Georgetown students cramming for finals, his one and only encounter with heroin, which, he claimed, almost killed him. "Felt like my veins were on fire. Then I threw up. Then I fainted. Never, *ever*, do that again."

THIRST

When Herbie played with her breasts she let him, when he ran his hand between her legs she let him do that too, because she knew it would lead to nothing.

Between snorts Herbie kept saying, "This is great, you know? I can't do this with Josie. If we're together I can't even do a little dope to cool myself out, she wouldn't stand for that. So this is great, being with you and all…"

Coked to the gills, he said, "Hey, you know? I got this deal working, I could maybe use somebody like you, somebody smart and pretty, we can make a fortune, guaranteed, whaddya think?"

Mollie smiled. She remembered one of the rare men she respected, this old guy who used to shoot pool in a bar where she worked. Between racks he talked to himself and one day she heard him mumble, "Never partner with an asshole. It's the dumb ones that'll kill you…" And that had stuck.

After a while Mollie was handling the razor blade, mincing and chopping and powdering the coke into fine tempting white lines. She could almost feel the rush but then she'd remember the blood spurting out of her nose. The young doctor's tired eyes and defeated gaze had moved her, so she fought it all the way and she'd won. It wasn't as hard as she'd thought and the payoff was worth the difficult moments. Herbie, the coked-out, runny-nosed, shiny-faced, impotent, and fucked up drunken fool that he was, told her everything. Everything. The drugs, the theft, the Zulu, the hiding place, the million bucks—every single thing. And by the time Herbie crashed on the floor full of beer, Laphroag, and Bolivian Marching Powder, Mollie Catfish knew her life was going to change for the much, much better.

Herbie stank like a distillery; his rank breath filled the room. A rivulet of spit ran down one corner of his lips. There could have been a turkey shoot in his living room, and he wouldn't have noticed. Mollie loosened his belt, stretched him out on the couch, and made him comfortable so on the off-chance he came to, he wouldn't need to move.

Then she began searching the apartment. She did it meticulously, putting things back just the way they were. She looked in all the drawers in the kitchen, beneath the folded shirts in the bedroom chest, in his shoes. There was nothing in his desk, nothing beneath his mattress, nothing anywhere.

The sun had come up. Herbie was going to be out for a few more hours, so she drew the curtains and kept looking. She was getting frustrated and angry, beginning to make mistakes, forgetting where she'd already looked. His cell phone rang once, twice, three times and she almost jumped out of her skin. Herbie stirred slightly. She was just about to give it up when she looked into his closet, saw his clothes neatly lined on plastic hangers, and began patting down anything that might have pockets. Inside a godawful olive green sport coat from Britches, she found a Radio Shack electronic address book, no bigger than a business card and almost as thin. She pushed the On button. The tiny liquid display screen blinked. She pressed Phone. The screen asked, "Name?" She pressed Index.

She got a pencil and a piece of paper from Herbie's desk, began copying names and numbers. There weren't that many, barely a dozen. Under "J" she found Josie, under "Z" she found Zulu. When she was done she put the thing back into the Britches sport coat and walked around the apartment three times to make sure nothing was out of place. Herbie hadn't moved. His breathing was shallow, labored. Maybe he'd die? That was a possibility, he'd done a monumental amount of dope, enough to kill a whale, and the fifth of Laphroag was almost empty. There were more than half a dozen empty beer cans lying on the floor. Combinations like that were lethal. She'd seen a guy OD on less and he'd never woken up, just huffed and puffed a little as he changed from flesh tone to white, and finally to light blue.

Thirst

Mollie went to the door, opened it, made sure no one was in the hallway, and then went down the stairs that led to the building's basement. There she found the exit into the alley next to the garbage bins. It was a quarter after eight in the morning; the rush hour traffic was blasting down Columbia Road. There was a bus stop three blocks away and she only had to wait five minutes. When the bus came, she got on after asking the driver if it stopped near the Dupont Circle metro. Her feet hurt. She could feel blisters forming on both her heels. Her eyes were gritty and she was lightheaded, but then who wouldn't be? It had been one hell of a productive night.

☙

In neighborhoods where reputations are wealth, Mamadou's name was powerful currency.

He was a black man who had undergone a tragedy common to black Washingtonian families. Death by bullet, needle, or pipe was part of life in the lower neighborhoods of the city. It rated no play in the evening news, though the nation's capital did earn brief international fame in the late eighties when the self-named Chocolate City began to be called Dodge.

The people of Mamadou's neighborhoods neither knew nor cared that the center of the Western world was a few miles away. Many residents couldn't have named the President of the United States, didn't know where the White House was, never went to the Northwest section of town, and couldn't read the morning newspaper. Decisions made a few miles away in the U.S. Capitol bypassed them entirely, except when laws passed there closed a free health clinic, or funding for food stamps and welfare checks decreased.

It was in such a place that Mamadou had first arrived as a new but not gullible immigrant. It was there he learned that honor could be bought from the poor as easily as from the rich, and for far less.

He was driving his newest limo slowly down numbered streets in the Northeast quadrant of the city. There were many boarded-up houses and stores, with here and there an oasis—a small, neatly painted two-story home festooned with bars on the windows and doors and adorned with flower patches and shrubs. The temperature was in the upper nineties, and the pavement shimmered. Most homes had curtains drawn, but Mamadou knew that in each and every building, eyes noted the passing of the long black car and hands reached for telephones to call neighbors.

He braked the limo in front of a cinder block and clapboard house with a tilted front porch and parked between a rusting Chevrolet and a spotless 1953 Buick convertible. He kept the engine running, turned the air conditioning to full, lit a Gauloise, and waited. Before he had finished the cigarette, his cell phone rang.

"You gonna come up or you gonna stay down there and fry?"

Mamadou laughed. "I wanted to make sure you were home, Aunt Mim."

The voice on the other end was a dry chuckle. "You ever known me *not* to be home? You come on up now. I'll tell Derrick to watch that car of yours. Did you bring anything to drink?"

Mamadou lifted the jug of Gallo burgundy and waved it so it could be seen from the house.

"Well that's good, shows you got manners."

Mamadou left the car unlocked with the motor running. Soon a small boy, one of Aunt Mim's relatives, came from the house, gave him a high five, and discreetly stuck his other hand out. Mamadou slipped him a ten. The boy smiled, sauntered to the car, and got in. Mamadou watched him turn the AC down a notch and fiddle with the radio until he found a pleasing station. The speakers boomed

Thirst

and the boy rocked up and down, a dwarf in the limo's seat, the entire vehicle vibrating to a hip hop beat. The car would be safe. Aunt Mim's boys could put Mamadou's dobermans to shame.

Aunt Mim was in the bed in the upstairs room, her huge shape swaddled in pink sheets. She wore a turban of the same color. Gray hair stuck out the sides in tufts. She was smoking a king-size Pall Mall, and the room was faintly hazy with smoke. Off to the side, Aunt Mim's lover, George, sat quietly on a chair perusing an old copy of *Utne Reader*. He looked up when Mamadou came in and smiled slightly.

Mamadou approached the bed and bent at the waist to kiss Aunt Mim on the cheek. He handed her the jug of wine. She looked at the label and said, "George?"

George nodded, stood, and found three high-stem glasses; he twisted the cap off and poured the wine carefully, handed the glasses around, and returned to his reading.

Mamadou said, "You're looking well."

The old woman harrumphed, pleased nevertheless. "Gained another ten pounds. I look at food and it sticks to me, don't have to eat it or nothin', just *look* at it. You're lookin' good too. You married yet?"

Mamadou shook his head.

"Din't think so, I'da heard. Your business still doin' good, I'm told. You getting richer, don' have time to visit, forgettin' the people that helped you…"

Mamadou shook his head again. "You know that's not true, Aunt Mim." He sipped from the glass. Aunt Mim drained hers, held it out to George for a refill. There was a long silence. Mamadou looked around the room.

He'd never seen Aunt Mim anywhere but in the huge bed, and George was always there, silent and attentive. The room itself hadn't changed from the last time he'd visited a year earlier. The rosebush wallpaper was slightly more faded, but the curtains, rugs, and furniture were the same.

"So how you doin'?"

"I'm well, Aunt Mim."

Aunt Mim squinted at him, sighed. "I still say a prayer every night for your sister. Poor little Amelie, don't I, George?"

George nodded again. Aunt Mim took a deep breath. "That was such a shame, young woman like that. Hope those boys are rottin' in hell. They *needed* killin'. But that's what happens when the drugs getcha. Ain't nothin' good to be *dee*rived from all that stuff. An' it's gettin' worse and worse, that's what people tell me."

Mamadou smiled, sipped. "People tell you everything, don't they, Aunt Mim? You know what they'd call you in French? They'd call you the *doyenne*."

The woman looked at him and laughed uproariously. The bed shook. "The *dwayen*? You still a *sweet-talkin'* man, ain'tcha? Ain't he, George? I like that word, dwayen. Sounds kinda African, though, not French." She drank from her glass and her expression changed. "Damn straight! They tell me *everythin'*. I won't tolerate no secrets. That's how I knew that boy took your sister, 'cause people came and told me. And that's why I asked George here to pay you a visit." She nodded in the direction of the elderly man, who did not look up. "Wasn't hard gettin' those boys to come to you. Hell, I knew that boy that hurt Amelie since he was little, knew his family too. None of 'em were any good. Ida been smart, I mighta could've prevented what happen to your sister, but I didn't see it comin', you know. I was gettin' old, even back then."

She made a show of sitting up in the bed and folded her hands on the coverlet. "So, what is it I can help you with this time?"

Mamadou told her. She listened silently, broke in only once, said, "AA? They tried settin' up a AA meetin' here once. I let 'em use my kitchen, but it didn't last. Most black people, men, they don' wanta talk about their drinkin'. They just want to do it. Or if they do talk, they boast, like it was somethin' to be proud of. Ain't that right George?"

Mamadou listened to Aunt Mim for forty-five minutes as she recounted births, deaths, marriages, abandonments. Before he left, he wrote the word *doyenne* on a piece of paper and handed it to her. Aunt Mim looked at it and spelled it out loud a couple of times. Mamadou said, "It means a great lady, one who's kind and helps people. A patron. A leader."

George spoke for the first time. "It also means the senior member, as in age or rank, of a group, class, or profession, etc. Webster's Unabridged. Page 431."

Aunt Mim nodded her head, unimpressed with George's scholarship. "That's a pretty word, ain't it George? Yeah. I kinda like that, bein' a *dwayen*. Gotta good ring to it. Maybe I'll get one of the girls to embroider a pillow for me, have it say, 'Mimosa Bell, *dwayen* of all she surveys.' That'd be right, wouldn't it?"

Mamadou put his glass down, took one of her heavy hands in both of his, and kissed it. "That would be absolutely right, Aunt Mim. A proper and fitting title."

Aunt Mim giggled. "Such a *sweet* talker, ain't he George?"

Chapter Twelve

The brunette one—whose name really was Clare Drake—said, "Well, I guess it coulda been worse. Do you think he really meant it? Throwing us off the ship? Could he really do that?"

The blonde, whose name wasn't Jennifer Jamieson, shrugged her shoulders. "Maybe. I remember in school reading about how ship's captains could do pretty much what they wanted. Bury people, have them whipped or put on a deserted island, stuff like that. But maybe that was just pirates. Anyhow, I think we'd better not screw up. That's all we need, getting tossed on some island full of spades and ending up in their version of jail. I don't think I'd like that much."

Outside the cabin's porthole there was nothing but blue-green water and bright blue sky. They could feel the ship humming beneath their feet, the sound of the giant engines not quite deadened. Clare Drake said, "He wasn't such a bad guy, all in all..."

Jennifer Jamieson opened the small closet door, selected three dresses, and tossed them on her bunk. "Far as I'm concerned, what we've gotta do is just not screw this up. There's fifteen grand waiting for us in Baltimore when we get there. That's in three days. Fifteen grand. We go to Florida, someplace near Disney World, get a decent

Thirst

apartment with a pool and a workout place. Start things over. No more hooking, no more dealing with assholes, 'cause I've got to tell you, I'm done with that." She held up a black dress, glanced in the mirror, made a face, and let it drop to the cabin floor. "It would've been nice to get a few extra bucks, but I told you that old fart's wife was all over him. We should've tried for that other guy, the one who came on to me by the pool."

"Except that he didn't have any money. I could tell that right away. He was a scammer, I know it. Did you see his shoes? What kind of guy wears shoes like that on a cruise? He had PayLess written all over."

Jennifer Jamieson shrugged, "Yeah, well. Next three days, we're prim and proper. Two teachers from an exclusive school, out on the cruise of a lifetime." She made it sound like a middle-of-the-night television ad. "Real exciting."

Clare Drake took her friend in her arms, hugged her hard. "Three days. We give Herbie his stupid package back, he gives us fifteen grand, we're outta here for good. Think of it. Right next to Disney World. We'll get to be pals with Mickey and Goofy, maybe even get jobs there. I'll be Snow White, and you can be one of the dwarves."

Clare Drake laughed. She was the smaller of the two. "Bitch!"

Jennifer Jamieson squeezed her harder. "Yeah. But you love me anyway."

ೞ

"Not much of a place." The words hung. Catherine had been quiet throughout the ride from Virginia, and now they were sitting in Colin's battered 924. The door to the garage housing Africorp's limos was shut, and no one had responded to their knocking.

"We'll wait a bit longer. The man I spoke with said Mamadou would be back around three." Colin looked at his watch. "It's almost that now."

"How do people live here?" Catherine nodded to the street, the building, the trash. "I don't understand how people can live like this and not do anything about it."

"I guess they have other things to worry about than whether their streets are clean."

They'd been there fifteen minutes and during that time had seen only a pair of young boys, who had eyed the car suspiciously and scampered down an alley.

"It's hard to believe this is Washington. I mean, this doesn't look like part of America."

"Inner city. Not that bad compared to some other places, like Detroit or the South Bronx."

Catherine looked out again. "I've never been to neighborhoods like this. Guess I've led a protected life."

"Be thankful."

Suddenly the car rocked. Catherine stifled a scream. A black face wearing large wraparound sunglasses was peering in her window. She drew back.

"Y'all lookin' for somethin'?"

Colin leaned over. "We're just waiting for someone."

The face considered this. "Unh hun. I see. But this here's a bad place to be waitin' for *anythin'* if you don' have business to transac'. Y'all sure I can't hep you out?"

Colin said, "Nope. We're fine. Thanks." And felt foolish.

The man straightened up and ambled away.

Catherine asked, "Was he selling drugs? Just like that, right in the open? Aren't there any policemen around here?"

Colin looked at her. "See any?"

She didn't bother to look around. "Scary place."

Thirst

The limo pulled up next to them so silently that neither noticed it until the garage door swung open. Colin started his car, followed the Cadillac in, and waited for Mamadou to get out. "Do you like this neighborhood, Colin? You're spending a lot of time here." Mamadou was not wearing his chauffeur uniform. He walked around the Porsche, opened the door on Catherine's side, and helped her out of the car. "You must be the young woman's mother. The resemblance is striking." He added, "Colin showed me her photo. I'm sorry for your plight."

"Plight?" Catherine repeated it, surprised by the choice of words.

Mamadou glanced at Colin. "Is that the wrong expression? I apologize. English is not my native language."

"Plight is fine," Colin said. "Mamadou Dioh, this is Catherine Stilwell. I thought the two of you should meet."

Mamadou bowed slightly at the waist. Catherine saw a tall, well-built man with the fine features and aquiline nose of an Ethiopian. She said, "Colin told me you're from West Africa?"

Mamadou met her gaze and smiled. "My grandmother was born in Addis, so I don't look like the classic West African. You've been there?"

Catherine shook her head. Mamadou shrugged. "I thought, perhaps, since your husband is with the State Department…"

There was a silence. Colin filled it, asked, "I know there hasn't been much time, but have you learned anything?"

Before Dioh could answer, Catherine said, "Colin told me about your earlier…encounter with drug dealers. And why it happened. I'm very sorry about your sister, and I'm grateful for anything you might be able to do to help with my daughter, with Josie."

"Which has not been all that much, so far, I'm afraid. But I've set some wheels in motion, and I'm hopeful."

The exchange petered out. Mamadou saw the exhaustion in Catherine eyes, the despair behind the false front. He added, "There are some people who know everything that happens in Washington. One of those people is my friend. More than a friend, actually." And he told them about Aunt Mim.

※

Catherine was fascinated. "How old is this woman?"

Mamadou laughed. "I'm sure I don't know. In her late eighties, early nineties, perhaps. Someone once told me that she and George—her companion—have been together more than sixty years. So between them they have almost two hundred years of accumulated knowledge about what's going on in the city. If you count the immediate family of sons and daughters, nephews, cousins, grandchildren, and other relatives, there's probably more than two or three hundred people, plus friends, who'll report to Aunt Mim."

Colin said, "I'd heard there were people like her. That's how the mayor was busted, fourteen or fifteen years ago. The drug thing. Nobody wanted to come right out and say it, but there were rumors of an old lady he'd offended. I remember a friend, a reporter for the *Post* who tried to do a story but nothing came of it. Was that her?"

Mamadou nodded. "It was. Aunt Mim isn't political, but the mayor did a number of things she found abusive. Budget things, cutbacks that affected the poorest. He closed a rehab and a halfway house in Southeast, then took patrol cars off the streets so they could go to the white neighborhoods. That didn't sit well with her. She tried to get to see him and was turned away. A comment he made about her came back—he called her an old Aunt Jemimah, and she was furious. She knew he was a drug user—everyone knew that. She found it shameful." He paused, smiled at a memory. "Do you remember the hidden camera that videoed His Honor lighting up? Remember the woman he was with?"

Colin nodded. Catherine said, "Vaguely."

"That was one of Aunt Mim's great-grandnieces." Mamadou found the story vastly amusing. "Aunt Mim set him up, you see? Indirectly, of course, but it was her handiwork."

Catherine said, "And you've known Aunt Mim since—"

"Since Amelie died."

৪১

"Shortly after Amelie died," Mamadou told them, "George came to my door. I didn't know him, he was simply a very old man dressed in the fashion of the forties, quite elegant. It was in the morning. I'd been up all night, and I was drunk and less than polite to him. The last thing I wanted was to see anyone. But George was persuasive. He made some coffee, right there in that hovel of an apartment, and waited until I sobered up. It took a few hours. I was *very* drunk. But he waited. He took a small dictionary out of his breast pocket and started reading it. I remember that very well; it stayed with me, the dictionary. Then, when I could walk without stumbling, he told me to get dressed as a gentleman would. He picked the clothes, found a tie and a clean shirt, and we took his car—that's another thing I remember, it was a 1953 Buick convertible, a beautiful thing, mint condition—and he drove me to Aunt Mim's house."

Mamadou closed his eyes. "She still lives in that house, incidentally...Aunt Mim was in bed. She's always in bed; I've never seen her upright. I think a couple of decades ago she decided there was nothing in Washington she wanted to see anymore, so she went to bed and stayed there. At any rate, she knew who I was. She knew what had happened. She knew the boy who was responsible for Amelie's death. She offered me revenge."

They were in the small office next to the garage. Mamadou had scoured the coffee pot and made a fresh batch. He lifted his cup. "More?" Catherine and Colin both shook their heads. Mamadou put his own cup down.

"I refused at first. I wanted to do it myself; I didn't need the help of some old black lady, and it didn't bother her at all. She just shrugged, and George drove me back home. I spent a week putting up wanted posters, talking to people, trying to get some information. I paid money to people and should have known better, because nothing happened. A second week was fruitless as well. Then George came back, asked if I wouldn't reconsider, and said he was quite certain Aunt Mim could help. By that time I was even angrier. I was a policeman in my former country, as I told Colin. I know that if a murder is not solved quickly, it will probably never be solved. Evidence vanishes. People vanish too. So I went back with George to see her."

Colin asked, "Why you? Why did she pick you?"

Mamadou rubbed his forehead. "I never asked and she never really told me, but George provided some hints. One was the reasons was that I was a former policeman. Aunt Mim knew that—how, I don't know. But I was a *good* policeman, a *very* good policeman, in fact. She knew I wouldn't panic if there was violence, guns. I'd dealt with that before. A second reason, I think, is that I had no record and had never been in trouble with the law. Do you know how rare that is for a black man who lives in the city? So that was a plus, you see. I wouldn't be an immediate suspect." He took a breath. "The last, and perhaps the most important thing Aunt Mim saw, was the level of my anger, and the fact that I wasn't defeated. People kill each other all the time here. But not where I come from. I wasn't *used* to such a level of violence as a lifestyle. I refused to accept it. Aunt

Thirst

Mim was aware of that. And, of course, she had her own reasons for wanting to get that boy off the streets." He fell silent. The hush lasted. Finally, Catherine asked, "So what happened?"

"She sent *him* to *me*. Told him where I was. And I killed him." Mamadou looked at Catherine without expression. He added, "Him and his friends."

Colin nodded. "And you were never arrested?"

"Hardly questioned. Released very quickly. I think she may have had something to do with that too."

"Powerful lady."

"Very."

Catherine was looking at her shoes. "You left out something. What did the boy do to her? What were *her* reasons?"

Mamadou smiled. "He was apparently a not very…nice boy. He got one of Aunt Mim's great-granddaughters pregnant and refused to support her afterwards. He boasted about it, which was a very bad idea. Aunt Mim is very traditional. She didn't approve of that kind of behavior."

He lit a Gauloise, blew out smoke. "And of course, Aunt Mim hates drugs, hates dealers. As I said, she knew of my background as a police officer. And she knew that I'd repay the debt."

"By giving her information," Colin said. Mamadou nodded. "Correct. I hear things she may be interested in, and I pass the information on. Not to her directly—mostly to George. And sometimes George asks me to speak to friends I've made, police officers he feels can be trusted. So you see, the information flow goes both ways. It's very effective."

Catherine said, "Do you think she'll help? Finding Josie?"

Mamadou smiled again. "Yes. Yes, I think she will."

Thierry Sagnier

❧

For Josie, there is no past, only a present and an indistinct future.

The beanbag chair is home. There is nothing else but that, that and the drugs. The drugs provide increasingly brief respites from what has become a slow-building agony. Josie has no notion of time save the moments elapsing between pipes. Her mouth, throat, and chest are raw, but whenever she fires up she refuses to cough; that might waste some of the salvation, and she could ill afford that.

She has become almost somnambulistic. She eats when told to, relieves herself when told to, and sleeps when the cravings allow it. The Zulu is God, and she is desperate to please him.

She misses sunshine, light. When she was just starting out, messing around with fruit wines and dope, one of her favorite things was to get lightly stoned and lie out in the sun, sensing each individual particle of light bounce off her face. She hasn't had that feeling in quite a while and wonders why.

She's drifting on a painful sea. Most of the time she's cramping, though it's not yet that time of the month; her period isn't due for a while, of that she's pretty certain. So the cramping is something else, and when she can give rise to an emotion other than want, that emotion is fear. She's not scared of death. She feels death will be a relief, and she's earned it. She's scared of something else, something she can't quite identify.

When she's high the memories rush by like express trains, and the jumble of them amaze her. Things she hasn't thought of in years, situations long forgotten—she can see herself in them, almost like being at the movies. There's even music and a cacophony of sound effects, voices, noises, slamming doors, rushing water. She thinks the song she keeps hearing in her head is Springsteen's "Born in the

Thirst

USA," it has that kind of a snarl to it. But then again the tune might be something else entirely. It doesn't matter.

The door opens and the Zulu walks in. She can tell he has a couple of rocks in a glass vial. He's shaking the vial in his hand; he always does that when he comes in, as if to announce his presence. It makes a noise like two pebbles rattling in a cup.

The Zulu says, "Miss Stilwell, my patience has just about run out. I am telling you this so you'll be aware of the situation you're in. These," he holds up the glass vial, "are it. There will be no more until my simple questions are answered. Do I make myself clear?"

Terribly so. Horrifyingly so. But the realization that she will soon be cut off comes second to the need of right now. So she nods—yes, she understands—and hands him the pipe that is now the sole link to an endurable life.

The Zulu shakes a rock out, drops it into the bowl, hands the pipe back, and fires a wooden match. She sucks it in like a true user, short intense gasps that hit her lungs like ball lightning. She wants to cough, tenses every muscle in her upper body to avoid it. And then it hits and life is okay again, more than ok but short of wonderful because now there's only one rock remaining.

The Zulu says, "Remember, Miss Stilwell. No more after this." As if she could forget.

∞

It took one phone call. Mollie Catfish thought she was smart and made it from a phone booth next to the Seven Eleven on Gallows Road, probably one of the last phone booths in Virginia. There was a lot of traffic, people pulling in and out of the parking lot to get coffee or wings, and she kept her back to the door so the customers wouldn't see her, wouldn't wonder why this woman was talking into the phone with a handkerchief wrapped around the mouthpiece.

She thought the man had a pretty sophisticated voice for a black guy, kind of English-sounding, like those movies on Channel 26. He didn't ask a lot of questions, said, "I see," two or three times as she fed him the story, and said, "Thank you," before he hung up, which she appreciated. She liked polite people. One phone call. One *million dollar* phone call.

When she hung up she was shaking, and there was a fine sheen of perspiration on her upper lip. Her stomach was churning, so she went into the store and bought a hot pretzel with mustard from the Pakistani guy behind the counter. And since she felt lucky, since she thought today was going to be a day that would change her life, she bought three Powerball tickets. The prize was up to $24.5 million—she couldn't even imagine that kind of money.

She waited at the bus stop and munched on the pretzel, which was too salty. She wished she'd bought a Big Gulp to go with it. She thought about what she would do with $24.5 million, but it was simply too large a sum to deal with. So she pared it down to what the phone call would get—a million, or $800,000 if she sold cheap, which she was willing to do. For $800,000 she could get a *very* nice car, say a fully loaded Jeep Cherokee, cherry red with a killer sound system and lights on the roll bar. And a *really* decent apartment with a pool and a sauna and a place in the basement to exercise. Should she buy or rent? She remembered a guy she'd spent two nights with who'd tipped her a couple of hundred; he was into real estate, and he'd said always buy, that renting was like flushing the money down the toilet. Okay, she'd buy; a one-bedroom condo would run, what? $300 max. so that would leave about half a mil.

The bus pulled up and she got on, found a seat in the back. When she sat she noticed her legs were trembling.

Thirst

With a half a mil she would have to be careful, not go crazy and buy diamonds or a Lamborghini. No, realistically, she would invest; that's how people got rich. She would try not to spend the capital and live off the interest. She'd read that in the business section of *Newsweek*, and the idea had appealed to her. She'd go to the library and read back issues of *Forbes* and *Money*.

She would move the dope through Benny, the bouncer at the club, who knew absolutely everybody. Give him twenty grand and he'd jump at it; he was always bitching about being a bouncer, always saying that if he had a nest egg things would be different. But she'd have to devise some sort of plan so Benny wouldn't rip her off. She made a mental note, *Work on Plan*.

The bus snaked down Gallows Road, cut right on Cedar Lane, melted into the traffic on Leesburg Pike, and passed the Tyson's shopping mall, which got her to thinking that one thing she would do when she got the bucks was treat herself to a full day's shopping at Tyson's II, where all the better stores were. Nothing too fancy, no mink coat, but maybe a decent watch and a Gucci purse. Spend maybe eight or ten thousand in one day, wouldn't that be a hoot?

The bus lurched, and there was a squeal of tires and a blasting horn. One thing, sure as hell— no more public transportation. She changed the color of the Cherokee from cherry red to midnight blue. Cherry red cars attracted cops; no sense looking for trouble, since it generally came without an invitation anyway.

Maybe she'd scam a little of the dope for her personal use. Probably no one would notice; she'd get a box of baby laxative and put two scoops of that stuff in, take two scoops of the China White out. Who would know the difference? And if someone bitched, she'd say it was Benny, that he did it, the cheating motherfucker. If they wanted their dope, they could take it out of Benny's hide.

Thierry Sagnier

∽

The Zulu put down the phone with a thoughtful but not displeased expression. He did not question providence, knew that occasionally events took place that were beyond human understanding, and knew as well that only very foolish people failed to take advantage of such moments.

It had not been a good day after all. A police sweep had closed the Sparrow Club and Dance Venue in the Trinidad neighborhood the night before. The club was owned by one of his best customers, and on a good weekend up to a quarter-pound of the Zulu's products was moved there. The Sparrow's owner was now in jail facing many charges, and that didn't worry the Zulu either, since there was a large buffer between him and the club owner, whom he'd never met face to face. Also, the club owner was a very wealthy man whose lawyers probably at this very moment were preparing counter-charges, since no doubt the man's civil rights had been violated during the arrest.

What worried the Zulu was that he wasn't apprised of the raid, and he should have been. He routinely spent a minor fortune lining the pockets of various people in positions of authority, and such things should not happen.

In another neighborhood the Immigration and Naturalization Services had nabbed ten illegal immigrants who were also dealers. A front page story in the paper described how ICE agents driving three unmarked vans had picked the people up off the street without a shot being fired. The Zulu should have known about that as well. The reporter's account said neighbors had cheered when one elderly woman managed to trip an escaping dealer with her cane.

The citizens' patrol in Shepherd Park was also becoming troubling. This was a recent development, residents forming their own posses to rid their neighborhoods of undesirables. The Zulu knew the dealers would find another block not far away and that business would proceed as usual—these concerted efforts were almost always short-lived—but they wreaked havoc with the distribution schedule, and this he didn't appreciate.

He drummed the fingers of one hand against the palm of the other. He looked at the notes he'd jotted while the caller was talking. Better safe than sorry, his great-great grandfather would say. Grasp the bull by the horns, anticipate rather than react. Colin Marsh, he thought. An Irish name? Or Scottish? Regardless of the man's origins, the Zulu thought, there was no need for some misguided paladin to foul up the works.

Chapter Thirteen

Colin dropped Catherine at her house. She hadn't spoken much on the way back from Mamadou Dioh's garage, had merely said that she liked the man and asked Colin, "Do you really think he can help?"

Colin had nodded. "He knows a lot of people. Washington's a small town."

He caught the last half of a meeting at the Serenity Club and bought a plastic container of salad and a ham steak at Whole Foods. He'd make it an early evening—a quick workout, food, an hour or two ambling the Net, weights, and then sleep.

As he came through the door to his apartment, something stunningly heavy hit him across the forehead. He staggered and dropped the Whole Foods bag. A second blow caught him just above the navel. He coughed and vomited. A fist bounced hard off the back of his head.

When he came to, someone had a handful of his hair and was holding his head upright. A voice said, "Looka that! Man puked on my shoes! On my *shoes*...man, that's disgustin'. Brand new shoes—my Momma gave 'em to me for my *birffday*. That's white man puke and now I'm gonna have to throw those fuckers *out*. Ain't nothin' more revoltin' than white man puke…"

Sharp aches, confusion. Colin wanted to say he was sorry, because he was. If someone had puked on *his* shoes, he would have been unhappy too. Especially if they were brand new and his mother had given them to him. It was a terrible, insensitive thing to do. He opened his mouth to apologize but the hand jerked at his hair, stretched his neck, and slammed his jaw shut.

"Whaddya tryin' to do," the voice said, "get me *mad*? Get me *angry*? Ain't pukin' on my shoes enough? You just shut the fuck up, hear? Else I'm gonna make you eat them shoes, puke and all."

But it was important to tell the voice how sorry he was so he tried anyway. His efforts were rewarded by another sharp tug, followed this time by a gentle slap.

"Yo! You ain't hearin' me, man? You don't understand: what we have here is a precarious situation." The voice pronounced 'precarious' with the accent on the first syllable.

"Very precarious," he repeated. "Cause, see, I'm just this far from really bein' pissed off over my shoes and all, and you ain't doin' nothin' to make me feel better. And I don't think Harold likes you much either."

A very large presence swam into view, a broad expanse of tight black shirt over acres of chest and belly. A second voice, deeper than the first, said, "Man! Yore shoes is a *mess*. I wouldn't put my feet in those shoes for *money*."

Colin couldn't understand why they wouldn't let him say he was sorry. He'd replace the shoes, buy the man a new pair if it made him feel better. He tried to move his hands, to show he understood how the man felt, but his wrists were tied to…He was seated, straddling the weight machine from Wards. Belts held his wrists to the crossbar, which was loaded with every weight plate he owned.

The deeper voice said, "Maybe the man's got a pair you can take. Looks to be about the same size feet."

The first voice bristled with disgust. "You want me to wear *white man shoes*? You crazy? Put my feet in some sorry fucka's shoes that's probably got some sort of white foot disease? Rot your feet off or something. Naw, man, this boy's gonna *buy* me a new pair o' shoes."

A hand groped at his pockets, removed his wallet. "Yo. What's this?" Howard held the large brass coin up to Colin eyes.

Colin said, "Chip."

Howard held it up to the light. "Worth anythin'?"

Colin tried to shake his head. "No. Chip. AA chip."

Howard addressed Harold. "Now the man's stutterin'. A—a chip. A—a chip of what?"

With his free hand, Harold took the chip from Howard. "AA. Alcoholic's Anonymous. That's what this is. Whoo! Looka this, boy's got ten years of no drinking. My dad had one like this, only it was for one year, and I know the sorry motha lied, he was *nevah* sober that long." He handed it back to Howard.

Howard asked, "So it's ain't worth nothin'?"

"Not to us. You remember? Zulu said the man was a drunk. Thass why he had us bring the booze. "

"Well, sheeyit." Howard tossed the chip away and it hit a wall and bounced on the floor. "So how's he gonna buy me new shoes?"

Harold grunted, said, "Let's forget the shoes, awright? Let's just ask this nice man a couple of questions, find out what we wanna find out. Cause I got other things to do than stand around in a room that smells like puke."

The hand holding Colin's head up found a new grip on the hair and pulled at it painfully. "Okay, lissen up. Watcha wanta know about the Zulu's lady friend? Why you asking all these questions? You ask us questions, we can probably tell you everything you want to know…"

Thirst

Colin croaked, "Josie?"

Harold said, "Yeah, Josie. The white girl. You been all over town asking about her, about that dumb fucka Herbie. What's your problem?"

Colin took a deep breath. His ribs hurt. His eyes were still looking at the first man's sullied shoes. "Herbie? He's dead."

Harold dropped to a squat so his face and Colin's were on the same level. "Well, no shit. Course he's dead. If he weren't dead, we'd be someplace else than here and Howard's shoes wouldn't be all messed up. What I want to know is, what do you want with poor old dead Herbie? He done something to you? Owe you money? Owe you dope, maybe?"

Harold and Howard. For some reason that sounded ridiculous. Black people aren't supposed to be called Harold or Howard. Especially not black thug type people. Colin shook his head. Every word he uttered left him breathless. He wondered if he was having a heart attack and decided he wasn't, but he probably did have a cracked rib or two. He remembered the dull ache from martial arts. "Her mother's a friend. Josie, I mean. That's all."

"Oh, man," Harold said. "Oh man oh man oh man. This guy's a hardass. Lissen to me, Mr. Marsh. You ain't in no *position* to be no hardass. Look at you, all those muscles and shit, probably work out a hunnerd times a week and look where you be? You got two plain ol' street niggers who just took you out, tied you up, and made you puke all over their shoes. There's somethin' here you don't understan'."

"A friend. Really. Didn't even know Herbie at all." It came out hoarse, between a croak and a whisper.

"No man, no man. *I* think maybe you did. And *I* think I'm losin' my patience with this shit. It's borin' me, and I got a whole shitload of things I'd rather be doin'." To Howard he said, "Gimme that thing."

Howard and Harold exchanged something glassy, square, and solid. Colin braced himself. This was it. He was going to die. A few wet drops hit him in the face.

Harold stood over him and pulled back hard at his hair until his face was upturned, jaws forced open. Harold smiled slightly, neither benign nor evil. In his free hand he held a slim glass flask. Colin recognized the label. Harold tilted the flask.

Colin saw the clear liquid move gently to the flask's opening and pause there. He saw the slight curve before the vodka's surface tension burst. He saw the stream fall in slow motion toward his lips, felt it bounce off his nose, into his eyes, into his mouth.

It burned.

He gagged.

He tried frantically to close his mouth but Harold held his hair in one fist, pulling, pulling, tearing the scalp from his skull. Colin whipped his head back and forth, retched, spit, tried to rid his mouth of the saliva, of the taste, of the elation.

Howard leaped back. "Motha*fucka!* You think you gonna do *my* shoes *too?*"

Harold guffawed and loosened his grip slightly. Colin jerked his arms up as far as the belts allowed, felt the Ward machine lift slightly and pulled harder. The machine swayed. Harder. It tilted. Harold's hand abandoned its hold, went to protect his face as the butterfly bars flew toward him. The machine was at a forty-five degree angle to the rest of the room. It stayed there forever for a second and slowly crashed to the floor, taking Colin with it. Weight plates scattered. A small one, a twenty pounder, came off the high side, sailed like a Frisbee, and hit Howard just behind the ear. Howard crumpled. His head made a nasty sound as it hit the floor.

The butterfly bar had caught Harold squarely across the nose and flattened it. He held two fingers to his upper lip as if trying to

Thirst

hold back the blood that already flowed past his chin and down onto his chest. He said, "My *shoes*! My *dose*! Now you fucked up my *dose*!"

The fall had torn loose the belt on Colin's left wrist. His left hand scrambled to free his right one. His mouth was still watering and he sprayed spittle across the room. There was a moaning sound. It took him moments to identify it as coming from his own throat.

He scrambled to the kitchen, the two men momentarily forgotten. He lunged for the sink, batted the water open, grappled with the dish sprayer and aimed it full at his face. The water was stunningly cold. It ran into his mouth, gagging him, and he felt his stomach muscles roll and heave.

Howard was in the doorway. He was laughing. "Motha*fucka*! You are a piece of work, ain't you?"

There was a knife in the sink. Colin's hand reached for it. His eyes didn't leave Howard's. Howard was still smiling. The gash behind his ear had bled more than it should have. He touched it with a tentative finger, rubbed the blood between thumb and index.

"Piece of work," he repeated.

Then he turned away. Through the door Colin saw him grab the back of Harold's shirt, lift him effortlessly to his feet. "C'mon, boy. Let's go home." At the door, still holding Harold, he looked back at Colin. "Man, you leave old dead Herbie in peace, okay? I really don't want to have to come back here." He shook Harold like a puppet. "And my man here, I don't think he' got another pair of shoes."

Chapter Fourteen

The door was still open ten minutes later when Joe the Cop walked in, a broad smile on his face. "Hey, Colin! I'm glad you're home, I wanted to tell you about—*Jeezus* Christ what the hell happened to you!" Joe stood in the doorway. He sniffed the air. "Oh man, it smells like a distillery in here. You okay? Did you..." He let the question hang.

Colin was on the couch. His head hurt and he was rubbing the back of his neck. "Just fine, and no, I didn't."

Joe's eyes were wide, taking in the tipped-over Monkey Ward machine, the weight plates on the floor, the puddle of water in the kitchen. "Holy shit! What happened?"

"Had a visit. Two black guys, wanted information about a dealer called Herbie."

Joe looked blank.

Colin continued. "Herbie was Josie's boyfriend, except that he's dead. I'm pretty sure it was the guy in the paper. These two guys thought I knew him. I didn't. They didn't believe me."

"What two guys?"

Thirst

"Don't know. Howard and Harold. Ever heard of someone called the Zulu? They were his people. He's got Josie."

Joe went to the kitchen. "Jeez. What a mess." He foraged in the refrigerator and came out with a quart bottle of ginger ale. "Zulu. That rings a faint bell. Listen, you all right? Want me to take you to the hospital or something? You look kinda rocky."

"They tried to pour some vodka down my throat."

Joe came closer, inspected Colin's face. "Oh jeez. That's shitty." He peered closer. "How'd you feel?"

Colin tried to smile, but it hurt his face. "I think that if I'm going to have another drink, I'd prefer to pour it myself."

Joe nodded. "Yeah. So. Want to go to the station? Try to ID them?"

Colin shook his head. "But can you go there and hit the computer? Search for Zulu, maybe find out who he is? I don't understand any of this, why they would come here, how they'd know we're looking for Josie…it doesn't make any sense. Only people who know about it are you, me, Cat and her husband. And that girl, Mollie Catfish. And the limo guy, Dioh."

Joe counted in his head. "That's what, seven people? Hard to keep a secret. You told the African guy? Shit, there it is. He probably told the other spade. Simple as that."

Colin thought about it and decided against. "I don't think so. Me and Cat saw him. He's straight."

Joe looked doubtful as he stood. "Yeah, I'll check. Zulu. That's Z-U-L-U. I'll look under the AKAs." Halfway to the door, he turned. "Almost forgot. Wanted you to see this. Maybe it'll cheer you up. It goes into the record books." He pulled a newspaper clipping from his notepad, found his reading glasses, and put them on his nose. "Today's *Post*. Listen to this. '*A man driving a stolen car was shot to death early yesterday by a man apparently upset that his frolic in an open fire hydrant was disrupted by the car's presence on the street, D.C. police said.* Blah blah

blah. *The gunman and a woman who disrobed to join him were enjoying the rush of water from an open hydrant* blah blah blah. *A short time later, a 1988 Chevrolet Cavalier that police later determined was stolen drove onto the street.'* This is where it gets good. *'Police said witnesses told them that the man enjoying the water became upset at the driver. He got up and took a handgun from a man standing nearby. The man walked to the car, fired several shots into the windshield, and then fired several more through the passenger window. The driver was dead at the scene.'* Can you imagine that? Running around naked with your girlfriend in front of a hydrant and just offing another guy. You gotta admit, that's rich." Joe folded the clipping, replaced it in his notebook. "I'm keeping that one. Nobody would believe it."

✽

With Joe gone, Colin tried to reach Mamadou, Catherine, and Orin. No one was home but Martha, Orin's wife. She listened to Colin's story and ordered him to go to the hospital.

Colin refused. "It's not that serious. And if I go there I'll have to explain what happened, and the police might be called. I don't want to get involved with that."

"Then come over," Martha said. "At least I can take a look at you, patch you up."

So he did. Orin was in Pennsylvania road testing a new gizmo for wheelchair users. "I have no idea how it works," Martha said, "but it allows people to use this little device and change traffic lights." She touched his head. "God, Colin, you've got a lump there the size of a goose egg."

She wrapped ice in a towel and pressed it hard against the wound. He winced and groaned. She shushed him. "You really ought to go and get checked out. You could have a concussion. What'd they hit you with?"

THIRST

"I don't know. I didn't see it."

"Well," she pressed the ice down harder, "you're lucky you've got a thick skull. But we knew that before, didn't we?"

He nodded. His neck still hurt. "What I'm trying to figure out is how they knew anything about all this. I haven't exactly been shouting from rooftops. Cat wanted to keep everything quiet. And I've never heard of this guy, the Zulu."

Martha bent down, inspected her work. "The swelling's going down. Well, I'd think the best thing to do is figure out the odds here. How many people did you tell, and how many can you trust."

"I've done that already." He recounted the conversation with Joe.

Martha was quiet for a moment. "What about Joe? He mentions it to other cops, they talk, and word gets around."

"No. I don't think so. Joe knew how important it was to Cat to be discrete. She didn't even want him involved in the first place. I trust him. He's been my pigeon for a while; I know him pretty well."

Martha asked, "So who are the people you *don't* trust?"

"Lars, Cat's husband. He's an asshole. But he has nothing to gain. Mamadou, the limo guy. He volunteered to help. It wouldn't make sense for him to set me up. Mollie Catfish—"

"Who?"

"A girl, Josie was her sponsor."

Martha smiled. "That's really her name?"

Colin nodded. "She knows Josie. Met the boyfriend, Herbie. Didn't like him, said he tried to hit on her." As an afterthought, he added, "She's a dancer. At a club downtown."

Martha looked thoughtful. "Lots of drugs in that kind of crowd. I used to know some dancers, back when I was working at a free clinic. They'd come in for tests, and some were trying to get drugs—Valium, Xanax, Prozac, pretty much anything they could get their hands on. Lots of them were users. The money's good; lots of tips, and a lot more if they were willing to do parking lot duty."

"Do what?"

"Parking lot duty. Go out with the customers to their cars. Quick sex." She looked momentarily embarrassed. "A busy girl could make a lot of money that way. Here." She took Colin's hand and put the ice pack in it. "Hold that there for a few minutes. Anyway, the women I met always knew who was selling what. Really well plugged in. So maybe it's the dancer."

Colin thought that might make sense, but wasn't sure. "But why?"

Martha shook her head. "Hey, I'm no psychic. I'm offering suggestions. Someone comes to your house and beats the heck out of you, there's got to be a reason, that's all I'm saying. And your friend Mollie is the weak link. I don't think this other guy, the drug dealer, Herbie? I don't think he rose from the grave just to get you roughed up."

∽

Mamadou dropped by later that day. "I tried to call but you were out. Things are all right?"

Colin nodded. "Went to talk with a friend."

"Catherine?"

"No. Someone else."

Mamadou nodded, then asked, "But Catherine, she's doing well? Bearing up?"

"As well as can be expected, I suppose."

Mamadou was thoughtful for a moment, said, "When I lost Amelie, I thought the purpose of my life was over."

Thirst

There was an awkward silence, and then Mamadou added, "I couldn't…protect her from the same thing that's threatening Catherine's daughter."

Colin sensed Mamadou wanted to say more. He waited, but the Senegalese had ceased speaking and was staring at something outside the window. Finally, Colin said, "I'm sorry."

Mamadou blinked, rubbed his eyes, and changed the subject. "So we have the same news. Yours came in slightly rougher form, I take it. Tell me about it; I'll fill in what I learned from Aunt Mim."

Colin did, but there wasn't much. "They were here when I came in, whacked me around and tied me to the machine," he pointed to the Monkey Ward device. "They asked me about Herbie, and I told them what I knew, which is nothing. They mentioned the Zulu, asked why I was interested in 'his woman'—their words. Then I managed to break free, and that's pretty much it. Oh, yeah." He smiled, "I vomited on their shoes. That made them pretty angry."

Mamadou laughed out loud. "Yes, I'm certain it did." He peered at Colin. "But you're all right?"

"A little sore."

"And quite lucky. The Zulu is a very nasty person, according to Aunt Mim. It's fortunate you're not a lot worse off."

"Aunt Mim knows about him?"

"Aunt Mim knows about *everybody.*" Mamadou paused, walked to the sofa, and sat. "So she knows about the Zulu, who really *is* a Zulu, incidentally. There's a man named Comfort who works for him, and Comfort has been buying take-out food and bringing it back to the Zulu's house. A lady neighbor noticed that because it was unusual to see Comfort at all. He doesn't socialize much. And suddenly he's coming home with bags from Burger King, almost as if there are guests at the house. And yesterday, this man, Comfort, appeared briefly on the front porch of the house with a young blond woman. The lady neighbor noticed that too, and more. The lady is a retired hospital worker; she spent twenty years watching addicts come in and out of where she used to work, and even from a distance she can see the young woman is under the influence of something. She guesses crack. That's what it looks like to her."

Colin closed his eyes and lowered his head. "Bastard."

Mamadou nodded, continued. "This isn't a neighborhood with a lot of white faces. A white one, a blonde one at that, stands out." He paused, added, "I think it's about time for us to intercede."

ಉ

Comfort didn't like Howard and Harold, the Zulu's new employees; they looked like thugs and had no finesse. He was vaguely pleased they'd been hired to do the strong-arm stuff. Truth was, Comfort really didn't have the heart for it anymore. He'd done it many years, in many places. It had been part of his job, and he took a certain pride in doing any job well, but in fact he'd never enjoyed it much, not really. He could remember the first time he'd killed a man. It had been far messier than he'd planned, and he'd learned some valuable lessons. The subsequent deaths he was responsible for had all been as surgical as could be managed. Until Herbie. He sighed and opened a window to let fresh air in.

He was in the efficiency apartment he'd been renting for close to two years, though he'd never spent more than ten nights there. The Zulu didn't know about it or, if he did, didn't care. The rent was cheap, the building nondescript and not as well kept as Comfort could have wished, but the neighbors never asked questions and at least the hallways were clean and didn't smell of urine.

It was sparsely furnished, sparsely decorated. The walls were bare save for a tourist poster from better times that entreated tourists to visit Nigeria. The poster showed a lakeside resort with

Thirst

white sands and mostly white people gazing at a red sunset. It read, "Come to Nigeria and Fall in Love." Comfort wondered if anyone in the past two decades had come to his country for that purpose. He doubted it.

An adequate stereo played selections from a Muzak station and a small color television was tuned soundlessly to a sitcom featuring a black family with a bellicose father and three hapless teenagers.

Comfort sat at his desk, a yellow legal pad before him. The numbers he was multiplying, adding, and sorting through, he'd already seen a hundred times. But it pleased him nevertheless to go through the calculations again. He did it twice, smiled to himself. Soon he could go home.

This pleasant thought was disturbed by the image in his mind of the young white woman in the Zulu's basement. He hoped she wouldn't die, or that if she did, he would not have to witness it.

It worried him slightly that she had not yet told the Zulu what he wanted to hear. Had he misjudged Herbie? Had the man really not shared his secret with his woman friend? The idea of helping her was tempting—a few words from him would do it, but Comfort was not yet completely at ease with the notion. He had not come this far to be led astray by a wisp of misguided compassion. He wondered whether leaving the girl alone with the two new thugs was a good idea. They probably wouldn't harm her; the Zulu had given orders she not be touched, but you never knew with such thugs.

Comfort glanced at his watch. The girl had been without drugs for eighteen hours now and her cravings would be fierce. He glanced at his watch again and nodded to himself. He'd finish his calculations and go see her, maybe give her some milk laced with sugar to lighten her suffering.

He wet the point of his pencil with a flick of his tongue, focused on the numbers once again, and hummed along with the music coming from the radio.

"Course I'll help. Whaddya want me to do?" Joe balanced a cup of Starbucks coffee on one knee, holding the top with two fingers. He'd been blowing on it for five minutes and it was still too hot to drink. He looked down into the cup with an unhappy expression. "You'd think they could figure something like that out, wouldn't you? I mean, it shouldn't take a genius to know that if you order a coffee to go, you want it so you can drink the damned thing, not juggle it."

Mamadou said, "Sir?"

Joe kept staring at the coffee cup. No one had called him *sir* in a long time, and it didn't register.

Colin said, "Joe, here's what we need you to do."

Later, Colin dropped by Orin's house. Martha was on the front porch, sitting in her husband's rocker and sipping Red Zinger.

"I wish Orin were here, Colin. He'd know how to handle this stuff. I can't reach him, though. I tried a bunch of times and left messages, but he hasn't called back." She sipped, thought, and sipped again. "But yeah, of course, you get Josie out, bring her here. It's been a while since I dealt with crack addicts. I used to get them all the time in the emergency room when I was with Fairfax Hospital. So you bring her here and we'll get her stabilized, find the best place to put her in for detoxing."

Colin nodded. He could hear the doubt in her voice. "We'll be careful, Martha."

She gave him a wry look. "Yeah, you'd better. Something happens to you, I'd never forgive myself. And Orin, he'd get even more impossible to live with."

Thirst

☙

Catherine's eyes were wide, and her lower lip quivered. "I mean, what do you know about this man Mamadou? How do you know you can trust him, Colin? What if something happens? You're going to break into this drug dealer's home and try to snatch Josie? What if she gets hurt? And Joe? Why would a policeman go along with something like that?"

Colin didn't really have answers and chose his words carefully. "You have to trust somebody, Cat, and unless you want us to bring back a corpse, we've got to act now." The image had the desired effect. Catherine closed her eyes, shuddered.

"We'll bring her to Martha and Orin's house. You know where they live, off Gallows Road? I'll call you when we get there. Martha's a nurse. She's handled druggies before and knows what to do." He fell silent and waited for Catherine to nod her head. "It'll be all right, you'll see. We'll get Josie back and she'll be fine."

Catherine nodded again. There really wasn't much of a choice, was there?

☙

When the Zulu came into the room, he found Comfort squatting in front of Josie. The girl was trembling, and her limbs palsied. Her eyes were closed and she was breathing heavily. The Zulu thought she might be unconscious. Comfort said, "She's coming down very hard, Dingane. I don't know what you've been giving her, but if you stop like this, it will kill her. I've seen it before." He said it without inflection; this was information the Zulu should know.

The Zulu sighed. It was taking far too long, and his patience was wearing thin.

"So what do you suggest?"

Comfort shrugged. "Her health is not my business, Dingane. But she needs to be weaned off. If you want her to live, that is."

The Zulu nodded, his face a mask. "I will get her something. She can't die yet."

As soon as he left the room, Comfort brought his mouth close to her ear and whispered, "Listen, Miss Stilwell. Listen very carefully." There wasn't much time. He hoped she was rational enough to hear him and understand. He squeezed her upper arm until she flinched and lowered his voice even more. When he was finished he asked, "Will you remember this? You must! It's your only chance."

∞

When the Zulu returned, Comfort watched him hand the pipe to Josie and light it. The girl sucked hard and held the vapors in her lungs, reluctant to let go. Her body relaxed as if a length of steel had been removed from it. Her eyes found the Zulu's and he lowered himself to a squatting position next to her. She leaned until her lips were inches from the Zulu's ear and said something Comfort could not hear, then repeated it.

A small smile broke across the Zulu's face, and Comfort noted not for the first time that his employer's teeth were extraordinarily numerous and amazingly white. The Zulu rose, searched a pocket, withdrew three small vials of drugs, handed them to the girl, and dropped a book of matches on her lap. Then he signaled to Comfort and they both left the room.

"Patience," he said, "wins out again."

Comfort raised an eyebrow. "She told you?"

The Zulu nodded. "Of course. I knew she would."

Thirst

Comfort feigned being impressed. "As usual, Dingane, you knew best."

"Yes. I did."

Comfort watched the Zulu climb the stairs ahead of him, watched the man's ample rear, and smiled thinly. The Zulu's final gift to the girl would kill her, but that, in the end, would be preferable to all concerned. Certainly it would be better for her than dying without, racked by pain and sweating blood. Comfort hoped she would not take too long to die, hoped her overdose would be quick and pleasurable.

Josie held the treasure in the palm of her hand. Her vision was blurred but she was cognizant enough to realize that her every problem had been solved, that unlimited happiness, total contentment, and an end to her pain was in her grasp.

Deep in the recesses of her brain, a small insistent voice tried to cry out a warning and failed.

With the nail of her little finger, she scraped clean the bowl of the glass pipe and turned it over to dump any residue. She fumbled with one of the vials, trying to open it, and finally stuck it in her mouth and pulled the stopper with her teeth. Carefully, she tipped the contents into the bowl. A part of her noted that it was different this time, powder more than solid. She struck a match and inhaled. The smoke hit her with the force of a fist. She dropped the pipe, watched uncaring as embers fell from the bowl abs burned through her jeans and into the flesh of her leg. She sighed once deeply. Her hands unclenched, and the two remaining vials rolled to the ground. With a monumental effort, she reached down to the floor and pushed them beneath the beanbag chair, where they would be safe from harm. Then she smiled.

Chapter Fifteen

"Goddamit!" The blonde girl yelled, slamming the door of the cabin shut. It made a hollow metallic sound that rang for a moment before being swallowed by the steady thrumming of the ship's engine.

"You promised!"

The brunette turned, a set stubborn look on her face. "I wasn't going to take anything. I wanted to look. Wanted to see what it was."

"Sure."

The silence hung between them.

The blonde wore a short bathrobe over a one-piece turquoise bathing suit. Her hair was damp and hung in streaks. The brunette was in a bra and panties. A pair of shorts and a bright yellow T-shirt that read "I ♥ Barbados" were laid out on the bunk before her.

The blonde took the bundle that was wrapped in brown paper and sealed in a CVS bag and inspected it closely.

The brunette looked sullen. "I told you. I didn't touch anything. I just wanted to look."

Thirst

"Look, my ass..." She turned the bundle this way and that. "Fucking addict. I should have known better. Jesus, how stupid can I get, trusting someone with a habit."

The brunette's voice flared. "I haven't used in almost a year! You know that! I wanted to *look*!"

The blonde took a deep breath, held it. "You wanted to look. And what would that get you, looking? Going to feel better if you *look*?"

"You never told me what was in there."

"You couldn't guess? You think someone's going to give us fifteen grand to cart a box of donuts halfway round the world?"

"You never told me!"

The blonde sighed. "Give me a break."

"You didn't trust me."

The blonde took a tote bag from the top shelf of the cabin's small closet, placed the bundle in it, zipped up the bag, and dropped it on the bunk.

"I thought we went through all that before, didn't we? Didn't I tell you that it was easier that way? Something happens, you don't know what it was, didn't even know it was there. I was trying to protect you. Jesus!"

The brunette's voice lost its edge, turned soft. "I forgot."

"Yeah, right."

"I wouldn't use. I'm through with that. I wouldn't do that to you. Or to me."

The blonde nodded. "Right. That's what you said."

"I meant it."

The blonde took the bag, put it into the closet, and draped a towel over it. "Just leave it alone, okay? Trust me. Just a little while longer."

The brunette shrugged. "I know what it is, you know. I'm not stupid."

"Never said you were."

"Bolivian Marching Powder." She giggled. "Lots of it."

"That's a good guess."

"I'm right. I just know I am."

The blonde shrugged again. "Does it matter? Fifteen thousand. Like I said, it's not donuts."

The brunette slipped into her shorts and pulled the T-shirt over her head. "I guess it doesn't. Matter, I mean. What do I know? Maybe it *is* donuts."

"Keep that thought," the blonde answered. "Very, very expensive donuts."

☙

Colin wondered why he was where he was, sitting in a car next to a black man he hardly knew, driving someplace to do something he was vastly unqualified to do. It felt like one of those early sobriety drunk dreams, when he'd woken with a shudder, gasping for air, terrified that the illusion had been fact. Those had lasted months, striking once or twice a week, so vivid they left the oily taste of cheap vodka in his mouth and an all-too-familiar stinging warmth in his stomach. Once, to his horror, he'd woken to find he'd wet himself.

Even the presence of Joe in the back seat had an unreal feel to it. Colin could hear him breathe, a faint in-and-out hissing sound. Joe had eaten garlic bread for dinner and was uncharacteristically quiet and fidgety.

Mamadou, by comparison, was made of wood; only his hands and head occasionally moved, monitoring the non-existent traffic and guiding the car exactly five miles above the speed limit.

Thirst

In the apartment earlier, the plan had made perfect sense. Wait until the middle of the night, drive in, snatch the girl, drive out. A simple thing, over in a matter of minutes. Now it seemed like unadulterated madness. The three hadn't exchanged a word since entering the District. Words would convey doubt, doubt would convey fear.

Colin wondered whether either Mamadou or Joe felt as he did, wrapped in cottony silence. His legs went tight when a police car detached itself from the curb and momentarily followed them, relaxed slightly when the cruiser turned off to the right and was lost to view.

"There's a gas station a block up," Mamadou said quietly. "If either of you want to use a bathroom, now is the time."

Colin smiled in the darkness. "Are we that obvious?"

Mamadou nodded. "It's normal. When I was a policeman—and I'm sure Joe will know what I mean—I used to get violently sick when I knew I was headed into a potentially dangerous situation. It lasted for the first six months I was in uniform."

"Then what happened?"

"Then I got calm. I realized that the outcome of whatever I was going into would have little to do with how I felt about it. It was a blessing to realize that." His hands moved the steering wheel slightly and the car jumped a lane. "But there's really no reason for your concern, Colin. All you have to do is strike one man, and he'll be sleeping. I would think you'd feel a certain sense of justice whacking Harold on the head. I would, had he done to me what he did to you."

"I already vomited on his shoes."

Mamadou smiled. "That is a vengeance of sorts. Perhaps not my first choice, though." He braked at a red light.

Earlier, Mamadou had offered Colin a gun, but Colin had refused the weapon. "Those things scare me." Now Colin thought of reconsidering. A gun, that most impersonal of weapons, might have added a degree of sanity to the situation. Joe was wearing his in a shoulder holster and had made a point of taking out the clip and checking it carefully. Mamadou had one also.

Mamadou picked up the cell phone from its cradle on the dash, punched a number, waited, and asked, "Anything new?" After a moment he flipped it closed and dropped it on the floor of the car. He turned to Colin, said, "One more time."

"I go up the steps. They creak, so I'm careful. Howard is asleep on the couch in the front room. I hope the neighbor is right about that, Mamadou. I don't want to tangle with that guy again…"

"Aunt Mim says the neighbor looked in their window five minutes ago. Howard's asleep."

"I bop Howard on the head."

"Hard."

"I bop Howard *hard* on the head, go downstairs, grab Josie, and get the hell out."

Mamadou said, "Joe?"

"I stay outside and watch. If anything happens, I punch *three* on the digital, and it buzzes both of you. I start the car and get ready to haul ass out." He paused, then added, "I still don't like this. I should be going in with you guys, help you out if you need it."

"Somebody's got to stay out here, Joe." Mamadou turned back to Colin. "And I'll take care of Harold and the Zulu. We shouldn't be in there more than two minutes, three at the most. How do you both feel."

Joe and Colin chorused, "Fine." Neither meant it.

Mamadou said, "Good." He fell silent for a moment, added, "There's not much finesse to a frontal assault, but more often than not, it works." After a moment, he added, "No ID, right, Joe? No badge or anything like that?"

Joe nodded. "Nothing at all. I left all that stuff at Colin's house."

"Colin?"

Thirst

"No papers. Ten bucks and a quarter to call a cab in case the car breaks down…"

No one laughed. They drove on, crossed the river, and headed into Anacostia.

Joe said, "Rough neighborhood."

Mamadou glanced in the rearview mirror and caught Joe's eyes. "There are people who spend their entire lives here; they get used to it. All the papers print about Anacostia is the crime rate, but there's a lot more going on than just crime. Some of Washington's best families—best *black* families, those that haven't sold out and bought houses on the Gold Coast or in Prince George County—live here. Some artists too."

Joe held up a hand. "Sorry. Didn't mean to criticize, or anything. It's just that—"

Mamadou interrupted him. "It's just that there aren't many *white* families living here." He slowed for a blinking yellow light. "Almost there."

The rest of the ride was spent in silence. Eventually, Mamadou slowed the car, pulled in close to the curb, and snapped the headlights off. "It's that house," he pointed. "Over there."

Colin peered into the darkness. It was a nondescript single family home set a few yards back from the street. Clapboard, peeling white paint, a single line of ivy climbing up the gutters. The first floor of the house was dark save for a faint light over the front entrance. On the second floor, one window was dimly lit. The house next door, by comparison, was brightly illuminated. "That's the neighbor lady, the one who's been calling Aunt Mim."

They sat in the car in the dark for many minutes. Eventually, Joe cleared his throat and said, "You're gonna love this, Colin, it was in the *Washington Times*." Colin could hear him unfold a piece of paper. "Listen. It's priceless." He began reading in a low monotone. "Here's the headline, 'Man Fatally Stabbed over McDonald's Order.'"

Colin whispered, "Joe, this isn't exactly the time and place."

Joe ignored him, reading, "'As he sat in the drive-through lane of a McDonald's restaurant in Northeast Washington yesterday morning'—Northeast, right? Where else is this shit gonna happen? Anyway, this guy realizes he doesn't have enough money for the order, so he tells the weenie behind the counter to take some stuff away…"

"Joe!"

"No, listen, this is *choice*. So this kid who's riding in the car gets pissed off, 'cause maybe it's *his* fries getting left behind, and this kid stabs him. Bam, just like that, right in the back. So"

Colin hissed, "Joe! Shut the fuck up!"

Mamadou was staring straight ahead. Now he turned to face Joe. "No, Colin, it's okay. I read the paper too."

Joe the Cop made a show of folding the scrap of paper, putting it back in his pocket. "Sorry. Didn't mean to offend."

Mamadou shrugged. "You didn't." He paused, turned again, said, "Tell us what happened."

Joe mumbled. "Nothing much. Usual violent crap."

"The boy who was stabbed. He died, right? You said, 'fatally stabbed.' Did they catch him, the other boy?"

Joe shook his head. "No. Not last I heard."

Mamadou nodded. "Shame."

"But they will."

"Undoubtedly."

With three men in the car it soon got hot, and Mamadou cranked open a window. In the house, the upstairs light went out. Mamadou said, "Soon."

Ten minutes later it started raining softly. Five minutes after that, the tempo of the drops increased on the roof of the car. Mamadou looked at his watch. "We'll wait another twenty minutes, unless something happens. I'll go out and take a quiet look around the

THIRST

house, just to make sure they're not watching television. I'm almost certain they're not. The neighbor told Aunt Mim these people go to bed early and rise late."

The rain beat a serious tattoo and just as suddenly ceased. Mamadou grunted. "It would have been nice if it had continued a few more minutes."

The street was shiny, as if coated with oil. Finally, Mamadou said, "All right. I'll signal you." He opened the car door softly, and Colin noticed the dome light didn't turn on.

Mamadou said, "Lock the doors."

Joe didn't like the idea. "Why?"

"Because I said so. Because I know this area, and I know the people, and even though it looks quiet, I don't want to have someone open the door, stick a gun in your very white faces, and steal the car."

Colin said, "Just do it, Joe. Don't argue."

Mamadou faded into the darkness, a faint black-on-gray shadow.

Joe said, "Man, he sure doesn't move like the other people around here. No elbows and knees on that man."

"Yeah," Colin said. "He's pretty unusual."

Joe nodded. "Former cop. Must have been kind of tough, in a place like Africa. I really hope I didn't offend him. I didn't mean to. Really. All I was trying to do was—"

Colin cut him off. "It's okay, Joe. Don't worry about it."

The clouds cleared momentarily. Colin cracked his window open an inch. An odor of mulch, wet tar, and spent electricity invaded the car. They waited. A few minutes later there was a tap on the side of the car and both men jumped. Mamadou's hair glistened with raindrops. Colin opened the door and the man slid in.

"Howard is asleep on the couch next to the foyer. He snores very loudly. The others are upstairs. Your friend is in the basement. There's a cellar entrance to the house but it's locked, so you'll have to go through the front door—I opened it for you."

Colin nodded. There wasn't anything to say in spite of the hundred questions he wanted to ask.

Mamadou turned to Joe. "Follow Colin, then go to the side of the house and stay out of sight. There are some bushes. You'll be able to watch the road without being seen. Remember the cellular. Just punch in *three*."

Mamadou reached under the driver's seat, pulled out an old-fashioned nightstick, and handed it to Colin. "I customized this. Is that the right word? A lead weight in the tip. Let's go."

Colin took the nightstick. It was top-heavy, the handle ribbed. Mamadou said, "That is a very big man sleeping in there, Colin, and he got the best of you once already."

Colin hefted the weight in his hand, felt a slight reassurance. Joe tapped his shoulder and walked quickly to the side of the house. Mamadou smiled and motioned Colin out of the car. Halfway to the house, Mamadou said, "Your turn." He vanished, and Colin felt insanely exposed. He approached the front steps slowly, feeling the grass give beneath his shoes. The lawn was mowed unevenly, tufts of green sprouting gray in the dim light. His legs felt weak. Only once in his life had he willfully struck someone in anger, and he had regretted it for months.

Five steps led from the sidewalk to an unscreened porch that begged for a coat of paint. He noticed the spout of the gutter was rusty and needed replacing. Two windows were open, one was closed. The house's breathing rang loud in his ears.

He tentatively placed one foot on the first step. The wood groaned and he froze, the nightstick dropping to his side. He waited for the front door to explode open, but nothing happened. He climbed the rest of the steps, crept to a window, and peered in. A black man he recognized as Howard was asleep on the couch. Horizontally, the man was massive, his chest and belly rising with every breath.

Thirst

Colin turned the door knob, pushed, and heard the hinges complain. Howard stirred, snorted, and turned on the couch so his back was to the door. He had undone his pants, and the elastic band of his underwear was disturbingly white.

Colin entered the room and glanced around. There was nothing there to personalize the place, not a single item to testify that people did indeed live there. The walls were bare save for a couple of yellowing Bob Marley posters. The furniture was Aaron Rents, large, functional pieces that took up too much space. There was no clutter, no newspapers on the floor, no magazines, no mail waiting to be read and answered, no stereo or TV.

Reaching Howard took forever.

Colin stood over him, nightstick poised, arm frozen, wondering how hard he had to hit. What if he missed? The man was such a large presence that surely one blow wouldn't injure him. What if he struck and it wasn't enough? What if he hit too hard and killed him?

Howard stirred, farted.

Colin's arm swung down in a short, vicious blow, and the nightstick made a fat, full sound as it struck Howard's head. Howard's entire body levitated from the couch. His eyes opened, and he looked straight at Colin with annoyed surprise. Then he relaxed, his eyeballs rolled, and he slid off the couch onto the floor.

The nightstick was a snake in Colin's hand. He dropped it, fumbled, and found a strong and steady pulse on Howard's neck. Whatever the blow had done to Howard's head, it hadn't injured his heart.

Colin listened for sounds, heard only the quiet cacophony of a house at night. The loudest noise was his own breathing.

He retrieved the stick and walked softly down the stairs to the basement. It was dark but his eyes saw with amazing clarity. He cracked open the first door he came to. It was a bathroom, still damp from someone's shower. A second door opened onto a remarkably neat study housing a computer screen with a Windows screensaver, a stereo glowing softly, books on shelves, a La-Z-Boy chair, and a potted palm. The room smelled faintly of sandalwood incense. A third door across the hallway was ajar. Colin crept in.

Even in the dark he could see long blond hair splayed out. There was no mistaking her. She was frowning, knees close against her chest, hands balled into fists. She was bone thin, the skin on the back of her hands almost translucent. From where he stood Colin couldn't see whether she was breathing or not, and for a moment he panicked. Then she moaned and a bubble of saliva grew at one corner of her lips. The room smelled like a dentist's office.

He shook her and she made a gurgling sound deep in her throat. She moved her legs slightly and the smell of dry urine wafted up to his face. She turned to her side, muttered something, and drew a small fist to her mouth.

Upstairs there were two sharp popping sounds. Colin held his breath, then lifted Josie up and slung her across one shoulder. She was remarkably light. The smell of urine grew stronger. Nightstick still in hand, he took the stairs two at a time and came face to face with Howard. The man was holding the back of his head with one hand, a large handgun with the other.

Colin swung the nightstick in a long arc that connected with a leaden thud. Howard's head snapped back. The gun went off with an extraordinarily loud sound. Howard fell to his knees, then on his face. Josie yelped, twitched, and struggled without strength. Colin held her tighter, struck out wildly at Howard again, missed. He kicked the handgun down the stairs, saw the black man trying to lift himself up, and struck again, this time on target, the stick singing in his hand. Suddenly he felt himself engulfed from behind in a bear hug, heard Mamadou shouting, "Let's go, Colin! *Now!*"

Thirst

From a corner upstairs window, Comfort opened the curtain less than an inch to watch the car that was watching the house. He didn't know who the three men were but doubted their presence meant anything good. In the dim light he could see that two were white and one was black, but that, in and of itself, didn't mean much. Everyone was in the drug trade, and color had little to do with it. Because they *were* in the trade, that was obvious. Who else would be surveying the place? They weren't law enforcement—the car was wrong, the method of surveillance too obvious. Their very presence implied something bad on the verge of happening.

Comfort decided it was time to act when he saw the first man leave the car and vanish from sight, only to reappear moments later. He had no intention of confronting the strangers. This was not a good time to get shot at, not a good time to have one's life plans altered by chance circumstance. In days—weeks at most, if things went right (and there was no reason to think they shouldn't)—Comfort would be on his way home.

He was just opening the back door of the house when he heard two shots. The sound was unmistakable. He fell to the floor, reached up to push the door open, and scuttled crab-like into the small backyard. There were no decent hiding places there so he crawled to the side fence and tried to melt into the shadows. He saw one of the intruders standing guard not fifteen feet away. The man, a corpulent white, had his gun drawn but was unsure of where he should be or where he should go. Comfort saw all this in a split second and hoped to stay unnoticed exactly where he was. When the man turned toward him he realized this was no longer an option.

Thierry Sagnier

☙

When Joe heard the gunshots, he whipped his pistol out of its holster and, in that defiant act, realized, remembered the cell phone. He took it out of his pocket and fumbled with it in the dark.

It had been years since Joe had drawn his sidearm. The weapon felt foreign in his hand, an unwanted and useless appendage that would probably malfunction. Joe couldn't remember the last time he'd shot the gun or cleaned it.

He turned to get his bearings and flicked the safety off, a sharp metal sound that filled the night. The shadows loomed large in the small space, and he thought he saw something there, a shape that maybe had a head, maybe didn't. He took a step closer to get a better look and the shape levitated from the ground, became a man that hit him in the face, the throat, the groin. Joe reeled back, yelled, felt a sharp pain in his wrist, dropped the gun and then the phone. With his good hand he managed to grab a shirt collar and pull down. The fabric ripped, gave way. Joe swung wildly where he thought his attacker's face might be and connected with something fleshy and satisfying.

☙

Comfort hated not having choices but it had happened enough times in his life that he knew how to react. In his mind he had already decided that the three men were assassins. They had come to kill the Zulu, a not unlikely turn of event considering his boss' occupation. They would kill him too, because that's how things were done in this line of work, and the thought angered him. People like that had been given plenty of opportunities earlier to kill him. Now was simply the wrong time. Home beckoned.

Thirst

When he heard the distinctive click of the safety, he rose from the grass like a black egret, every gram of his being intent on escape.

In slow motion he saw the round face of the white man explode into surprise, fright, terror. Comfort's own arms, legs, and fists moved with aching deliberation but he knew this was an illusion. Another part of him could feel and appreciate the swiftness of it all. He struck the man's face, launched an elbow to the Adam's apple, a knee to the groin. With the cutting edge of his right hand he smashed into the gun-bearing wrist and saw the weapon drop. He scooped the gun up, brought it to where the intruder's head should be, and fired three times. The noise deafened him and he felt his face splattered with droplets of something warm and semi-liquid.

&

In the moments before losing consciousness, Joe the Cop had a flurry of thoughts. The first was mild surprise that his gun indeed had worked. The second was that if *he* had been the one using the weapon, it probably would have jammed, such was his luck lately. The third was that he hadn't led a very interesting life but that he was dying sober.

&

Comfort wiped at his face, stuffed the gun in his pocket, and scrambled over the fence, ripping his pants. He cut through the neighbor's yard and into the alley. When he heard the first siren, he decided it couldn't be the police yet. 9-1-1 calls from this neighborhood were generally put on hold. As the sirens approached, he revised this opinion and slowed his running to a purposeful walk. A block away, he carefully wiped the gun and dropped it into an open dumpster. He made his way to a house he knew was abandoned and boarded up and entered it through a gaping basement window. He sat in the dark, hugging his knees for warmth and waiting for daylight.

༄

"Now, Colin! *Now!*"

Mamadou shoved Colin forward. Colin stumbled, felt Josie sliding from his shoulder. Her ankles bumped hard against a doorjamb and she whimpered once.

"Get to the car, Colin! Quickly! *Quickly!* I'll get Joe."

Josie's still form was almost weightless. He stepped over Howard, who lay on the floor, arms outstretched. In the front yard he looked around quickly, noticed the window shades of the next door neighbor's house were all drawn. He opened the car's rear door and tried as best he could to arrange Josie on the back seat. He heard himself panting loudly and felt his chest heave. The palms of his hands were sweaty, and he wiped them on the legs of his pants.

Mamadou came leaping out of the darkness an instant later and slid into the driver's seat.

"Where's Joe?"

Mamadou shook his head. "We can't help him." He turned on the ignition and the engine caught. "Wait a minute! *Wait a minute, goddamit!* What the hell are you saying? You can't leave—"

"He's gone, Colin. Dead. Someone shot him. There's nothing we can do. We have to get out of here." Mamadou's hands trembled on the steering wheel. Sirens wailed in the distance.

"Mamadou, we can't—"

Mamadou turned to face Colin. His voice was just above a whisper. "You want to stay, you stay. There are four dead people over there. Stay and explain that. Be my guest." He reached across Colin and moved to open the passenger door. Colin stopped his hand. "Four?"

"The Zulu. Another man upstairs—Harold, I think. Howard. Your friend Joe."

"Howard's not dead!"

Mamadou put the car in gear and slid away from the curb. "Yes, he is."

Colin looked back at the house just in time to see flames explode out of the upstairs windows. Glass fell like pointed rain, and black smoke billowed.

"Jesus, Mamadou! Did you—"

"Yes. Now be quiet. Let me drive."

Chapter Sixteen

In the final edition of the paper the next morning there was a small article about a house in Anacostia that had burned down in the early hours of the morning. Bodies were recovered, but none had been identified to date. The firemen had been unable to quench the blaze; it was an old house, the clapboard was dry, and the nearest fire hydrant had been tampered with. It took minutes for the firemen to get water, and minutes were all the flames needed. The next-door neighbor, an elderly lady, said there'd been no warning. The fire had started spontaneously, and though she'd not known the people next door well, she would include them in her prayers.

Colin read the story and felt nauseous.

Not a word had been exchanged during the ride back. Colin had thrown a jacket over Josie, who remained semi-conscious through it all. Mamadou had dropped them off at Orin and Martha's house and driven away, still silent. Martha had taken over, a sad and serious expression etched across her face.

"She should be in a hospital, Colin. I think it'd be wiser."

Orin had agreed. The sight of the girl had shocked him. "Jesus, Colin, she's a walking skeleton, except she isn't walking…"

Thirst

Martha had put the girl immediately to bed and rigged an IV. "She's dehydrated, and it looks as if she hasn't eaten anything in a week. Her pulse is steady, though, and that's a good thing. But she needs more care than I'll be able to give her here."

So Colin asked Martha to call Catherine, but he left before Josie's mother arrived.

Mamadou had said Joe was dead, but Colin called the police station anyway, asked for Joe by name. Maybe he'd only been wounded, maybe he'd escaped. The cop on duty told him Joe wasn't there but that he'd take a message. Colin said he'd call back.

There was no one to call, to tell of Joe's heroism, his sense of humor, his grin. Colin wondered if Joe had relatives, remembered him once mentioning a cousin who was a cop in a small Florida town.

In the middle of the afternoon he fixed himself a sandwich, ate a single bite, and threw the food away. He made a pot of coffee, picked up the phone to call Catherine, punched the first three numbers, and then put the phone down.

The fact was, the multiple killings would probably not elicit much interest, would be seen as part of the city's never-ending drug wars. He wondered what the coroner would do with the discovery that one of the dead men was white. Probably nothing.

In the evening he watched the news. The fire had already been relegated to a mere mention at the end of the show. A three-second shot of the house showed a blackened and still smoldering ruin. The front porch had collapsed and the front door was gone. The camera panned to two children with very white teeth looking straight into the lens. One waved and said, "Hi, Grandma!"

He wondered how Josie was, and found he didn't care; her fate was out of his hands—if it ever had been there in the first place.

Shortly before ten p.m., Catherine knocked on his door and called his name several times. He didn't answer. After a few minutes, he saw a scrap of paper slide beneath the door. He didn't pick it up.

An hour or so later, he took a shower, shaved carefully, and put on a clean pair of jeans and shirt. He selected an old hound's tooth jacket he hadn't worn for years but the thing was far too tight around the shoulders, so he found the least tattered sweatshirt and put that on instead.

He remembered Orin's admonition to call before he did something foolish, but that didn't seem like a good idea at all. Orin would probably try to talk him out of it, and Colin felt he'd been waiting a lifetime for this moment.

The bar was a dark and cheerless place with neon signs advertising beer and a TV tuned to an all-sport station. Colin ordered a double vodka (Absolut), a shot of Glenfidich with a Michelob draft on the side and, just for the hell of it, a margarita.

He drank them quickly, waited a moment, and ordered a second round and then a third.

Chapter Seventeen

The assistant *sous-saucier* had been harboring a low-level fever for three days. It wasn't enough to go on sick call—not that he ever would, the *saucier* was a slave driver—but it clouded his judgment. He had added too much white pepper to the *blanquette de veau au persil*, failed to sample the *rémoulade de canard*, and been unable to detect an overabundance of ginger in the *coquilles St. Jacques à la Vietnamienne*. These subtle failures had annoyed his immediate supervisor, but not to the point of reporting the oversights to the *chef administratif*.

Jean-Marie Berger, the *sous-saucier*, felt his stomach rumble ominously. He swallowed once, twice, closed his eyes, breathed deeply through his nose, and exhaled through his mouth. That calmed him somewhat. He went about his business efficiently, checking on the work of the three sub-assistants for whom he was responsible; nothing was amiss. He ducked out for two quick puffs of his Gauloise cigarette and blew the smoke out through the overhead vent. The no-smoking rule was rigidly enforced in the galley; the *chef administratif* was a born-again teetotaler and reformed pack-a-day smoker with little patience or compassion for the unfortunate many whom, unlike him, could not control their addictions.

Jean-Marie focused away from his stomach and concentrated instead on how he would feel two hours hence when his shift was over and he would be able to have a quiet smoke in the designated area before going to bed. He thought about his girlfriend in Brittany, whom he would be seeing in two weeks, and how she would like the trinkets he had bought her at the ship's gift store. He thought about how her breasts would feel in his hands and smiled at the faint stirring.

He glanced at his watch. Time to make the *sauce marinière à l'ail des îles*. He rubbed his hands together. Creating sauces always made him feel better. He went to his locker and removed the packet of spices he had purchased three days earlier at a small fishermen's restaurant far from the tourist trade. The cook there had served a dish that had been spectacularly piquant, and Jean Marie Berger, ever on the lookout for undiscovered ingredients, had managed to secure a small amount of the mixed herbs that had made the cook's creation so distinctive. He shook a teaspoon of the mélange from the plastic bag and sniffed it. The diners would be pleased; the spices truly reflected a tropical personality.

In a large metal bowl he spooned the ingredients of the *sauce marinière* without measuring, doing it by heart and feel. He added virgin olive oil, a half-cup of tarragon vinegar, sherry, and garlic paste. His stomach rumbled again and he held his breath, willing it into submission. He dumped the island spices in, mixed slowly and evenly with a large wooden spoon. He wondered if he had picked up some sort of intestinal flu. He'd been feeling poorly for seventy-two hours; it had started on his return from the fishermen's restaurant and undoubtedly would go away once it had run its course.

When the sauce's consistency was to his satisfaction, he called one of his assistants, handed the man the bowl, and told him to brush the mixture lightly onto the chicken breasts prior to broiling them. The man nodded and walked away.

THIRST

A wave of sickening heat rose from the pit of Jean Marie Berger's stomach and rushed past his chest, up his neck, and lodged in his mouth. The intensity of it took his breath away. He staggered and held onto the edge of the large butcher block with both hands. His legs suddenly felt boneless and he crumpled quietly to the ground. His eyes were swollen in their sockets, and his tongue was parchment paper. He took a deep breath and forced himself to stand, look around. No one had seen him fall. Good.

A second wave of nausea swept through him, and this time he was ready for it. With all the dignity he could muster, he walked slowly to the small toilet reserved for the kitchen employees. The light in there was very bright and hurt his eyes. He tried to focus on the sign admonishing kitchen workers to wash their hands but the words swam. He fell to his knees and vomited, tried to aim for the toilet bowl and missed. The *chef administratif* found him there two hours later. Jean Marie Berger's hands were clammy and his breathing slight and rapid. He did not respond to the *chef administratif's* questions. When two men from the medical dispensary took him away on a stretcher, they had to strap him down. His legs and torso were trembling spasmodically. One of the men, a young Ugandan from Kampala, had seen such a thing before. He commented that it looked a lot like a case of food poisoning he had encountered once in Mali, where the cook in a no-star restaurant had sought to brighten the taste of his creations with powdered mangrove root.

Within seventy-two hours, fifteen people had suffered severe food poisoning, and four had been hospitalized. The young Ugandan thought of mentioning his suspicions to the ship's physician but did not. He had never cared for the physician who that very morning had made disparaging remarks about the state of former British colonies. The man was old, dour, and, the young Ugandan knew, did not well take to suggestions from lesser medical personnel.

Chapter Eighteen

He opened one eye, then another, and closed them both. There were people talking in the background. The conversation rose and fell, stopped, started, and stopped again like a faltering engine. He could identify two voices and tried to concentrate, but what the talkers were saying was a mystery. His head hurt. The pounding came from inside and radiated out like a malevolent heat source.

"He's waking up. Colin? Colin!"

He felt his head being lifted and scalding liquid hit his lips. He tried to turn aside.

"Colin! Drink this. Now. Don't be more of a pain in the ass than you already are."

He opened his mouth and the liquid seared his tongue. He swallowed and immediately felt sick.

"Way to go, hotshot."

He recognized the voice and it filled him with dread. "Orin."

"Right."

From the corner of an eye, Colin saw the spokes in the wheels of Orin's chair. The spokes whirled and made him dizzy so he closed his eyes again. He heard the wheels' shushing sound get closer to the couch.

"Bang up job, Colin. Couldn't have done it better myself. I always said if you're gonna go out, do it in style." The chair moved again. "Certainly hope a couple of those drinks you had, you had for me, considering I had to pay the fucking tab."

Colin sat up. His stomach heaved and he made a concerted effort not to show it.

"I don't think you got anything else to puke. It's all in my van."

Colin shut out the light with both hands across his eyes. "Oh Christ. Sorry, Orin." His voice was small.

"Yep, so am I." Orin's tone was conversational but hid a deep threat. "It's gonna take weeks for that van to smell normal."

Orin leaned closer and Colin could smell a trace of salami, sour milk, and cheap pipe tobacco. He held his breath. Orin took a turn around the living room, paused, and lit his pipe. "Aren't you the least bit interested in knowing how you got home? I would be."

Colin's face was even with Orin's lap. He didn't look up.

"Generally," Orin continued, "I've found that it's a good idea, if you decide to get plowed at a bar, to have some money. You had four dollars and change, mostly pennies. Oh, and your chip, of course. Your tab came to $127.55, without tip. You told the bartender to call me. Do you remember any of this, Colin? No? Well you told him to call me and even gave him my phone number. You know it by heart, I guess, and I should be touched but I'm not." Orin drew on his pipe, relit it.

"So he called me, the bartender did. Martha's staying with your friend Josie's mother for the night. It wasn't sage to leave that girl alone yet, so they took her to the ARC earlier today. The upshot of it is, I had to drive here and you know how much I love driving, don't you. It's a lot of fun when you don't have legs." Orin paused for emphasis and shook his head in disgust.

"So I drove, double-parked, almost got a ticket. Went into the bar, paid your tab—you owe me a hundred and fifty bucks. You were in the john. Nice sight, man really looks his best when he's passed out in a toilet stall with his dick hanging in the bowl. The bartender got you into the van. Then you puked, but hey, no problem! I just drove with the windows open."

Colin said, "Jesus, Orin. I'm so sorry…"

"Just shut the fuck up, okay? So when I got here, there was this little problem, getting you out of the van. I tried to call Joe but there's no answer. Came up here, used the key you gave me, called your other friend, Mr. Dioh. His number was on your kitchen counter. Mr. Dioh was kind enough to meet me. He carried your sorry ass from the van. That was nice of him, don't you think?"

Mamadou came into view. Colin avoided his eyes, said, "Joe?"

Mamadou shook his head.

Colin looked at Orin. "Joe's dead."

It took a few seconds for Orin to understand. He said, "What? What?" Then he said, "That's why you got drunk?" When Colin shrugged, Orin looked momentarily bewildered. "I thought you knew better. Really. I did."

"It's my fault."

"You killed him?"

Colin looked at Mamadou for help. The black man turned away.

"Did you?" Orin was insistent.

"No. But it's my fault anyway. I dragged him into it, and I shouldn't have. He didn't know what he was getting into. I didn't either."

Mamadou broke in. "Colin is mistaken."

Mamadou's description of the night before was brief and to the point. As he went on, Orin's body seemed to deflate, get smaller in the chair. He listened silently, blowing out clouds of smoke. At the end he threw Colin a disbelieving look, wheeled his chair to the

THIRST

balcony window, and gazed outside. "You'll never cease to amaze me, Colin. I guess that's why I've been your sponsor all these years. It's been…interesting."

He drew a deep breath and shoved the still lit pipe into the pocket on the arm of the wheelchair. Smoke seeped out but Orin paid no attention. "So there're four dead. Three nasties and one good guy. No police, right Mr. Dioh?"

"We were gone before they got there."

"And it's a shit neighborhood; cops aren't gonna pay a lot of attention to a bunch of dealers offing each other. You kinda counted on that, didn't you?"

Mamadou nodded. "I did."

Orin looked at them both, then focused on Colin. "Martha says the girl's gonna be all right. Physically, anyway. Gonna need a serious detoxing, supervised. Whoever had her pumped some new form of nastiness into her. They're doing tests. She knows what's going on, or at least some of it. Her mother's a mess, though. Her father came by too. Jesus, what a shithead. Came in, looked at her, shook his head, and left. Didn't say a word."

Orin reflected on that for a bit, wheeled his chair back a couple of feet so it faced Mamadou.

"So you guys committed the perfect crime, it looks like. Congratulations."

Colin rubbed his eyes with a thumb and index. "Except for Joe."

Orin nodded. "Right. Except for Joe."

"I've got his stuff. His badge, his ID. He left it here."

Orin looked away. "Keep it. Maybe next time, it'll remind you not to do something completely idiotic."

He turned, faced Colin again. "You know, they don't make a book for sponsors, an instruction manual. I guess a sponsor is expected to wing it. Do the Big Book, and the Promises, and all that other AA crap—I guess that's supposed to help keep you out of trouble. But the truth is, Colin, some people see a turd in the middle of the road and they'll dodge traffic just so they can step in it. Which is what you do. You haven't realized yet that it's a selfish program. You're supposed to help others, but you're supposed to help yourself *first*. 'Cause if you don't do that, you're gonna have a hell of a time being anyone's white knight." He looked sad, the first time Colin had seen such an expression on his face.

Orin's voice turned uncharacteristically kind. "Well, shit. Come on, Colin. Get yourself cleaned up. Take a shower. Shave. Put on some fresh clothing. My night's shot all to hell anyway and if I go home now, I'm sure not gonna get any sleep. We'll go have breakfast. There's an early bird meeting at the Serenity Club and you're going there to tell everyone how much you drank last night. That should be kind of amusing."

As an afterthought, he turned to Mamadou. "Thank you for helping out, Mr. Dioh."

Mamadou bowed slightly at the waist and looked at Colin. "I'm sorry about your friend, more so than I can tell you. But he was a policeman, and he died getting rid of bad people, which is something policemen learn to live with." He paused, squeezed Colin's shoulder. "I'll call you in a couple of days."

Chapter Nineteen

Later that day, Orin said, "Well, Colin, you make a great alcoholic but a piss-poor human."

Martha was pouring tea. She looked up. "Hush, Orin. He feels bad enough. You don't have to make it worse."

Orin threw her a menacing look. "You stay out of this, Martha, it's between me and him. Just 'cause you married an alcoholic doesn't mean you know everything about 'em. Colin's smart enough to know that even on your best day, you don't fry bacon naked." Orin lit his pipe and spit a piece of tobacco out. Martha's eyebrows knit. She opened her mouth, thought better of it, shook her head, and walked out of the kitchen.

"Now she's pissed at me too." Orin puffed furiously, his tomato-red face enveloped in a blue cloud of smoke. Colin sat on a chair and stared out the kitchen window. It was raining and mist covered the tree tops in Orin's backyard. The last two days' events were distant, but by concentrating he could still feel the tingle of the nightstick in his hand.

"You listening to me, Colin? Or am I just flapping my gums."

Colin turned to face his sponsor. "Sorry, Orin."

Orin rocked back and forth in his wheelchair. "I used to boast to the other old farts about you. I'd tell 'em that after sponsoring God knows how many losers, people that went out after a week, or a month, or a year, I'd finally been asked by somebody who looked like he had his shit together. And you did, in your own fashion. So maybe that's why I'm taking all this kinda personally. I shouldn't, I know that." He paused and spat out more tobacco. "Now I'm gonna have to tell these guys you went out, and they'll all give me a bunch of program crap tryin' to make me feel better, and I just *hate* that, people tryin' to make me feel better..." His voice drifted off.

Colin watched a crow being chased by a blue jay. The smaller bird harassed the bigger one's tail feathers. The jay's wings beat furiously as it dove and swooped, but the crow was unconcerned, unwilling to evade the attack. It struck Colin that there was an analogy to be drawn somewhere but he didn't pursue it. What he wanted was a drink.

He wasn't surprised by the urge, by the fact that it had resurfaced full blown after a decade of abstinence. He had expected that. Even as he sat in Orin's house, as Orin's voice droned rising and falling in the background, Colin felt a liberating sense of normalcy come with the unwanted desire, a sentiment of things being as they should be. He had expected a war of emotions, but there was nothing more demanding than a minute unease he could attribute to an overdose of sugar and spirits. The dull headache, the heaviness in his shoulders and legs, the vague sourness in his gut—all were old friends.

Orin said, "I know what you're thinking."

Colin nodded. "I'm sure you do."

Orin closed his eyes. "I was in and out for years before I got tired of it. For you, though, it's new. You haven't felt like this in a long time. There's a big part of your mind that's saying that you can do this until all this crap is laid to rest, and then you'll be able to stop. And there's a little part—the sane part—that's saying it's

Thirst

bullshit. That little part, deep down, it knows how good you are at fooling yourself." He touched a match to his pipe. "Truth is, a man like you, in great health, who exercises all the time, you'll be able to last a while. You'll be able to pace yourself better than some other asshole whose idea of exercise is pumping the old lady once a month. You've got a lot of willpower and it'll kick in, and that'll be self-defeating too 'cause you'll think maybe you *don't* have a problem, maybe you never *had* a problem. But that little voice is gonna stay there, Colin. You'll never quite kill it off." He paused, turned his chair around, added, "But shit, Colin, you're welcome to try, you know. I ain't gonna stop you, wouldn't even if I could. Ain't my job."

Colin eventually found his jacket and draped it across his shoulders. He looked out the window again and saw Orin wheeling his chair on the ramp that led to the backyard. The quarter-acre lot was crisscrossed with concrete walks so Orin could get around and check on his tomatoes, his fishpond, his three apple trees that never bore fruit larger than cherries. Bolted to the back of his sponsor's chair was a bright yellow golf umbrella.

The clock on the kitchen wall read just past noon. From the living room the television set put out bouncy, muted music—Colin guessed it might be a game show. He wanted to leave the house quickly, quietly, but the front door was across the living room and Martha was there, while the kitchen door led directly to the backyard and to Orin. He had selected the kitchen as the safer exit when Martha called, "Colin? Catherine's here."

ೞ

He thought she looked haggard; her eyes were old and her lips made one thin line. She was wearing jeans and a short leather jacket and her hair was disarrayed. Martha smiled, said, "You two have got a lot to talk about," and left the room.

Catherine lit a cigarette and sank into a large armchair that Colin knew was Orin's favorite piece of indoor furniture. "Thank you."

Colin shook his head. "Not necessary."

There was a long moment empty of words during which they avoided each other's gaze.

"I'm sorry about Joe. I can't tell you how much." She drew deeply on the cigarette, exhaled. "I wish I'd known him better."

Colin saw she was near tears but couldn't move.

"And I know about…what happened with you. Martha told me. I guess I can understand it, but I'm not sure. I can't tell what was in your mind." She exhaled again. "But I wish you'd called me."

Colin didn't look up. "I didn't really think that was a wise idea, and you had other things to worry about. Anyway, I wanted to be by myself. I figured if I was going to relapse, I'd be my own best company."

She nodded. "Yeah. That, I can understand. I don't imagine I'd want to take a drink with AA friends around."

The conversation wavered, stopped. Finally, Colin asked, "Josie?"

Catherine sighed. "Hooked. Angry. Cries a lot. Wants a fix. Doesn't want a fix. Can't figure out why it happened to her. Right now she's really pissed off at God, but that'll pass. She'll be okay. Martha and I put her in the ARC yesterday. Funny, isn't it, how things turn out? She's where you and I were when we rehabbed. Orin knows some people there; he pulled strings so she could get in right away. She's looking at twenty-eight days at a minimum, maybe more." Catherine looked up, met Colin's eyes.

"She's not too clear on what happened. Doesn't remember most of it, though she says she's been having nightmares about gunshots, like people are shooting at her. I told her you'd gotten her out but she doesn't know who you are. I didn't tell her about Joe. I figured that was news she could live without." She paused, canted her head. "She wants to see you, to thank you, I guess."

"How's Lars handling it?"

Catherine smiled without humor. "It's hard to tell he's her father. He's relieved, of course, but not for the right reasons. Mostly he wanted to know if the police had been involved; I told him no, that it was all your doing. That made him happy. Or relatively happy...it was the best of two bad choices, you or the police. He doesn't like you much, you know that, but now he's indebted. He doesn't like that much either."

She found an ashtray, ground the cigarette out. "Jesus, he's such a freak of nature. I don't think there's ever been a man born with less parental feelings. He said that when Josie gets out of the ARC, he wants her out of the house." She fumbled in her purse for another cigarette, for a lighter. "I'm going to file for divorce, Colin. I can't take him anymore, and me and Josie would better off living by ourselves. I could take care of her better than I have been."

Colin suddenly felt the conversation was taking a dangerous curve, getting away from him. He pictured Catherine, Josie, and himself in a small apartment; he saw himself fleetingly as if in a mirror. "You don't have a job, Cat. Making ends meet, it's tough."

She shook her head. "I don't care. That house, it's a mausoleum. I never liked it, ever. I'll get money out of him, I know I can. And I'm not that dumb, you know. I can work. Do something at the mall; real estate. I can take courses and get trained. Pretty much anything would be better than staying there with him. This last thing with Josie...you know. He hasn't even gone to see her yet."

Colin remembered that when he and Catherine had first found each other, when they'd lain naked and embarrassed on his futon, he'd wondered if there might be anything long-lasting, perhaps even permanent. The notion had scared him. He said, "I'll do anything I can to help."

She nodded, but a frown remained on her face. "So. Visiting hours at the ARC are over for today. I'll pick you up at your place tomorrow morning. Ten. You be sober, hear me? One person in my life falling out is all I can handle at a time."

☙

Colin lowered the dumbbells slowly, counting one Mississippi, two Mississippi, three Mississippi, four. It was night and he hadn't had a drink though he desperately wanted one. Earlier he had eaten a bad meal at a fast food place, come home and drawn the drapes, then methodically attacked the weights, starting with the biggest ones and working his way down. The veins of his arms and chest stood out like bootlaces and he was covered in a thin sheen of sweat.

He had skipped the meeting he and Orin were supposed to attend together and he could imagine his sponsor's anger, but right now that didn't matter much. He closed his eyes, rubbed his face hard, and felt stubbles scratch his palms. Outside the traffic had died down to the whisper of a car now and again. He glanced at the clock in the kitchen and saw it was well past ten, which meant the only meetings available would be downtown. A perfect excuse not to go.

He had spent the better part of the evening trying *not* to think of Josie and Catherine. A futile exercise. He remembered someone once saying that trying to not face up to a lie was more demanding than coming clean, and he knew it was true. He thought of ten years trying to work the steps, and then one night *not*, and how the one night had won. Incredible.

Thirst

When the phone rang he looked at it for a long time before answering. The voice on the other end wasn't familiar. "Colin? My name's Ed Kuminsky. I'm a friend of Joe. You know, the cop?"

Colin muttered, "Yes?" Held his breath.

"I'm in the program too. Like Joe. The reason I'm calling is, Joe and me were supposed to get together and he never showed. I tried his apartment, tried the station. No one's seen him." The man had a high reedy voice, almost breathless. "I thought maybe—he told me you were his sponsor, that's how I have your number, in case of emergencies I'm supposed to call you—maybe you'd seen him?"

Colin held his hand over the phone's mouthpiece, thought furiously. "Not in a couple of days." That was almost not a lie.

The man said, "Ah. Well. It's just, it's unusual, you know? We always drive to the Thursday meeting together, a step meeting at Fairfax Hospital, and afterwards we have dinner. He picks me up, usually, and this time he didn't so I waited around because sometimes he's late, being a cop and all, but now it's almost a quarter of eleven and I've been waiting since eight..." He let the sentence hang.

Colin closed his eyes. He knew the caller indirectly. Joe had spoken of him. Dumb as a post, in Joe's own words, but strong sobriety. Someone to hang out with and talk about the Redskins, politics, the weather.

"No, I'm sorry, Ed. I haven't heard from him today." He added, "But if I see him I'll give him the message." Self-loathing washed over him.

"He said you and him were doing something together yesterday, so I thought maybe—"

"Sorry, Ed, I can't help you. Haven't seen him. But I'll tell him you called." Colin hung up, his hands shaking.

That night he slept without dreams and without rest.

In the morning, the news channel reported a new development on the fire and related deaths in Anacostia. One body, that of a white male apparently shot in the head several times, had been identified as that of a Falls Church policeman. The name of the officer was yet to be released.

The commentators, an overweight white man and a young black woman who looked like a pop singer, made much of the report and ventured unsupported opinions, guesses and rumors of police officers on the take. Colin watched until the coverage segued to a feature on a successful graffiti-eradication program in Southeast Washington.

He dressed slowly, put on and took off a tie, brewed a pot of coffee, and drank three cups in quick succession.

&)

Catherine picked him up in front of his apartment building and her first words were, "I know what you're thinking."

Colin smiled. "That's what Orin said yesterday."

She shook her head, "No. Yesterday, that's something else. What you're thinking now, this morning, is whether Josie will remember your…encounter with her. And if she does, how are you going to handle it. That's what you're thinking right now. And you're also wondering how *I'm* going to handle it, I know you are." She took a breath, lit a cigarette, continued. "So let me give you some relief, because I was up most of the night thinking about this." She swerved to avoid a dump truck, pumped the horn. "Asshole! Here's what we're going to do. I'll go in first, stay a few minutes to see how she's feeling, and I'll tell her you're here. Then I'm going to leave the two of you alone, get in the car, go to the nearest Starbucks, and have a quintuple espresso which I'll nurse for a half an hour or so. That should give you enough time to get through whatever it is you've got to get through." She nodded her head, as if agreeing with herself.

Thirst

"After that, I'll come back to the hospital and pick you up and we'll talk about the weather, about the program, about anything except you and Josie, because the truth is, I don't want to know. Really, I don't. If Josie chooses to talk about it in the future, that's something else, that's her prerogative and I'll listen and deal with it then. Today, I'm feeling grateful that she's alive, and grateful to you for being the one that got her back. I still feel horrible, terrible, about Joe. That's going to take a while to get over, even if I didn't know him well. But you and Josie, what you did years ago? I don't want to hear about it. Fair enough?"

"Fair enough. And thank you. But you know—"

She cut him off. "But nothing. I meant it. I don't want to know. Nice day, isn't it?"

☙

Someone had washed and cut her hair, that was the first thing Colin noticed. It had been sheared at shoulder level and hung straight like a sheet on a drying line.

She was seated on her single bed in the small ARC room she shared with another female patient. The walls were totally bare and Colin knew there were no locks on the door and that the windows were sealed. In the past there had been a couple of suicides at the ARC, patients who knew their stay at the rehab was pointless and decided to take the easy way out. And in the beginning, when the ARC opened its doors, three patients had died of alcohol withdrawal. So now it was policy for a nurse to check on the patients hourly and make sure they didn't hoard or refuse their medications, or ingest drugs smuggled in by friends and family.

The floor was highly polished linoleum—the patients swept it every day and a service waxed it once a week—and above each bed was a reading lamp bolted to the wall. Josie had on new jeans and a tee shirt that read 'Powerless Over People, Places, & Things.' Colin smiled when he saw it. She smiled back.

"A friend gave it to me when I got my first one-month chip, but I've never worn it."

He nodded and sat on the opposite bed. "How are you feeling?"

She made a face. "Horrible. Shitty. Massive cravings. I kind of hurt all over and I have a headache. Half the time I want to puke, the other half I get the shakes. And since they have me on lithium, my head's all spacey and my legs feel wobbly. I almost fell down the stairs on the way to breakfast. So, all in all, about normal for what I'm going through…"

Colin searched her face, tried to see recognition in her eyes, and was both relieved and saddened to see none. He said, "Yeah. I remember all that. I was here too, ten years ago."

"With my mother." It wasn't a question.

He looked at the girl and nodded.

Josie laughed, a bright sound, and clapped her hands together like child. "I *knew* it! You're the mystery man! You're the one!"

She gave him a long, frank stare. "I've always wondered who it was. I knew it had to be someone in the program. Had to be, they're the only people Mom sees anymore. I used to sit in meetings and look at the men and wonder, 'Okay, which one of you is it?' Now I know." She laughed again. "This is so *cool!*"

Colin let the moment wash over him.

Josie stood and came to sit next to him. "And you pulled me out of that place, so I guess the entire female side of the family owes you. Mom asked you to do it, didn't she?"

"She asked me to help, nothing more. It really wasn't that much."

She stood again, bent down, and planted a feather of a kiss on his lips. "Thank you."

Thirst

"You're welcome."

~ ~ ~

Shortly before noon Catherine came back to the ARC to pick Colin up, but he told her he was going to be staying around until after Josie ate lunch with the rest of the patients. He'd catch a bus home, since it wasn't that far. Catherine gave him a long questioning look, which he chose to disregard. She thought he was strangely cheery and that surprised her, but she had dictated the rules of the day and chose to abide by them. She drove home, took a long bath, and constructed a sandwich of ham, Camembert, and sourdough bread.

She wondered whether anything would come of that evil night, whether this time her daughter would be able to shake off the chains and not merely rattle them. It didn't look good, not really, and all her experience, strength, and hope were feeling pretty puny. She recited program mantras to herself but couldn't shake the thought of Josie maybe not making it, and it frightened her, left a dreadful empty feeling in her stomach.

She shoveled the sandwich into the garbage can beneath the kitchen sink and looked at her watch. Almost one-thirty. She walked to the hallway mirror to inspect herself and peered at her own face. Still pretty, she thought, still capable of attracting people, men. A face wholly capable of starting everything over. She decided that with Josie back and safe, she would make an appointment with a lawyer next week. She didn't know exactly who to call, but she had plenty of female friends who'd gone through divorces and come out the better for it. She wondered if Lars would be shocked. Probably not. Surely he too must realize by now that his lack of concern, of sympathy, had proved beyond a doubt there was nothing left in their union worth salvaging. Who knows, she thought, he might even be grateful. The bastard.

※

The counselor was peeved. His name tag read Lester Shakey and he was a generally nice man, the only professional staff at the ARC who was *not* in recovery. This shortcoming had long ago ceased to irk him—he had been dealing with alcoholics and drug addicts for years and come to the conclusion that it was not necessary for the inmates to run the asylum—but today he was in a bad mood not made better by the man seated before him.

Lester Shakey's office was uncluttered and sunny; his desk nicely proportioned and arranged to be in the exact center of the small room. He wore pressed blue jeans, a message-less sweatshirt, and white boat shoes with no socks. His face was round with very light blue eyes that now focused on Colin's mouth.

"It's important that you understand, Mr. Marsh, how very crucial a time this is in Josie's treatment." He smiled, showing evenly gapped teeth. "Crucial. Josie has to get familiar with her new environment. This is all very different for her, it's—"

"Her fourth rehab."

Shakey frowned, annoyed at the interruption. "Fourth? I thought it was the third." He shuffled papers, found a blue folder, opened it, and read something slowly, lips moving. The fingertip of his right index traced a line. "Right you are. Fourth. Says so right here in her records." He smiled again, paused as if to make a point, and continued. "Josie is very confused, she—"

Colin cut in again. "She knows exactly where she is and why. This is not a new dance, Mr. Shakey. Josie has been through this before. She probably knows some aspects of this treatment better than you do. And I think there are some things I can tell her that I truly believe will be helpful. All I need is another fifteen minutes or so with her. After that, she's yours."

Shakey shook his head, lips pursed. This was highly irregular and he didn't like it. "I wish you had consulted me before talking to her, Mr. Marsh. You know the rules, no contacts with outsiders unless it's supervised. It's for their own good, you know."

Colin nodded, acquiescent. "I apologize. I should have checked in with you. Fifteen minutes. Please."

Shakey decided this had gone far enough. He rose from behind his desk and motioned for the door. His visitor, however, did not rise, which forced Les Shakey to pretend he was actually going to do something else and resume his seat. He sighed and glanced at the full inbox on his left. He said, "Now I really must get back to work, Mr. Marsh." And tried the rising trick again. Marsh didn't move. Shakey sighed a second time, more loudly.

"Fifteen minutes, Mr. Marsh. I'll be watching the clock."

⁂

They sat on the front steps of the building housing the ARC. Josie shook her head, nodded, and looked confused. "Yes, I mean no, I didn't even know Herbie was a dealer, not really. I kind of suspected it—he always had money and didn't have a job—but it's not like I really *knew*, you know?"

She pulled an already half-smoked cigarette from a pack of Marlboros and lit it, and Colin saw her inhale exactly as Catherine did. She held the smoke in, let it out slowly. He said, "Okay, so a friend took you to their place, and the Zulu fixed you up."

She inhaled, nodded.

"But you didn't know about the missing drugs? Herbie had never told you anything about that?"

She looked at the cigarette, fixed her eyes on the glowing ember for a moment, inhaled a last time, and flipped the butt into the parking lot. "No. Herbie was always kinda secretive about almost everything. I mean, he liked to show off, liked to flash money and pay for things, but it wasn't that kind of a relationship, you know? Like, we didn't talk a lot about stuff, real stuff. Mostly we went out. Took cabs, ate at restaurants, went to clubs, places like that. I think he liked to show me off." She held up her hands, looked at her nails, and smiled crookedly. "I looked kind of better than this a few days ago…"

Colin took her elbow. "Josie, listen, this is important. I know it's not pleasant to think about, but you've got to. He thought you knew, the Zulu. That's why they took you. That's why they gave you the drugs, right?"

She nodded.

"But you *didn't* know?"

She nodded again.

Colin rubbed his forehead. "So why would he keep you alive, Josie? It doesn't make sense."

She opened her mouth, said, "I…" and fell quiet. Colin watched her watching cars moving in the parking lot. She took another cigarette from the Marlboro pack rolled in the sleeve of her tee shirt, stuck it between her lips, but didn't light it. She said, "Comfort."

"What?"

"The other black guy, the nicer one. His name was Comfort. You know, like 'calm'; like 'serenity.' He was the taller one. He came into the room where they were keeping me; he came in and told me what to say."

"I'm not getting this, Josie. There's something missing here."

Thirst

Her voice became insistent. "He told me what to say! Like he knew. He knew where—oh, Jesus!"

Colin leaned close to her. "What did he tell you, Josie? Word for word. Try to remember. Try real hard."

◈

Mollie Catfish squared the pile of bills before her. It wasn't as tall as she'd hoped. She had closed her checking account, maxed out both her credit cards, and sold the stuff she'd bought with them for twenty-five cents on the dollar to another girl at the club. She'd borrowed $500 from Benny the bouncer. There was $3,472.32 and it was all she could come up with. She remembered the Rolex she'd lifted from a trucker, found it, and rushed from her apartment. An hour later she was back, seething. The pawnshop owner had offered her a tenner for it. "It's a fake, honey. Twenty bucks on K Street." She'd taken the ten, balled the loan ticket in her hand, and tossed it angrily into the gutter.

$3,482 would have to do. There was no time to plan anything, no time even to turn a few tricks. In spite of herself, she felt vaguely thankful for that.

◈

So it was all about drugs. Colin whipped the old Porsche onto the Rte. 66 access, drifted into the left lane, and took the third Arlington exit. A get-rich-quick rip-off that had gone wrong and cost the lives of four people. No, five. Herbie was gone too. Small loss.

And Josie hadn't remembered Colin. There'd been nothing in her eyes save exhaustion; the hour or so the two had spent that one-and-only time long ago had been washed away. Colin wondered whether he should feel mildly insulted, but decided his relief far overshadowed any bruise Josie's negligent memory might inflict to his pride. And, if he were truthful, he had to admit that the encounter had become vague in his mind as well; the commotion of the moment left little save a hazy recollection of blonde hair and pale skin. He wondered whether Catherine would ask and how he would respond. Maybe she'd laugh. No, she wouldn't.

It would be easy enough to track the ship's whereabouts. A few phone calls would do it. Any travel agent would be more than happy to supply a potential customer with information on the Royal Scottish Line.

Colin parked the Porsche, rode the elevator to his apartment, and checked his voicemail. Two messages from Orin, one from Ed Kuminsky. "Colin? Ed. Joe was my sponsor, you remember? I talked to you a couple of days ago. I guess you must have heard by now, about Joe, I mean." There was a silence, a long sigh. "Jesus, I can't believe it. I don't know what he was doing out there. It's insane. Some people are saying he was into it, you know, that he was scoring, but I know that's not true. So, you know, if you hear anything like that…" The words trailed off and picked up again. "Anyway. I know you were his sponsor. He respected you a lot, he told me so. I don't know why I'm telling you all this. Unloading, I guess. But I thought you should know. I guess what really gets me is that he could have been saved, you know? If he'd gotten help, an ambulance, he coulda been saved. Jesus. He died in the street like some sort of animal. Jesus." Pause, sharp intake of breath. "Well, look, I'm sorry. I shouldn't be telling you all this stuff. It's part of the investigation. I needed someone to talk to, and you're my grand-sponsor, even though we never met. I was wondering if maybe we could get together sometime? Joe'd been wanting us to. He thought it might be good for me. Maybe he mentioned it? So if you'd like to, get together, that is, give me a call, okay? Jesus. Just fuckin' left

Thirst

him out there in the night. Jesus. I'm sorry. I'm really out of control about this, makes me want to find the cocksuckers myself and watch *them* die real slow. Shit. I'm sorry, I shouldn't burden you with this. Call me, okay? Here's the number, in case you lost it."

Colin hung up the phone slowly. The breath ebbed out of him, his throat closed, and a flood of saliva pooled in his mouth. A great weariness enveloped him and swathed him like a blanket. He gagged, rushed to the bathroom, felt his gut constrict. He knelt in front of the toilet bowl (the porcelain god, Orin called it) and retched acid fluid, smelling the acrid odor of his emptying stomach. After a while he stood, washed his face, rinsed out his mouth, and spat foulness into the washstand. He had believed Mamadou in their mad flight from the scene, blindly allowed the African's whispered entreaties to sway him, and they had run and Joe had been alive and they could have saved him. A minute or two, no more.

Colin peered at his reflection in the bathroom mirror, raised an arm, smashed the glass. It exploded around his fist, bright shards showering the floor tiles, breaking again and scattering. He held his hand up, saw glass splinters embedded in his knuckles, but felt no pain. He watched drops of blood form there, turn into rivulets that pooled between his fingers and ran down to his wrist and forearm.

He stood there for a very long time as the blood fell to the floor, no more than a trickle of dirty red between his shoes. He imagined the blood flowing out of his friend's body and wondered if it was the exact same color. He turned on the cold water tap and ran his hand beneath it until it regained sensation, a vague indistinct pain that failed to focus his anger.

The phone rang and Colin walked to the living room, picking it up without thinking. He heard Mamadou's rich West African voice. "Colin? Are you all right?"

Colin shook his head.

"Colin? Are you there?"

Colin nodded twice, whispered, "Yes."

"There's something you should know, something I didn't have time to tell you before. When we were in the Zulu's house…"

Colin cut him off. "No. There's something *you* should know." He sat, switched hands on the phone, and felt sticky liquid across his palm. "When we left him, Joe was alive. You forced us to leave and we could have saved him. One or two more minutes and—"

Mamadou's voice hardened. "We didn't have one or two more minutes."

"That's not true. We'll never know that."

"The police—"

"The police took their time coming. You counted on that, factored it in. We could have taken him to a hospital."

"And said what, Colin? Explained it how?"

Colin felt a weight against the back of his eyes. "I don't know. It wouldn't have mattered."

"You're upset."

"Upset?" The word struck Colin as ridiculous. He felt the relief of anger sweep him, sensed the flight of reason. He said, "We're murderers." And hung up.

∽

She had a key to the travel office. The manager had given it to her so she could come in early or stay late and work the computers, learn the trade.

It was quiet there, the glow of the monitor a splash of dim light in the dark room. Mollie booked a flight to Nassau, first class, what the hell. When the computer asked her if she wanted a round-trip, she hesitated a moment, tabbed over to the "yes" box, punched

Thirst

"enter," and cleared the screen. She checked the printer to make sure the ream of blank tickets was in place and hit another key. The printer hummed, zipping back and forth. A moment later a second machine came to life and printed her itinerary in triplicates.

She found an American Airline ticket folder, the kind with the little slash on the inside for the boarding pass, folded the paperwork, and carefully inserted it. She blew a kiss at the screen before turning the computer off.

∞

Mamadou Dioh sat in his darkened apartment sipping a large Wild Turkey. It was his third and he was stone sober. The liquor was no longer sweet on the tongue and he could feel it churning acids in his stomach. Another death. Another victim.

He took out his wallet and unfolded the small piece of paper he had found on the Zulu's body, looked at the elegant cursive script, read the words, and then replaced the note between two credit cards.

The girl was alive, that was something. Better than Amelie. Whatever he felt about the death of Colin's policeman friend was at best mixed. What Mamadou had told Colin was true: people who enforced the law woke up each morning with the dim notion that this day might be their last. Or if they didn't, they should. The policeman had been fat and poorly dressed, hardly in keeping with the image necessary to uphold the law. He was a racist, that was obvious from his conversation in the car, from his gleeful quoting of the article from that morning's newspaper. His gun probably had neither been cleaned nor fired in ages. He'd been taken by surprise; those were the breaks, as Americans said.

And Colin? Colin had been totally unprepared and weaponless, a stupid choice, no matter the philosophy. One did not enter the den of the lion naked. One took precautions. All in all, Colin should have been thankful not to have been the one left behind. Mamadou sipped his drink, drained it, and poured another, smaller one. If he himself had committed an error, it was by involving others in his affairs, by not having the necessary wherewithal to handle the Zulu alone, as he'd sworn he would.

Allies, Mamadou thought. More often than not ill-chosen, and rarely up to the task.

And now, of course, there was this quandary; that things never quite worked out as one might hope. Killing the Zulu was supposed to be the end of it. He had anticipated relief, elation, some sort of catharsis; instead he was now faced with yet another moral choice, this one involving a great deal of money. Very strange.

Mamadou Dioh took his glass to the kitchen and emptied the remaining amber liquid into the sink. He felt a bit lightheaded, troubled by the conversation with Marsh, and not at all vindicated by the events of the past few days.

ᛒ

Captain Roderick Stuart's mistress said, "I think we may be having a minor problem with one of the Gray Panthers?"

The captain's eyebrows rose slightly. He was entering the events of the past twenty-four hours in the day's log. He did this by hand at the same time every evening, shunning the computer in his cabin. At the end of this trip, he would personally deliver the log to the company archives and accompany the records officer to make sure the volume was placed where it should be, on the shelf bearing his own name engraved on a small brass plaque.

"Or maybe not so minor," his mistress continued. "It depends."

Thirst

"On?" The captain did not turn around, continued writing in the even hand he had learned in public school and developed over years at sea.

"On whether this particular gentleman is actually doing what one of the bartender suspects, which is selling small quantities of cocaine to some of the younger passengers."

"Which bartender?"

"Julio Castro."

The Captain paused and thought for a moment. He knew the name of each member of his crew as well as the number of years spent in the service of the Royal Scottish Line. Finally, he nodded.

"Castro. Won an award two years ago, saved the life of a passenger. Heimlich maneuver. "

"That's the one."

"Good man. And the Panther?"

"Earl Thorogood Miller. Seventy-one. First trip."

The Captain once again thought for a moment. "American, from Georgia or somesuch. Tall man. Full head of hair, military mustache?"

"Former professor, Renaissance Literature. Very popular with the ladies; his dance card is full every evening."

As on every other ship belonging to a major cruise line, female passengers—mostly single, widowed, or divorced—outnumbered the males by an uncomfortable margin. To correct this disparity, the ship employed a dozen or so males—the Gray Panthers—ranging in age from their late fifties to late seventies. These men—always presentable, well-mannered, and above-average conversationalists capable of playing a decent hand of bridge and dancing the fox-trot, tango, and rumba—traveled free of charge. They neither smoked nor drank overly much and were expected to devote their time to entertaining—quite properly, for the most part—clients of the opposite sex. If a shipboard romance thrived, so be it. It was not the Captain's duty to enforce morals among his passengers. It was, however, his responsibility to see that the Gray Panthers behaved in a fashion befitting his ship's good name. Dealing cocaine, even in minute amounts, was an unforgivable offense.

"Castro saw Miller do this?"

The mistress shook her head. "Not exactly. First he saw a passenger giving Professor Miller some bills. He thought this was odd and a couple of days later witnessed the same thing again, this time with another passenger. And yesterday evening, three men asked him whether Miller was around. The Professor apparently spends a lot of time in Castro's bar. Later that night, one of the men had too much to drink and spilled a drink on himself. He emptied his pockets and dumped everything on the bar, and Castro thought he saw a small plastic bag with some white powder in it. Obviously, it could have been anything, but he said the man snatched it back and walked away—or staggered away—very quickly."

The Captain carefully replaced the cap on his Mont Blanc fountain pen, blotted the latest entry, closed the logbook, and placed it on the shelf above his desk. "That's all?"

His mistress nodded.

The Captain sighed. According to Interpol, virtually every cruise ship at sea carried between twenty and 200 pounds of illegal drugs at any given moment. Even senior citizens were not above making a few thousand dollars by shepherding caches of drugs—usually not more than a pound or two—from one port to another. The smugglers were often women in their sixties who had been on cruises at least once before. They were rarely caught.

The Captain sighed again and rubbed his forehead. "Have Professor Miller's cabin searched. If you find anything, have one of the men bring him to me."

Chapter Twenty

The grocery cart had a gimpy wheel and pulled to the left. Every few steps, Colin picked up its back end and straightened it out. They were in the houseware aisle, and Catherine was selecting cleaning products. She dropped a large orange box of Tide in the basket and said, "Well, I did it."

"The separation?"

"Went to see a lawyer two days ago; he drafted the papers. Lars wasn't even surprised. Said he was expecting it. Got down to business right away—what did I want, how much for how long, that sort of thing."

"That was quick."

"I've been thinking about it for a long time. The thing with Josie, well, that was the deciding factor. The fact that Lars *really* didn't care. I used to think maybe it was because he didn't like to show emotions, kept things in, but the truth of the matter is, he didn't—doesn't—give a damn."

Colin lifted the cart's back end, set it straight. "So what now?"

"He keeps the house, which is just as well. It's a mausoleum. He said he wants to entertain more anyway," she raised her eyebrows, "which struck me as kind of strange for Lars, who's not a big people person, but that's not my problem. I'm sure he won't have any difficulties finding hostesses." There was only a trace of bitterness in her voice.

She selected Windex, Comet, and Dove soap, flirted with a box of Brillo, and returned it to the shelf. "We haven't worked out the financial details, but I'm sure it'll be satisfactory. I gave him a ballpark figure and he didn't blink. I should've said more, and maybe I will when the lawyers get together. He didn't mention Josie until I did, and his concern was future college tuition, so that'll be taken care of too."

She scooped up a carton of Light Days and said, "You know what else I did? Went to Books-a-Million in McLean. They had a help wanted sign in the window. I talked to the manager, and I got an application form."

"I didn't know you liked books."

She gave him a sidelong glance. "Lots of stuff you don't know."

They went to the fish section and Catherine picked up a salmon steak. "Here. Buy this. They're easy to cook—I'll show you how—and good for you."

He accepted the fish. "Have you told her yet?"

"No. I'm not sure whether I want to wait or not. Maybe I should find a place for us first. There are a couple of buildings I like—I want to rent an apartment, a house would be too much—and I have to price them. It's kind of exciting, actually. Two women on our own. What do you think, about telling her?"

"I don't think it'll surprise her much either."

As they filled the cart, the wheel began to squeal. Catherine said, "This is silly." She went to the checkout, selected another cart, and transferred the groceries. "Yeah, that's true. We didn't hide much from her, me and Lars. Never tried to. She's a smart kid in spite of everything. She's known things haven't been going right for years." She stopped and moved in front of the cart, blocking its way. "Here's a question, Colin, an important one. Your answer won't make much of a difference, I'm going to get the divorce regardless, but I'm curious. I'm going to have a lot of free time. Am I going to see you more?"

It took him by surprise, the shift. He paused before answering and saw in her eyes that it *would* make a difference. He said, "Yes, yeah. You will."

She smiled and took his arm. "I wasn't sure. We're still going to have to work a bunch of things out. But I'm glad. It's a good thing."

༄

Comfort spent two days in the efficiency apartment taking stock of his situation. The Zulu was dead, as were the two hired thugs. Obviously, the girl had not perished in the blaze. Comfort had watched the early and late news each on his small TV set; he had purchased the *Washington Post* and *Washington Times* every day. Nowhere was there a report of a female body found in the burnt out house. He wondered if that had been the intent of the raid: to rescue the girl. He wondered to whom the blonde addict could have been so important; addicts so seldom were.

Obviously the man he had fought with in the yard had been a policeman. And the policeman had died. Comfort felt no responsibility for this particular death; the man had a gun, they'd struggled, shots had been fired. Had he pulled the trigger? His recollection of the fight was hazy. It had been over so quickly, not even a blink-of-the-eye moment. Death, he knew, came to many just that way.

It worried him that it had been a policeman because he knew the man's demise would lead to a much greater investigation than would the death of almost anyone else. Policemen were the same all over the world—the murder of one brought out the fury of their brotherhood. But it had been dark, and there'd been no witnesses—none, at least, who would cooperate with the authorities. And if one did, what of it? What had made Comfort the excellent acolyte was his total anonymity. He was a faceless black man in a city of faceless black men.

Still, during the two days, he'd come to one basic conclusion. It was time to leave, to go home to Nigeria and live the life he'd been preparing for.

There was nothing in the apartment worth keeping save the gray pinstripe suit the Zulu had bought him in a rare fit of generosity. He'd never worn it; it hung in his closet in the original Macy's garment bag. There was also a pair of soft black leather shoes Comfort had purchased for himself for no other reason than he'd never had such shoes. A few shirts, socks, some underwear—that was it.

He made a small pile of the clothes he would wear during the trip and packed the rest in a Wal-Mart suitcase. Traveling overseas without luggage might arouse suspicions.

He spent the next day going to the twelve separate banks where he had accounts and withdrew one-quarter of what he had in each. He asked that one-third of what remained be wired to an account with the Banque Nationale de Lausanne in Switzerland. Another third went to Afribank Nigeria Plc. in Lagos.

Not a single teller seemed interested in the transactions except for a Nigerian woman at First National in Tyson's Corner. She'd smiled at him and asked, "Going home?"

It pained him to leave the rest of the money behind, but that had always been his intention. Closing out all the accounts might arouse suspicions.

Thirst

When he added up all the money, he found he'd underestimated the sum by $182. He'd forgotten to tabulate the interest earned in a month on five of his accounts. That was a good omen.

※

In a bright blue turban that matched the bedspread, her hands folded above the covers and a half glass of dark red wine on the night table next to her, Aunt Mim looked a like a dark primitive painting, an African queen by Goya.

She said, "A lot of people in the neighborhood are calling me that *dwa-yen* word. I just don't know how that got around." She shot the elderly George a suspicious look, which George ignored. Mamadou noticed that today Aunt Mim's paramour was reading a hardback version of *Grey's Anatomy*, poring over the words with an old-fashioned magnifying glass.

"Man refuses to wear glasses," Aunt Mim chided. "How silly is that, but whatcha gonna do? I tell him, 'Pride goeth before the fall,' but he don't listen to me. Never did."

George looked up briefly, said, "Glasses, huh?" and returned to his reading.

Aunt Mim reached over, found her wine, and took a dainty sip. "So you got that white child out? "

Mamadou poured himself a little of the burgundy and drank two swallows. "Yes. She'll be all right—as all right as any addict can be, in any case."

"Lotsa death, though." Aunt Mim sipped again.

"The Zulu. Two of his men."

"And the white policeman."

Mamadou nodded. "And the white policeman." There was a note of resignation in his voice.

"Bad business," Aunt Mim intoned.

"Very."

"Lucky for you, nobody saw anything."

Mamadou looked up. Aunt Mim met his eyes. "Don't worry yourself. That nice neighbor lady, she's a friend of mine, her name's Mrs. Thornton. Bethany Thornton. Got seventeen real nice grandchildren. Imagine that, seventeen." She paused, sipped, and continued. "She told me, soon as things started happening, she went down to her kitchen—it's in the back of the house, on the other side—and started making pancakes and bacon and eggs. All that frying sound, pans clanging, and the teevee on too, she didn't hear a thing. Fire worried her, though. She was afraid her own house might burn down."

George looked up. "She didn't have a thing to worry about. Her house is on the east. The wind was from the northwest. She wasn't in any danger at all."

Aunt Mim shook her head, annoyed. "Hush up, George. Wasn't talking to you. Why you always gotta know everything, anyway?"

"That's what the weather channels said. Both of them," George persisted.

Aunt Mim ignored him.

"One man got away," Mamadou said. "The man who shot the white policeman."

"That so? Does it matter?"

Mamadou took a second to think. "No. I guess it doesn't. The Zulu's gone. He was the one. The last one. Amelie—"

"Your sister, she can rest in peace now."

George looked up, nodded, and resumed his reading. Aunt Mim lit a Vantage cigarette. The smoke hung in the room like hazy curtains. "These things got no taste at all. None."

George shook his head. "Doctor said for you to stop altogether. Said your lungs probably look like smoked hams."

Thirst

Aunt Mim snorted. "Doctor? I put that boy through school; look what he does to me now? I don't have that many pleasures left in life." She stubbed the cigarette out in a crowded ashtray. "Anyhow. That's it. It's over, ain't it?"

Mamadou drank the rest of his glass in one swallow. "Just about, Aunt Mim. Just about."

☙

The ship was in Freeport and would sail the following afternoon on its last leg, a straight shot to New York. The travel agent Colin knew from AA said the trip would take about forty-eight hours. "It can hug the coast this time of year, do maybe thirty-six knots an hour," the man said, pointing to a map on the wall of his office. "Now during winter, there's too much current off Hatteras, right here; a ship gets caught off Cape Fear, well, it wasn't named that without a good reason. Some 2,000 ships have foundered there at one time or another. So your boat would have to make a large loop," he traced it with a finger, "go out to sea, and come back in. That's in winter. It takes longer. But right now? No storms, current's nice and friendly. Two days at the outside."

☙

Mamadou would take one of the limos. He glanced once again at the scrap of paper found in the Zulu's home. Clare Drake and Jennifer Jamieson, aboard the *Isadora*. The ship's arrival date in New York, complete with pier number, were underlined. The Zulu had been thorough.

Thierry Sagnier

With the limo, he'd be able to get close to the ship. No one would question his presence there, just another chauffeur holding up a sign bearing the names of his clients.

ஐ

Perched on a stool at the bar in Dulles Airport, nursing a Coke and nibbling on pretzels, Mollie Catfish once again chided herself for getting there way too early. It had set her back almost fifty bucks to take a limo from downtown, and she still had two hours to wait before boarding. It galled her that the limo hadn't even been a real limousine, which was what she'd been expecting. Instead, she rode in a cheesy gray van with tinted windows, sharing the middle seat with a thickly accented businessman from God-knew-where. He'd tried to make conversation in a thick guttural voice but she'd ignored him, and after a while he'd fallen silent, watching the traffic flow along the Dulles access road.

She looked at the digital clock over the bar. Time to go. She gathered her carry-on bag and purse and double checked to make sure the ticket was in the back pocket of her jeans. At the security check-in she took her shoes off and placed the bag and purse on the conveyor belt. She'd made sure to empty both the bag and purse of anything metallic, had no liquids in plastic bottles. She stepped up to the metal detector. A bored security agent waved her through.

In the plane she placed the carry-on beneath her seat as the card instructed, fastened her seat belt, and closed her eyes. She hated flying. When the plane took off she held on to the armrests, promised God that if she got through this, she'd never do anything bad again.

The flight went quickly. She ordered coffee twice, ate the pretzels—they didn't even serve peanuts these days—and read the

Thirst

airline magazine. She wanted to check the carry-on, make sure all the money was still there, but resisted the illogical impulse. Of course it was still there. And what if someone saw her? All those bills, fifties, twenties, and tens. $3,482. Less the money for the limo.

When the plane began its descent into Freeport, she forced herself to look outside. From that high up, there wasn't much to see. The water was a shade bluer than she'd seen elsewhere, though not as blue as on the TV ads. There were palm trees, just like in the south. As the plane made its final approach, she saw the harbor and the five cruise ships anchored there. She squinted, tried to make out names, but couldn't.

She walked through the airport to the taxi stand, a nondescript young woman in blue jeans and a University of Maryland Terrapins sweatshirt that was far too hot for the Bahamian weather that day.

Chapter Twenty-one

They were taking a nap when the commotion broke out. It was a somewhat cloudy day and the winds were gusting. Though the ship was berthed, its roll had become more pronounced and the sea was frothed with white. Outside their cabin a man's outraged voice said, "This is intolerable! I'll not permit it! This is a gross infringement of my rights!"

A calmer voice answered, "Captain's orders, sir. If you'll stand aside, this will only take minutes. We'd appreciate your cooperation."

Jennifer rose, opened the door, peeked outside, and turned to whisper to Clare. "It's whatshisname, our neighbor, the professor. And there's a bunch of the crew there too."

More voices, this time more restrained. "But I don't understand this. Perhaps if I could speak with the captain, I'm sure we could straighten this out. There's no reason for this intrusion. I'm a passenger—"

The calm voice said, "You're an employee of the line. Consider this a direct order issued by Captain Stuart. Stand aside."

Clare rolled off her bed. "Let's see what's going on."

Thirst

In the corridor, the man who'd introduced himself on the first day of the cruise as Earl Thorogood Miller, formerly Professor of Renaissance Literature at Georgia Southwestern College, was standing in the doorway of his cabin, arms outstretched, looking slightly ridiculous is a pair of jockey shorts and a Rock Til You Puke tee-shirt. Four crewmembers in dress whites faced him. A shapely woman in her fifties was being escorted from the cabin by a fifth crewmember. Her hair was disheveled, and the back of her unbuttoned sun dress revealed a tanned spine and two inches of white skin below the waist. She tried unsuccessfully to keep the dress in place as she was hurried away.

"This is intolerable!" said the professor.

The crewman in charge of the detail shrugged. "Captain's orders, Mr. Miller."

"Professor Miller!"

"Fine. *Professor* Miller. Now stand aside, *Professor*, so we can do our jobs and then we'll be on our way, *Professor*."

The professor stood aside, turned to the two women. "*Outrageous* behavior! Why, in all my years spent traveling, I've never—" Something happening in the cabin caught his eye. "You sonofabitch! Get your hands out of that!" The crew had turned over the mattress and were rummaging through a worn plaid suitcase. "I said leave that alone!" The professor rushed the crewmen. There was a brief flurry of arms and legs, a chorus of yells. One of the crew kicked the cabin door shut. Down the corridor, more heads appeared. A short, heavy woman shot a furious glance at the retreating female passenger, whose sundress was unbuttoned. "What in the world? Ethel? Ethel Schwartz, is that you? You said you didn't like him, that he wasn't good enough for me! Ethel, you bitch!" And the heavy woman burst into tears.

The professor's door opened. He stood framed in it, face as pale as the corridor walls, his hands held behind him by two crewmen.

He was led out without a word. The last man out carefully closed the cabin door and made a show of locking it. Then he turned, winked at Jennifer and Clare, held a finger against one nostril, and snorted loudly.

The heavy woman gasped. "Drugs! I saw them do that in *Pulp Fiction*. It means he was doing drugs." Then, at the top of her voice, "God damn you, Ethel Schwartz! I hope you get what you deserve! I hope you get the clap!"

☙

"How are you, sweetie?"

They hugged, and Catherine could feel her daughter shaking and beginning to sob. She stroked Josie's hair, touched her forehead, and leaned back to look into her eyes.

"It's nothing, Mom, just a slight fever. The doctor said it's normal, part of the detoxing." She laughed, a dry sound. "My body's telling me it's unhappy, as if I didn't know."

"It'll get better, darling. I promise."

Josie nodded and pulled back. "I know. Everybody tells me that. I'll get through it. It's not like it's the first time. And I'm pretty tough, you know?"

Catherine smiled. "Oh yes. Yes, I expect you are."

They were in the hospital cafeteria where the ARC patients took their meals. Josie's plate, pushed to the side, held the tattered remnants of salad and chopped meat. She toyed with a melting scoop of ice cream, her spoon turning small circles in the bowl.

"He's nice, your friend Colin. We had a talk. Did he tell you?"

Catherine shook her head, no. "Whatever the two of you had to say to each other is private. I promised him I wouldn't ask."

Thirst

Josie shrugged. "Nothing very special; he asked me what I remembered, and I told him. He wanted to know about Comfort, the thin one who brought me food. What he said to me. At first I couldn't remember, and then it started coming back…" She let the sentence trail.

"That's all?"

"It's not like we had a long relationship, Mom. I don't remember Colin getting me out. What else were we supposed to talk about?"

Catherine didn't answer for a moment, then said, "I thought maybe you knew him, maybe you'd seen him at a meeting or something."

Josie nibbled at the ice cream, pushed it away, changed her mind, and took another bite. "He's your lover, isn't he?"

Catherine stared at her daughter, closed her eyes, and opened them again. Josie put the spoon down. "Don't look like that. I've known about it for a long time."

"About what?"

Josie gave Catherine a sly look. "C'mon, Mom."

"Ah. About Colin."

Josie picked up the bowl, depositing it carefully in the center of her dinner plate. "No, I mean, not specifically. I've just known there had to be somebody, and that it wasn't Dad."

Catherine looked down at the table, gathered her thoughts, and blurted, "We're getting divorced."

Josie smiled. "Yeah? That's so cool!" And hugged her mother.

≪≫

He wrote the options down on paper, feeling foolish, finding no other way to focus his thoughts.

He could just let everything go; Orin would suggest that. Whatever drugs were involved were an infinitesimal amount compared to the tons smuggled in daily, broken into kilos, ounces, grams, stepped on, stepped on again. Another two, three, ten pounds…meaningless.

He could call the police and tell them everything. And be held responsible for Joe the Cop's death.

He could go to New York and find the two women.

And then what? And then somehow destroy the drugs. That would end it, would make Josie's ordeal at least serve a purpose. It might even make Joe's ghost fade.

ॐ

There was a subtle satisfaction to knowing that the late Herbie had somehow managed to swindle the Zulu. Mamadou, who did not particularly believe in an afterlife, nevertheless hoped that somewhere the Zulu's soul was raging at the theft. Not that it really mattered. They were all dead now, Amelie's assassins. The Zulu had been the last of them. There only remained one final act to put the universe back into a semblance of order, and that was to wrest the drugs back. By doing that, the shame and horror surrounding Amelie's last days might at last be put to rest.

ॐ

Comfort was ready. He took a last, brief look around the efficiency apartment, went into the kitchenette, and removed the ice trays from the refrigerator. He dumped the ice into the sink, then unplugged the appliances. He had cleaned the place meticulously and doubted anyone could find a trace of his tenancy. He was going home after a long time away and did not want to leave behind so much as a speck of himself. He wasn't quite sure why this was important to him, but it was.

He sucked his stomach in and patted his shirtfront. He wore a money belt with $5,000, and this was allowed. He removed his watch, satisfied that this was the last item he wore that might set off a metal detector. The zipper of his pants was plastic—he'd bought the slacks with that specifically in mind—and even the eyelets of his shoes were non-metallic. Change still jingled in his pocket, but he'd get rid of that in the Friends of The National Zoo box at the airport.

He drove to Dulles airport in a 1991 Dodge Colt bought for the occasion from a Nigerian acquaintance who never signed the title over and would declare the car stolen in a week.

Everything was wonderfully, magnificently in place, and he could forgive himself a small smile that grew and turned into a grin, and then a quiet, delighted laugh.

∞

The one thing Mollie Catfish had gotten from trying to work the steps of AA was an unshakable belief that if one tried to make luck happen, it would.

She never gave a second thought on how she'd contact the two women whose names were written on the piece of paper she was now cupping in one sweaty palm. During the cab ride to the dock, she'd gazed at the passing scenery with feigned interest but was actually concentrating hard on making her luck work, and it did. When she got to the pier, the covered passageway from ship to shore was guarded by a Royal Scottish Line sailor who told her that, no, she could under no circumstance go aboard. She looked at the man, he looked at her, and he grinned, holding his right hand out. He rubbed his thumb against his index and forefinger in the age-old sign. She dug in her bag and brought out five twenty dollar bills.

She found a pen in her purse, asked him for a piece of paper, and wrote, "For Passengers Clare Drake and Jennifer Jamieson. I'm a friend of Herbie's. I'll wait for you tomorrow morning at ten in the lobby of the Sunspree Resort Holiday Inn. It's very important." She'd seen the hotel on her way from the airport to the ship.

The sailor nodded and put the piece of paper in his pocket. She shook her head and found another twenty. "Now."

Chapter Twenty-two

That same day at the evening meal the ship buzzed with rumors and allegations concerning the professor who had been forcibly removed from his cabin for allegedly dealing drugs.

Some claimed he wasn't really a passenger. A gigolo, said a few who'd been on cruises before, actually hired by the line to keep older female clients happy. Some of the ladies resented this, particularly those who had spent a few entertaining hours with the fascinating man. The man's female companion at the time of the arrest was not to be seen.

He had been dealing cocaine; no, heroin; no, surely it was marijuana and crystal meth. At the captain's table, one guest broached the subject, but Captain Roderick Stuart politely shunted it aside, commenting instead that the salad that evening was quite tasty, which it was. The *saucier*'s kitchen staff had obviously outdone themselves.

People spoke of the professor at the bar, on deck, during the floorshow, between number calls at bingo, after the feature film. Clare Drake did not mention that she had seen the entire incident, and that it had frightened her. As the man had been led away, she had seen the defeated look, the vanquished eyes, and mostly the handcuffs. The passenger seated next to her at the dinner table spoke of an earlier cruise where a similar incident had occurred and the entire ship had been searched while at sea. "They combed through each and every cabin. I remember it well—I was terrified. It was my first cruise and naturally I'd bought more than my allotted share of liquor aboard after a stop in the Caymans. Cigarettes and Cuban cigars as well. I was certain, absolutely positive, that I would be arrested and whipped or keelhauled or some such." He laughed and forked a morsel of veal into his mouth. "I wasn't, of course. They were hardly interested in my bit of amateurish smuggling. But they did find some drugs in the cabin of twin sisters, seventy years if they were a day, can you imagine? And both acting as innocent as newborn babes! Well, it goes to show, doesn't it? Appearances are deceiving!"

Clare Drake returned to her cabin knowing there would be hell to pay for what she was about to do, but determined to do it anyway. Two days earlier, she'd seen a man lose a thousand dollars on one roll of the roulette wheel and it had struck her at the time that $15,000 wasn't really going to change her life. But getting arrested for possession would.

She found the parcel Herbie had given them and cut a corner open with a pair of cuticle scissors, then squeezed a small stream of the white powder into her palm. She scooped a small amount with a fingernail and rubbed it on her gums. Then she took a pinch and snorted it, sneezed, and snorted again. She made a face and shook her head. She sneezed and tears pooled in her eyes. It took her a moment for the full impact to hit.

She threw back her head and laughed hard, suddenly feeling good, no, great. Then she took the parcel, placed it in a beach bag, covered it with a towel and, still laughing, put it back in the closet.

Thirst

She found the unsigned message taped to her door as she left the cabin.

❦

The next morning Clare Drake and Jennifer Jamieson arrived at the Holiday Inn a few minutes after ten. They were mildly worried. The message hadn't said who they were supposed to meet. "What if it's a bust?" Jennifer said. "What if it's a setup and not from Herbie? What if Herbie gave us away? You know, sold us out, made a deal or something?"

That was always a possibility. It had worried Clare from the second the deal with Herbie had been struck. She thought for a moment.

"Just in case. You never know, it could be a set up. If things are okay, I'll come out and get you. If I don't come back in ten minutes, you go to the ship and get rid of the stuff. Throw it overboard or something."

So Jennifer waited outside while Clare went in. A few seconds later, Clare returned wearing a curious expression.

"It's not Herbie. It's a woman."

Jennifer made a "so?" gesture and asked, "Who is she?"

"Mollie something. She says she's a friend of Herbie's. She says Herbie sent her, that plans have changed. She wants the package."

Jennifer shrugged. "She's got the money?"

"Some. She's got $3,000 and says Herbie will pay us the difference when we get to New York."

That didn't make sense. Jennifer said so. "No deal. We're supposed to get $15,000. We can call Herbie, set him straight. We—"

"I told her we'd do it. Go get the stuff."

"But why? Herbie'll never show up! He'll—"

Clare took Jennifer by the shoulders. "Trust me on this, okay? I know what I'm doing and I'll explain later. The ship's leaving in a couple of hours and I want us free and clear of all this bullshit. It's the best thing we can do. Just take my word for it. It'll all work out."

Jennifer wanted to argue but was deterred by the look in her friend's face. "I don't like this," she said. "We're getting ripped off and I don't like this at all." But Clare was already going back into the hotel, so she returned to the ship anyway.

※

Twelve hours later, the first passenger to report to the infirmary complained of acute stomach cramps and, while she was being given a tiny cup of Pepto Bismol, got sick on the attending nurse. Two more passengers, a first-class couple, came in shortly thereafter. They were pale, their hands clammy, and they also suffered from cramps. The nurse logged these complaints, and when twelve more passengers appeared in a twenty-minute span, she called the ship's physician, Dr. Subramanian Purushotham.

Dr. Purushotham was a regular at the Captain's table. Tall, graying, a urologist by training who had studied in Delhi and the United States and come to despise his specialty, Dr. P., as he was known, inspired an effortless confidence. He had been serving on the *Isadora* seventeen months and, prior to that, had attended to passengers' needs on two other Royal Scottish Line ships.

He had seen every conceivable manifestation of sea-sickness, agoraphobia, and motion disorders. He had set broken bones, treated fibrillating hearts, purged gastrointestinal parasites, and closed the eyes of more than a dozen cardiac arrest victims. He could and often did prescribe antidepressants, beta-blockers, and occasionally opiates.

Thirst

He had never, in his long sea-borne career, witnessed anything like the tumult that soon took over his infirmary.

The first patient had come in shortly after one that morning. By five a.m., more than three hundred passengers were clamoring for Dr. P.'s attention. The corridors reeked of regurgitate and other effluvia he hardly dared name. Three of the ship's four nurses were as ill as the passengers they were trying to treat.

Dr. P. knew that, twenty-four hours earlier, the ship's *sous saucier*, Jean Marie Berger, had complained of agonizing pains in his bloated stomach. Dr. P. had diagnosed an inflamed appendicitis in need or urgent removal and remanded the man to Freeport's community hospital. Perhaps the diagnosis had been wrong.

Captain Roderick Stuart, made aware of the pandemonium, checked in by phone every thirty minutes. As the news grew worst, he consulted his charts. By seven that morning, 417 passengers at last count were seriously ill. One elderly woman had lapsed into a coma; three tourist-class fares were vomiting blood. Few crewmembers were affected, a blessing. All hands not crucial to the immediate running of the ship were on clean-up detail, swinging mops and buckets throughout the four decks.

Shortly before eight, Captain Stuart, having explored all available alternatives, changed the ship's course. They were too far out of Nassau; turning back was not an option. Even had it been possible, there were probably not enough hospital beds there to treat the epidemic.

Even at maximum steam, the *Isadora* would not reach New York for twenty-five hours. He consulted his charts again.

His mistress had joined him. "What does Dr. P. say?"

"Food poisoning, almost certainly. Perhaps botulism. Two more passengers are in a coma." He massaged his eyes. "Nothing like this has ever happened."

She stood behind him, rubbing his back. He was standing erect at the chart table and she thought she could feel a slight tremor beneath her fingers.

"A Coast Guard helicopter is on its way to ferry the coma cases out, and the cutter Seawitch will be here within three hours with half a dozen doctors. There aren't enough helicopters to transport everybody."

She kneaded his shoulders, the muscles unforgiving as stones.

Captain Stuart said, "Baltimore. It has to be Baltimore."

※

When Mollie got to the airport a stream of gaily painted cabs was disgorging passengers. She'd planned it that way, had made it a point to get there when traffic was at the highest. The ten-pound package weighed much more than she'd anticipated. It was in the carry-all and the strap pulled at her shoulder so that she felt lopsided.

She was bumped hard; she stumbled, almost fell, and felt herself being pulled around. Then the strap of her bag broke. She yelled but someone pushed her and this time she did fall, landing on her hands and knees. She heard the sound of feet running and looked up from the floor to see a pair of black legs and worn Reeboks weaving through the crowds. Then she heard a police whistle. Four men in uniforms dashed past her, a shiny military boot barely missed her head. She struggled to a sitting position on the floor, felt hands on her neck, on her shoulders.

"Miss? Miss, are you all right? Miss?"

Not much later, as she sat on a hard plastic chair in the congested office of the airports customs office, it struck her that her luck hadn't held out after all, AA notwithstanding, and that no matter how things worked out she was in a great deal of trouble.

Thirst

She stood, put her hand on the doorknob, and tried to turn it. The door was locked. She sat back down and looked at the tourist posters advertising a much more pleasant country than the one she was in. She lowered her head into her hands and started crying.

Two doors down from the office in which Mollie was sequestered, Major Charles Townsend opened the travel bag. He was a tall black man of military bearing, born and raised in Freeport and proud of the services he'd provided to his country. His men had cornered the thief—a mere boy—in a toilet, thoroughly pummeled him, and whisked him away to a small holding cell usually reserved for quarantined animals. They had deposited the travel bag on the Major's desk.

He unzipped it, reached in, and felt a heavy parcel wrapped in paper. He pulled the package out, slit the paper with his pen knife, found a layer of plastic, and slit that. The white powder gleamed at him. He moistened a finger, poked it into the powder and brought it gingerly to his lips. He frowned, did it again.

The Major was due to leave the Customs Services in a week. His good-bye party was already planned. He thought about the paperwork involved in this particular seizure. It might take weeks to interrogate the suspect. He had already purchased two airplane tickets to New York for the day after his retirement so he and his wife could visit their eldest son living there.

He found that morning's newspaper and spread it carefully on his desk. Then he slit the parcel completely open.

He tasted the powder again.

He flattened the mound of powder across the newspaper with a ruler, poked his finger here and there throughout. He smelled it and tasted it again a half-dozen times. He inspected the powder and used the eraser end of a pencil to push it around, looking for anything that might have been concealed there.

After a while he gathered the corners of the newspaper, folded them together, and used several feet of Scotch tape to wrap the bundle tightly.

In one of the bag's side pockets he found Mollie's wallet. There was $318 in cash, plus change. He took $250 out, folded it, and placed it in his shirt pocket. He dropped the parcel in his trashcan.

Mollie had stopped crying when he opened the door, but her face was red and splotchy, mirroring her thoughts. He handed her the travel bag and led her out of the room. "I'm afraid you've missed your plane, Miss. You'll have to make other arrangements."

She nodded, not really hearing him.

"I'm very sorry this happened," he said. "I hope it won't stop you from visiting Nassau again." He pointed toward one of the airline counters. "Delta has a plane leaving in two hours. If you hurry, you might be able to get a reservation."

He gave her a gentle push in the direction of the Delta counter. When she was a few feet away, he said, "Miss?"

Mollie turned to face him. He wore a stern look.

"I believe U.S. laws expressly forbid the importation of foodstuff from the Bahamas. That includes fruits, meats, lactose products, and flour."

Chapter Twenty-three

"I am not quite sure that I'm satisfied with your answers, Mr. Okwuike. May I call you Comfort? Of course I can. At this point, I can do virtually anything I want, can't I?" The man smiled as if he found the statement amusing.

Comfort breathed through his mouth. He thought his nose might be broken but wasn't certain.

"Good. Let's begin again."

The Nigerian State Police officer was a bulky man with café-au-lait skin. He had removed his Armani jacket, unbuttoned the top of his white Caleche shirt, and rolled up his sleeves. He had big hands and two pinkie rings, one set with a diamond, the other with a ruby, and a heavy silver and gold watch on his left wrist.

There was one chair, one table, one lightbulb, no windows, and a bucket of water on the floor. The NSP officer occupied the chair. His elbows rested on the table. Between his elbows was a child's ruled school notebook and a Lacrosse pen. The room was blindingly hot. Comfort was naked and tied by ankles and wrists to four iron rings set in the wall. Two wire leads ran from his limp penis and testicles to an old-fashioned crank generator the man held in his lap.

Both of Comfort's thumbs were broken and his hands had swollen so they looked like winter mittens. One of his eyes was closed, the lid bruised and bleeding.

"We shall begin again." The policeman pondered a moment, then gave the generator's crank a vicious turn. Comfort jumped and moaned.

"My God that looks painful," the officer said. "Personally, I'm sure *I* couldn't take it." He turned the crank two more times. The shocks made Comfort whimper.

"Now that I have your attention, let me say that you may be Comfort, but my middle name could be Patience. I have all day, Mr. Okwuike. As a matter of fact, I have all week. I'm on leave, you see. The government gives me twenty days a year. I have spent two of those days finding you, which was longer than I anticipated. I would prefer not to spend any additional vacation time in such a hostile environment, but if is to be, *Insh' Allah.*"

He sighed and turned the crank. "You know," he said, "your case is positively unusual. People pay me to help them *leave* Nigeria, and you come *into* the country after wiring an extraordinary sum of money—in American dollars, no less—to Afribank. And no one knows who you are! You're not a politician or a minister or even a businessman. My sources tell me you're not bribing anyone. I don't think I've ever heard of anything quite like it. *Nobody* retires in Nigeria if they can help it."

Comfort's speech was blurred by his thickened tongue. He said, "I've told you everything."

"And I do not believe you, which puts us in a quandary. So we begin again. Your name is?"

Comfort's breath rattled in his throat. "You know my name."

A turn of the crank made his back arch.

"Your name is…"

"Comfort Okwuike."

Thirst

"And you came from…"

"The United States. Washington."

"And you got this money by…"

Comfort hesitated. The man's hand pressed lightly on the crank.

"Drugs. I stole some drugs."

"Good," said the man. He stood, took a cupful of water from the bucket, and threw it in Comfort's face. Comfort tried to catch some with his tongue and got a few drops.

"You obtained $587,000 and some-odd dollars by stealing drugs. We are now getting somewhere. Here," he refilled the water cup, held it to Comfort's lips, and allowed him to drink.

"What sort of drugs?"

"Heroin," said Comfort. "Very good heroin."

"Which you stole from…"

"From my boss. From the Zulu."

"Earlier you said it came from a man named Herbie."

Comfort nodded. His legs had gone from unbearably painful to numb. "Herbie. Yes, I'm sorry. The drugs came from Herbie, but he got them from the Zulu."

"Your boss."

"Yes."

"So you took the drugs from Herbie?"

"No. Yes. No. Herbie stole them from the Zulu. But it was my idea."

"You're confusing me, Mr. Okwuike." The crank turned half a circle. Comfort's legs spasmed.

"Herbie stole them from the Zulu. I told him how to do it. But he didn't, not really. I had switched them. He stole a bag of flour. Flour and lactose."

"Baby formula?"

"Yes."

"What a resourceful fellow you are, Mr. Okwuike." The man's voice dripped sarcasm. "And what a stupid man this Herbie must have been…"

"Not stupid. I tricked him." Comfort tried to swallow but couldn't. He asked, "May I have some more water? Please?" He was burning up. The lamp above his head was drilling a hole in his skull.

"In a moment. How did you trick him?"

"I gave him some heroin. From an earlier shipment. It made him very sick."

"And why was that?"

"Rat poison. A tiny amount mixed in. Very tiny. It was his first time with heroin. And he thought…"

The man nodded. "He thought all heroin might have the same effect."

Comfort nodded.

The man dipped another cupful of water. Comfort drank too greedily, choked, and coughed. The man jumped back, wiping at his shirt angrily. Comfort closed his eyes and steeled himself for another turn of the crank. It didn't come.

"So you sold the heroin, the real heroin."

"Two dealers I knew. They bought it. A good bargain for them."

"And Herbie?"

"Lactose. Flour. He died."

"From the fake drugs?"

"No." Comfort shook his head. "No. Zulu. Zulu had him killed. After he found out." Even in the midst of his pain, Comfort knew better than to admit his participation in a murder, or his role in engineering it.

"This is getting to be a fascinating tale, Mr. Okwuike. I'm enthralled." He placed his hand back on the crank. Comfort stiffened. "I'll put this away now." He unclipped the leads from the generator and let them fall to the ground. Comfort's entire body went soft.

THIRST

"Thank you."

"You're quite welcome. Please do go on. So the Zulu killed your poor friend Herbie for a bag of flour. There's something almost Biblical about that, isn't there? And how did he react when he discovered the subterfuge?"

Comfort tried to stand up, but his legs were without feeling or strength. "Will you untie me, please? I couldn't escape, even if I wanted to."

The officer smiled but shook his head. "Perhaps in a moment, when you've finished your tale."

Comfort took a deep breath. "Herbie gave the fake drugs for safekeeping to some other people. The Zulu never learned of the switch. Until it was too late."

"Your idea, of course."

Comfort nodded.

"Brilliant." The officer shook his head in admiration. "Simply brilliant. Now. Let us talk about your assets and how we may share them."

༄

The *Isadora*'s plight made the seven o'clock news. The ship had sped to Baltimore where medical teams had ambulanced afflicted passengers to city and suburban hospitals.

The Center for Disease Control in Atlanta, Georgia, had come up with a preliminary finding it felt confident in announcing to the media. Passengers had ingested minute quantities of mangrove root which, for reasons unknown, had been added to a *sauce marinière à l'ail des îles*. The dish upon which the sauce was served had proved quite popular among the guests.

There were no fatalities, though one man remained in critical care following cardiac arrest that may or may not have been caused by the poison. The comatose patients all survived.

The ship's physician, Dr. Subramanian Purushotham, was interviewed by the local news channel and quite enjoyed the experience. Passengers who were not ill were put up in various hotels throughout the town, their bills for the day in port graciously covered by the vastly embarrassed company.

Colin spotted Mamadou's limo and muttered, "Shit." Encountering the Senegalese was not in his hastily formed plans. Keeping out of sight behind a parked truck, he watched as the African held up a cardboard sign. Passengers from the ship eddied around the man, and Mamadou raised the sign higher.

Soon, two women approached. Colin saw they were young, dressed demurely. They were pleased at first to see the limo, then grew agitated as Mamadou spoke with them. One, a tall blonde, kept shaking her head. The other, a shorter brunette, stood slightly back and fidgeted with her purse. Mamadou opened the limo's door for them but they refused to get in the car.

Curiosity won out. Colin came closer, heard, "…know what you're talking about. We thought the school had sent the limo. If it hasn't, then there's been some mistake."

Colin edged behind Mamadou, withdrew Joe the Cop's police badge, and held it up in the air. The blonde woman saw him first. She said, "Officer, this man is bothering us. He wants to…"

Mamadou turned and Colin stepped back, badge still held high.

If the African was surprised, he hid it well. "Mr. Marsh! Or is it 'Officer Marsh'? Perhaps you can be of assistance. I believe these young women are perpetrating a felony, importing a great deal of illicit drugs—"

Clare Drake cut him off. "That's bull—*nonsense*. My friend and I are passengers on the ship and…"

THIRST

Colin shook his head and stepped past Mamadou. "Your friend Herbie is dead. There's no one to protect you. Nothing will happen, no police, no authorities, if you just hand over the package. That's all we want and we're out of your life."

Jennifer Jamieson gave Colin an odd look, turned to her friend, but said nothing. Colin added, "A lot of people have already died because of this. Five so far."

"Six," Mamadou said. "You're forgetting Amelie."

Still they didn't respond, though Colin thought he saw Clare Drake stiffen.

Passengers were still flowing around them. An elderly couple asked Mamadou if his limo was available. He shook his head without taking his eyes from the two women.

Finally, Jennifer Jamieson said, "Ah hell. What you're looking for, it's gone. We gave it to a woman in Freeport. She said she was a friend of Herbie's and that he'd told her to pick it up. But we don't know what it was. We weren't involved in any of this."

Clare Drake let out an exasperated sigh. "Oh, fuck it! This is ridiculous! Let's end it, okay?" She looked at her friend. "Herbie's dead, and even if he isn't what the hell does it matter anyway?" She turned back to the two men. "You know what it was that we gave that woman? It was lactose and flour. Like maybe ten pounds of it. And I know because I thought it was coke, and I thought I'd try some, except that it wasn't. So Herbie, alive or dead, well, he got taken, is what I think. There never was any dope, not now, not ever."

She paused, sighed, and shrugged. "So, what do you want to arrest us for, smuggling? Smuggling what? There was never anything to smuggle!"

Mamadou rubbed a hand across his chin and scratched his cheek. "I don't believe you. Colin, these women are lying, they're trying to—"

"Who did you give it to? The woman, what was her name?"

In unison, the women said, "Mollie. She said her name was Mollie."

And to Colin, it made all the sense in the world. He started walking away when Mamadou caught his arm. "Talk to me! What is going on here? Who is Mollie? Where are the drugs?"

Colin shook his arm free. "Maybe another day, Mamadou. Not now. But I think you can believe them. There's no drugs."

"Are we all straight now?" Clare asked. "Can we all go on with the rest of our lives?"

Colin nodded and started walking away. Clare looked at Mamadou, "Since you're here, can you take us to D.C?"

The forklift came toward them at an idle, its driver perched high in the cage. He wore a hardhat, sun glasses, orange overalls, and work gloves. One arm was in a sling, but he nevertheless managed to work the controls of the vehicle. As he passed the limo, he swung the forklift sharply to the right and accelerated. Mamadou heard the roar of the engine and caught the movement out of the corner of his eyes. The two women stood staring with their mouths in big oval "ohs." Then Clare Drake screamed, grabbed Jennifer's arm, and yanked it so hard the woman was pulled out of her shoes. Mamadou dove, his shoulder catching Colin in the chest. The forklift hit the limo broadside and the windshield and passenger windows exploded, showering them both with glass.

The forklift backed up, the driver slamming it into reverse. Mamadou rolled and rose to a crouch, a gun in his hand. He fired once, twice, three times. The forklift driver's sunglasses shattered. He jerked and threw his arms into the air. His movement flung the cage door open and he collapsed to the side, then slowly began sliding headfirst out of the cage. His shoes—they weren't work boots—somehow got wedged in the forklift pedals and he hung upside down, his head bobbing just above a giant tire. There was the sound of tearing metal as the forklift hit the limo again and lurched, its huge wheels spinning, then stalled.

Colin got to his feet, picking shards of glass from his hair. "Jesus!"

Mamadou shook his head, brushed himself off, and smiled a grimace. "No. Not Jesus. The Zulu."

※

After the crowds drifted away and both Mamadou and Colin had answered questions from the police, the port authority, the company representative of the firm that owned the forklift, the customs people, and the Coast Guard, Colin said, "I thought he was gone."

Mamadou shrugged. "I guess he wasn't. It was dark in the house…"

There wasn't much to say.

The two women had been questioned as well, then released, and opted to take the first available flight out of Baltimore-Washington International directly to Florida. Colin drove Mamadou back to his garage in D.C. There wasn't much to say during the ride either.

※

The extremely fat tourist waved a fistful of dollar bills in the air and hooted, "Over here, honey! Over here!" His voice carried easily over the gut-deep thumping of the music, but no one paid attention. Mollie felt the sweat trickle between her breasts, closed her eyes, and thrust her hips in his direction. The man yelled, "My heart! I'm dyin', honey! Come and make me alive again!" Molly glanced at the boss, who was tending bar, and saw him nod. She finished her dance and found her camisole. The man stood as she approached.

"That was just beautiful! Beautiful! Wanna drink? Two? Three?"

He still held the bills clenched in one hand, the wad folded over to look larger. "Wanna share some of this later?" He pulled a small clear plastic bag from his shirt pocket and waved it in front of her nose.

She shook her head. "No. I don't do that stuff anymore."

She wondered how much money he had. Every time there was a paying customer, every time she saw a handful of cash, she wondered. She had paid $3,000 for a ten pound bag of flour, and now every bill took on a different significance. It could have been, should have been, hers.

The fat man said, "So, how much?"

She looked at him. His face shone in the heat and his eyes bulged. "For what?"

"Everything, honey. The whole shebang. Up, down, and sideways…how much?"

She looked at the money in his fist, looked up. A bubble of saliva was forming in one corner of his mouth.

"Three thousand dollars," she said.

The man looked at her and grinned as if he'd just heard a bad joke.

She gave him her most fetching smile and ran a hand around the neck of his shirt. "Or five hundred bucks and a ticket out of here."

The End

About the Author

I was conceived in an army truck and born on the radio.
Well, almost.

I was actually born in the freight elevator of the American hospital just outside of Paris, France. A rookie policeman delivered me between the third and fourth floor during a rare snowstorm in the City of Lights.

My parents met at the end of World War II. Both were soldiers with the Free French, the breakaway remnant of the French military that refused to surrender to the Germans after the capitulation of France. Their eyes met and that same evening—or so I was told—they consummated their union in a US Army truck. The one-night stand would last a lifetime.

After the war, both found jobs as actors in a soap opera aired on Radio France. My father, who spoke English, portrayed a not-too-bright American GI married to my mother, a wily French maiden. The show was live, wildly popular, and broadcast daily. One evening as they were reciting their lines to the microphones, my mother went into labor. She never quite made it to the delivery room.

THIRST

My mother was an artist, a musician and an author. My father was a journalist who had studied violin at the Versailles conservatory. I was destined to write or play music. I do both.

My first literary work was an out-and-out theft. I was six years old and envious of a child celebrity, Minou Drouet, a little girl whose poems had been published in French magazines. Her name was on everyone's lips. She was a genius, an *enfant prodige*, and the decorated pride of the nation.

I decided to be the same. I copied some poems from a book in my parents' library, appropriated authorship, and proudly showed the works to my mother. She was thrilled and immediately summoned the media. My subterfuge failed and a fiasco ensued. I was seriously chastised and I'm not sure my mother ever really forgave me for not being the wunderkind she thought she deserved.

My family moved to the United States when I was ten. By age sixteen I had written a series of short stories in English—my chosen writing language—on the unfairness of society and the tribulations of being an immigrant. I wrote songs, poetry, essays, fiction, a play, and complicated letters to an imaginary friend who, I think, got bored. One day he left.

I struggled through both American high school and the curriculum of a French *lycée*. I went on to attend Georgetown University's Foreign Service School but dropped out when offered a copyboy position with the *Washington Post*.

In time I became an in-house free-lancer specializing in the nascent hippy movement. I wrote about radicals, Yippies, Black Panthers, drug dealers, thieves and scammers, bikers and rock stars. I was in the newsroom during Watergate. I participated ever-so-slightly in the scandal's coverage by fielding telephone calls from Martha Mitchell, the demented wife of Richard Nixon's duplicitous Attorney General, John Mitchell. I left the paper after a noisy disagreement with the then-editor, Ben Bradlee, who did not approve of a story I

Thierry Sagnier

had written for the Sunday *Post* about being a conscientious objector to the Vietnam War.

By then, I had written *Bike! Motorcycles and the People Who Ride Them*. Harper & Row published it, but unfortunately, the book hit the shelves the same week as another bike book that became an overnight classic—Robert Pirsig's *Zen and the Art of Motorcycle Maintenance*. I got a shining review from *Rolling Stone*, did a quick book tour, and some radio and television talk shows. My future as a writer was assured.

I free-lanced compulsively. I wrote for newspaper and magazines both here and in Europe. I produced short television documentaries for the Canadian Broadcasting Corporation, and authored weekly columns for *Le Devoir*, Montreal's leading newspaper, and other publications. I had regular shows on Radio Canada and Radio Romane. I got married and divorced. I learned how to play the guitar and the Dobro and played in blue grass and rock 'n' roll bands. I was commissioned to do a tourist book for *Washingtonian* magazine. I traveled cross-country to help a French reporter for the *Le Figaro* newspaper write a series of articles on American youth. In short, I had a blast.

I wrote and sold *The IFO Report*; the novel was optioned for a movie that was never produced. I was hired by a UN organization to help start up a magazine and given the opportunity to travel all over the world writing about the organization's projects. I stayed there for more than a decade, and then decided to strike out on my own.

I returned to school and got the necessary creds to become a drug and alcohol counselor. I worked for several area rehabs and ended up in the world's most depressing job—dispensing methadone to heroin addicts. For hours on end I sat behind a bulletproof plate glass window, taking in soiled five dollar bills and buzzing addicts in so they could get their daily fix. This gave me the incentive to write

THIRST

Thirst (formerly titled *The Girl, the Drugs, and the Man Who Couldn't Drink)*, a novel dealing with the dangerous lives of recovering addicts.

Last year, I was nominated for a Pushcart Prize following a story published in *Chrysalis* magazine. I didn't win but, still and all, it felt good.

I write because it's what I know how to do, and what I do best. I don't necessarily believe in God-given talent; in fact I'm pretty sure putting words to paper is nothing more than a craft. You become good and better at it by practice, much as a cabinet-maker gets more skilled the longer he's at the trade. My favorite saying is, "Writing is the art of applying the seat of the pants to the seat of the chair." Mary Heaton Vorse, a labor writer, said that a century ago and it's still true.

I write every day. I write blogs, novels, short stories, non-fiction books and the occasional play. It's feast or famine with a preponderance of famine, but that's okay.

I believe you need an enormous ego to write, and monstrous *chutzpah* to really believe that one's thoughts and ideas will be of interest to others. Thick skin is a prerequisite; writers live amidst rejection, from agents, publishing houses, editors and readers. This being said, writing is also the only endeavor where I refuse to indulge in false modesty. I think I'm pretty good.

Thierry Sagnier, March 2015

Made in the USA
Middletown, DE
25 September 2017